TURN BACK TIME

TURN BACK TIME

Elisabeth McNeill

This first world edition published in Great Britain 1998 by
SEVERN HOUSE PUBLISHERS LTD of
9–15 High Street, Sutton, Surrey SM1 1DF.
This first world edition published in the U.S.A. 1998 by
SEVERN HOUSE PUBLISHERS INC of
595 Madison Avenue, New York, N.Y. 10022.

British Library Cataloguing in Publication Data

McNeill, Elisabeth
     Turn back time
     I. Title
     823.9'14 [F]

     ISBN 0-7278-5398-8

Typeset by Palimpsest Book Production Ltd,
Polmont, Stirlingshire, Scotland.
Printed and bound in Great Britain by
MPG Books Ltd, Bodmin, Cornwall.

Chapter One

Lambeth, London, April 15th, 1878

It was warm outside, the first sunny day of spring, and Lambeth Crown Court was stuffy and airless. On the crowded public benches men and women of all classes were packed in close, leaning their heads towards each other and talking animatedly, exchanging gossip about the wicked woman they had come to see sentenced.

Silence fell abruptly when she was brought up by two policemen from the downstairs cells. Every eye in the court was fixed on her, every spectator held their breath when she stood up, straight as a tall, elegant poplar tree, to answer the charge of murdering her mother.

She gave a shudder as she first faced the bewigged and robed judge but only those closest to her noticed this sign of nervousness. As far as the others at the back could see she was perfectly controlled and emotionless. She was fighting hard to maintain an expressionless exterior, trying to keep her dark eyes blank, her gloved hands calmly folded on the ledge in front of her.

This hard-found impassivity and apparent indifference won her no friends however and, in fact, alienated many of the people who sat watching her. The most hostile pair of eyes belonged to the presiding judge.

She did not realise that this calm exterior was doing her cause a good deal of harm. Lessons on how a lady ought to behave, lessons that had been dinned into her since childhood, had been well learned and, though on the verge of fainting, she presented an appearance of composure. Who could have guessed that her ears were singing, her eyes were misted with unshed tears and her brain was so numb that the words directed towards her by a court official only sounded like a senseless gabble.

"You are Mrs Amelia Portbury and your age is thirty-five?" he said, reading from a paper in his hand.

She stared bleakly at him and said nothing, so, after a few seconds pause, he repeated in a slightly exasperated tone, "You are Mrs Amelia Portbury and your age is thirty-five?"

This time, with a struggle, she understood what he was saying and managed to reply "Yes" in a voice that was cultured and clear.

The clerk went on reading, "Mrs Portbury, you are charged that on January 30th, 1878, you struck your mother, Mrs Julia Ares, aged fifty-seven, of Victoria Park House, Dulwich, so violently with a fire-iron that she succumbed to her injuries and died on 2nd February of the same year." Then he paused, looked up at her and asked, "How do you plead to the charge of murder – guilty or not guilty?"

Conscious of the concentrated stare of every pair of eyes in the courtroom, and knowing that they were all waiting for her to answer the question, she straightened her shoulders, licked her lips, twisted her hands together, swallowed and at last found her voice.

"I am not guilty," she said.

The last two words rang out so loudly that they startled even the speaker with their assurance, and the judge looked up quickly from the papers he was studying to stare hard at her. In that moment she met his eyes and with sickening certainty knew from their cold stare how much he disliked her. Without a shadow of doubt he had no sympathy for someone he considered to be a base, spoiled and wicked woman.

Their eyes had met for only an instant however before he gestured with his pencil to tell her to sit. She was so frozen with fright that she could not move and the warders at her side had to push her, none too gently, down into the chair where she sat, staring sightlessly ahead, while the terrible process of the law ground into action.

It seemed that grim-faced men had been hurling words of accusation at her for weeks and nothing was required of her other than to follow her lawyer's advice, which had been to act like an imbecile and say 'not guilty' whenever they asked her a question. In fact, she knew perfectly well that she was guilty of killing her mother but what was important now was to persuade the judge and the prosecuting lawyers not to hang her. She must make them realise that the death of her mother had been a terrible mistake.

"I didn't mean it, I didn't mean it, please don't hang me," she longed to cry out, to throw herself on their mercy, for horror at the thought of being hanged never left her for a moment. Through long nights spent sleepless on a hard cell bed, she had thought about nothing else and, even now, as she sat in the dock, she could not stop herself putting a hand up to her throat as if to loosen the hangman's noose. She cringed inside as she imagined it being looped over her head and slipped down her neck like a macabre necklace. At this thought a wave of terror, which seemed to turn her whole body to water, swept through her.

Suddenly she realised that her defending counsel, Mr James Abbott, who had visited her many times while she was in prison on remand, was prancing about on the floor of the courtroom, sweeping his gown around like a bullfighter in an arena and staring across at her.

"Mrs Portbury," he intoned, "I would like you to tell the court about the last meeting you had with Mrs Ares, your mother, on the day she became ill." He emphasised the word *ill* because on it he intended to build her defence.

It took a huge marshalling of will-power for her to collect her wits. The black pupils of the eyes she turned to Abbott were enormous and staring like the eyes of a terrified animal. What a handsome woman, he thought, not for the first time. Amelia Portbury was tall, slim, and dark haired with eyes of a peculiarly lustrous and thrilling velvety-brown sheen. Her skin was cream coloured and, because of her pallor, her strongly boned face looked like a carved cameo. Abbott hoped that her good looks, fashionable clothes and her air of affluence, would not prejudice the judge and jury against her – such things sometimes did.

4

He and she had rehearsed how she was to answer his questions. When she began to speak, he breathed a sigh of relief that she had not forgotten his instructions, for he had not been sure how much she had actually taken in during their interviews in the prison. Speaking clearly and staring straight ahead with those sightless eyes, she began. He was relieved that she appeared composed because when he had interviewed her in the cells she had frequently been on the verge of hysteria, asking him over and over, "Will they hang me, will they hang me?" A question he found difficult to answer for the truth was that they might.

"I went to see my mother at her home about eleven o'clock on a Tuesday morning. It was January 30th, I think, yes it was.

"It had been snowing all night and outside it was very cold. She was in her morning room, sitting by a big fire. My children, Edward and Daisy, were with her because they were staying at my mother's house . . ."

At that point her voice died away and she stood very still, staring ahead as if in some sort of a trance.

He prompted her when he realised that she was not going to start again unless he broke into her reverie, "Why did you go to see your mother that morning? Was there any special reason?" he asked.

Life seemed to come back to her; he could almost see the blood flowing into her face, as she rallied.

"I went to plead with her to give me back my children. She was keeping them away from me. She said that my late husband, Dr Muldona, their father, had appointed her as their guardian in his will and so she was keeping them.

"But how could he do that? I'm their mother. How could he give them away to someone else? She said the law was on her side and she was keeping them."

At this impassioned outburst a rustle swept the court. Some of the women in the audience even looked as if they sympathised with her, and Abbott pressed on.

"On that morning your mother again refused your request to be allowed to take away your own children?"

"Yes. She said she was going to keep them for ever because I was not a suitable mother."

"What did you say to that?"

"I don't remember. I was so angry. I think I said that she wasn't any better than me because she was a thief. She was keeping some things that belonged to me and she wouldn't give them back, either."

Abbott wished his client hadn't equated her children with more mundane possessions but he had to ask, "What sort of things of yours was your mother keeping?"

She furrowed her brow. "There was some silver, a little boule cupboard and a crystal decanter which had been given to me as wedding presents when I married Dr Muldona. When I asked my mother for them she became very nasty. She said that not only could I not have the children but the other things were hers as well . . ."

"They don't sound very valuable."

"They weren't really but they were mine. I wanted them back."

As she spoke she blinked her beautiful eyes and her mind went back to that terrible January morning over two months ago. Once again, she relived her agitation when she remembered how, as she stepped into the room, her mother had looked up with the familiar sneering smile on her face to say, "So you've come back with your tail between your legs again, have you?"

"No," she'd replied. "No, I've only come for my babies."

"Well you can't have them. They're staying here with me."

"I'll go to law about it," Amelia had said, and her mother had laughed sarcastically.

"The law's on my side, you'll find. Your husband gave your children into my care and there's nothing you can do about it. No court in the land will give you custody of those children after what you've done. You're a wicked, wanton woman."

Abbott's voice broke into her memories again. "Where were the children when you and your mother were arguing?"

"Edward, my son, he's nine, was kneeling on the hearthrug staring into the fire. He wouldn't look at us. I think he was afraid because he doesn't like it when people start shouting. My baby, Daisy, she's only three, was on a footstool at her grandmother's feet. She kept staring up at me and I could see she wanted me to kiss her so I held out my arms and she came running into them."

When she said this Amelia Portbury's voice quavered and tears began to slip down her pale cheeks as she remembered her anguish as she held out her gloved hands beseechingly in the child's direction. "Daisy, come to Mama!" she'd cried.

The little girl had risen from her seat and rushed over, sinking her face into her mother's rustling taffeta skirt.

Then she had spoken to her son, "Look at me, Edward!" she'd said but he never turned round and had continued to stare into the fire.

"What did your mother do when you caught hold of your daughter?" asked Abbot, bringing her thoughts back to the present moment.

"She came over and tried to pull us apart. She told me to leave the child alone because I was only upsetting her. She said that if I loved the children as much as I pretended I'd never have married again."

"So part of the trouble between you and your mother was over your recent remarriage? How long were you a widow?"

"Nearly two years."

"How long had you been married for a second time when your mother died?"

"Nine months."

"Your mother didn't like your second husband, did she?"

"She hated him. She said he was a ruffian."

"When she tried to pull your daughter away from you, what did you do?"

"I called for the maid to take the children out of the room. I didn't think it was right for them to hear the sort of things my mother was saying about me."

"Did the maid do as you asked?

"Yes, the one who answered my call was a housemaid called Alice, little more than a child herself really. I told her to take the children downstairs where they couldn't hear our argument because they were both upset, especially Daisy who was crying."

She remembered watching the three of them going out of the room, each child holding onto one of the maid's hands. They looked so defenceless, so precious to her. She was jerked back again from this memory to the reality of the courtroom by the insistence in Mr Abbott's voice.

"Please tell the court what happened after the children were taken away," he said.

She sighed, a long, deep sigh of resignation. "We went on arguing. Neither of us was going to give in. She said some very cruel things to me. She made me cry . . . she usually did when we argued."

"This was not the first time you and your mother had argued, was it?"

"Oh no, we'd been arguing a lot, especially recently. My mother was a bully, you see. She liked her own way and if she didn't get it she could be very nasty."

"You had been on bad terms for some time, I believe? Would it be correct to say that your mother exercised power over you because she controlled the family money?"

She nodded silently and he prompted her to speak. "Am I right?"

"Yes."

"How bad were the relations between you? Would you say that the breach was unmendable?"

"They were quite bad but I thought we could make it up if she'd only be reasonable. There were times when we got on very well. You see, after my first husband died, the children and I went back to live with my mother, but when I married again she disapproved so much of my new husband, Mr Portbury, that she put me out of her house."

"What did you do then, where did you go? Did Mr Portbury have a house that you could live in with your children?"

"Oh no. He had nothing. But I was able to buy a house – or at least my mother allowed me enough money from the sale of the house I'd lived in with my first husband to buy another, smaller house in Dulwich – and we went there."

The audience in the courtroom were hanging on every word for this was what they had come to hear.

Abbott turned his back on them and spoke directly to his client, "You left your second husband and went home to your mother. How long after your marriage did you do this?"

"Six months."

"So then you and your mother made up your differences?"

"Yes, for a while. She was very pleased that I'd gone back; come to my senses, she said."

"How long did you and your second husband live apart?"

"About two months – sixty-four days exactly. Then I went back to him again and she was very angry about that. Worse than she'd been before, in fact."

"Why was that do you think?"

"My mother was a snob and Mr Portbury was not from our class of society . . . and I think she was jealous."

"Jealous of you?"

"Yes. Perhaps. She didn't like getting old . . . She'd been very beautiful and she hated losing her looks. I was young and I had married again – she didn't like that. She wanted me to stay with her."

"So it was your second marriage that caused the worst trouble between you and your mother? It wasn't really about who kept certain pieces of furniture?"

"Yes, I suppose it was, but we'd had arguments in the past as well, even before my first husband died. He always took her side. The last real trouble between us was about my children though. I wanted them with me."

"What did you fight about when your first husband, Dr Muldona, was alive?" asked Mr Abbott.

"Just silly things like spending too much money and sometimes my mother didn't like my friends . . . she wanted to rule my life even though I was a married woman – because I was her only child, you see."

Abbott nodded and said in a gentler voice, "Now, I want you to try to remember exactly what happened after your children and the maid left the room. Describe the course of the argument between you and your mother that morning."

Amelia leaned forward in the dock and her face became haunted and tragic as she recalled the events of the most terrible day of her life.

"When the children were taken away, my mother got up from her chair and ordered me to get out of her house. I said I wouldn't go without some of the things I'd left with her – especially the crystal decanter which I particularly loved. I pointed to it. It was standing on a table in the window. She was keeping port wine in it.

"She said I couldn't have it because my dead husband, Dr Muldona, had given it to her but that was a lie, and I told her so. We both began really to lose our tempers then, I'm afraid.

"I went to take the decanter and she ran over to prevent me. When we both reached for it, the stopper fell out, it toppled off the table and broke. The port ran over both our skirts . . ."

She paused and brushed one hand downwards from the waistband of her black taffeta gown as if wiping spilled wine away.

"When it smashed to pieces on the floor my mother started to screech like a fishwife and something seemed to explode in my head—"

As she spoke she put up a hand to her forehead for she remembered only too vividly the veil of scarlet, like blood, that had flowed over her eyes and interfered with her vision that morning. She remembered the wild roaring in her ears as what was left of her self-restraint snapped. It was as if she had gone mad.

Abbott broke in and said again, "But the decanter can't have been very valuable. Why was your mother fighting so bitterly over it?"

"I don't know. She had many other decanters, and nicer ones too. My mother was a very rich woman, she had lots of lovely things. I think she was determined to keep it because she saw I wanted it. It was because it was mine that she refused to give it to me It was a symbol, I suppose."

He coaxed her gently. "Tell the court what happened after the decanter broke and the port was spilled."

"She hit me. She lashed out at me with her clenched fists, she struck me on the face."

Her mother had been as tall as her and they had stood shoulder to shoulder pushing at each other like bare-knuckle boxers.

"She hit you," Abbott prompted again.

"Yes, and she was screaming loudly by this time, so loud that the gardener came running in. The maids had gone out for him because they were afraid of what was happening between my mother and me."

"It must have been a nasty scene for the servants to try to break it up."

"I suppose it was." She didn't sound surprised or ashamed and Abbott got the impression that screaming scenes had been fairly common in Mrs Ares' Victoria Park mansion.

"And then what happened?" he asked quickly, hoping to stop the judge from having the same idea.

"The maids cleaned up the broken glass and took it away. When they left I turned to go too because I realised there was no point staying but my mother said something that made me turn around . . . I ran across to the fireplace and picked up the brass poker which was lying on the fender and threatened her with it. I told her to be quiet or I'd hit her."

"What had she said that made you react like that?"

"I don't remember exactly." Amelia's face closed up tightly when she said this, but he persisted, "What did she say? Try to remember because it must have been something very bad to make you want to strike her with a poker."

"I wasn't really going to hit her with it. I was only

13

threatening her, trying to make her stop calling me those names. I didn't intend to injure her. I really didn't."

"Did she stop miscalling you?"

"No. She called me more terrible names. She said awful things about me going back to Sam." The woman in the dock hung her head and stared down at her hands clenching and unclenching on the wooden shelf in front of her.

"So was that when you hit her?" Abbott's question hung in the air like a challenge.

She looked up, stared bleakly at him and nodded. "Yes, I hit her but it was only a slight blow. I shouted that I would hit her if she wasn't quiet and she laughed at me. Then she took a candlestick off the mantlepiece and I thought she was going to hit me with it, so I struck her first, on the top of her arm. I could have struck her on the head if I'd wanted to do her a real injury but I didn't. I only wanted to stop her calling me names and to protect myself, to stop her hitting me. I didn't want to hurt her. I certainly didn't want to kill her. Oh, I never for a moment meant to murder her."

"What was she calling you that you found so upsetting?"

She gulped and it was obvious that she did not want to answer that question. "She called me frightful names – a whore, a harlot, a slut . . . Things like that, terrible things. She said that Sam Portbury had only married me for my money, and I'd married him because I wanted him in my bed . . . she laughed at me and said that I reminded her of a bitch on heat. She compared Sam and me to dogs coupling in the street."

When the words came tumbling out the whole courtroom went strangely still.

"That was all she said?" asked Abbott calmly after a little pause.

"She said other things too but that was the worst. I only wanted to stop her shouting things like that at me. My children might have heard her and so might the servants."

"So you hit her. Then what happened? Did she stop calling you names?"

"She screamed and fell backwards into her chair. The servants must have been listening at the door because they came running in and so did Bryce the gardener. They sent for the doctor and carried my mother to bed."

"Why did they think it was necessary to fetch a doctor? Was she badly injured?"

"No. I don't think so. She wasn't bleeding or anything but she was gasping and gulping and she said she was dying – so they sent for her doctor. When he came he said he thought she'd be all right but she was distressed and should stay in bed till she felt better."

"The doctor will give his own testimony later, Mrs Portbury, just tell the court what actually happened between you and your mother that day."

"I helped the maids take my mother upstairs and she stayed in bed as the doctor said she should."

"How long did she stay in bed?"

"Four days."

"And then?"

"Then she died."

There was another significant pause while Mrs

Portbury wiped her eyes with a minute handkerchief. He'd told her to do that and was glad she'd remembered his advice. He recommenced his questions.

"Where were you during your mother's illness?"

"I stayed in her house. I wanted to look after her but she said she didn't want me in her room so the maids did everything for her until my cousin Isabella came."

"Your cousin is your nearest female relative? You have no sisters or aunts?"

"No. Apart from my mother and my children I have only one cousin. I had a brother, but he died when he was four years old."

"Were you with your mother when she died?"

"No, my cousin kept me out of the sickroom because she said my mother didn't want me there and it would only upset her if I showed my face."

"But you didn't leave the house? You didn't go home to Mr Portbury?"

"I stayed because I thought my mother would change her mind and see me. I wanted to tell her I was sorry for hitting her."

"Did you manage to do that?"

"No. On Friday morning she died. I hadn't expected her to die. I don't think anyone did. As soon as the doctor came and confirmed she was dead, my cousin sent for the police and they arrested me. I couldn't even go to her funeral because I was in custody."

There was another significant pause but, though Mrs Portbury crumpled her handkerchief in her hand, she did not weep again.

Eventually Abbott asked her, "Were you glad your mother was dead, Mrs Portbury?"

"Definitely not. I've grieved sorely for her. She was my mother and I loved her in spite of everything that happened between us."

"She was also a very rich woman. You always knew that her death would benefit you financially, I presume. Did you know exactly how rich your mother was?"

"I never thought about it. I knew she had a considerable income because she talked about money quite a lot. It mattered to her, you see, and she was always threatening me that if I didn't do what she wanted she'd change her will. But I never anticipated her dying. I certainly never wanted her to die so I could inherit her money. Anyway I've money of my own, left to me by my father and I was also left an annuity by my first husband."

"So money could not be considered as a motive for you killing your mother?" Abbott said soothingly.

"Of course not! I didn't kill her! She died because she had a bad heart. I didn't kill her, I really didn't. I only hit her slightly in self-defence. I loved her, please believe me."

"You struck your mother in self-defence. You did not murder her," said Abbott looking at the jury as he spoke.

She seized the suggestion eagerly. "Yes, yes, she was going to hit me with the candlestick. I was terribly afraid of her."

And that last sentence, at least, was true.

Chapter Two

The frankness and apparent composure of his client cheered Abbott. He was also pleased that she had managed to turn herself out so smartly, although this could not have been easy for she'd been in prison for over two months. The impression her impeccable clothes made on the jurors – a line up of susceptible-looking men – would be very favourable, he was sure.

However, his euphoria began to disappear when his opponent, Sebastian Busby, the prosecuting counsel, took the floor. Busby began in a low and sympathetic key, at first giving the accused woman an easy time by plying her with innocuous questions until he saw her relax. Then he dismissed her, saying, "I have no more questions, Mrs Portbury," with such a kind look that it would have been possible to imagine he was on her side. Only too soon, however, he would be going in for the kill, like the accomplished court dueller that he was.

Edward Bryce was the first witness for the defence, because it had been obvious to Abbott that this man was fond of Amelia and would not condemn her unfairly. Stocky and well set-up, with receding sandy hair and a kindly face, Bryce gave such an impression of honesty and trustworthiness that no juror would ever suspect him of distorting the truth or being activated by malice.

In response to questions he said that he had worked as gardener for Mrs Julia Ares for twenty-two years, and it was he who the terrified maids had called when his employer and her daughter began fighting violently in the morning room.

"When I went into the room it was in a terrible mess with broken glass all over the carpet, spilt vases and upturned chairs. Like a bar-room brawl, sir," he said, shaking his head.

"What did you do?" asked Abbott.

"I told Miss Amelia – Mrs Portbury, I mean – not to make so much trouble for her mother because the old lady had a weak heart. I told them both to calm down."

"And did they?"

"No, sir. About ten minutes later I had to go back again because they were still fighting and the mistress was taken ill. I thought she'd had one of her bad turns."

"You weren't surprised by this?"

Bryce's eyes beneath bushy eyebrows were shrewd but not judgemental as he looked across the courtroom floor at the woman in the dock. "Not really, sir. I'd asked them to stop fighting because I was afraid Mrs Ares would be upset by it, but I don't suppose I expected they'd pay any attention to me. I was only the gardener."

"Had this sort of thing, this fighting, happened before in your hearing?"

Bryce nodded his head. "I'm afraid it had, sir. Mrs Ares and her daughter have been on very bad terms recently and they didn't try to hide the trouble between them from the servants. We all knew how things stood."

"So this last quarrel was only one of many?"

"Yes, sir, it was."

"But this time your employer was badly hurt?"

"Like I said, I thought she'd had one of her collapses. When I went into the room the second time she didn't look too bad at first. She was sort of slumped in her chair, with her head hanging down. Then when I got near to her I saw that her face was dead white and her breathing very rough, all wheezy. She'd been taken ill like that before when she'd had a temper tantrum in the garden."

Abbott jumped in at this and asked, "So she was prone to attacks like that?"

"Well, yes, sir, though not quite as bad as that last one. She did have something wrong with her heart and when she got excited or angry she used to get wheezy and once or twice she fainted away. The maids used to come for me then to help carry her upstairs because she was a big woman and heavy."

"Did that happen often?"

Bryce pondered. "Only when she got angry, like I said . . . maybe four or five times in the last couple of years, I'd say."

"Would you also say your employer, Mrs Ares, was a bad-tempered woman?" asked Abbott.

"She was quick-tempered, sir. She liked things to be done right, if you know what I mean, and she let people know if she wasn't pleased." Bryce was obviously being diplomatic.

"But would you say she was a bully?" persisted Abbott.

A shutdown look came over the gardener's face. "I've known worse employers than Mrs Ares. She was paying our wages and it was up to us to do what she told us, wasn't it?"

"Did she bully her daughter, in your opinion?"

The gardener sighed. "She liked Mrs Portbury to pay her respect and she liked to be the one who made the decisions. I got the feeling that she was old-fashioned when it came to relations between mother and daughter, if you get my meaning. And she held the purse strings, didn't she?"

"Where was Mrs Ares' daughter when you went into the morning room the second time the maids called you that morning?" asked Abbott.

"She was standing in front of the fireplace with the long brass poker in her hand. She was weeping and her hair was falling around her face. She kept saying that she hadn't done anything to her mother." Again Bryce looked across at Amelia Portbury and this time there was visible sorrow and sympathy in his regard.

"Could Mrs Ares still speak at this stage?" prompted the barrister.

"Yes, sir. She looked up at me and said, 'Don't believe her. She tried to kill me, Bryce.'" The words came slowly and almost reluctantly.

"Those were her exact words: 'She tried to kill me, Bryce'?"

"Yes. They were."

"Didn't that surprise you?"

"Yes. I didn't really believe it but, you see, Mrs Ares could be quite dramatic sometimes. She said things she didn't mean. I looked around and there wasn't any blood to be seen or anything . . ." The gardener was now deliberately not looking across the courtroom at the solitary figure in the dock, but his probity was so strong that he was still determined to tell the truth as he remembered it.

Abbott changed tack as a diversionary move. "Let's go back to the beginning, Mr Bryce. Why did the maids run to fetch you out of the garden?" he asked.

"I've told you that. The housekeeper was out and the girls were frightened by all the shouting and crashing in the morning room. After I'd spoken to Mrs Ares and Mrs Portbury, I went down into the kitchen and was just leaving there when Alice came running down to say Mrs Ares was ill. The maids are only girls, they didn't know what to do."

"What did you do?"

"I helped her to sit up straight in her chair and told one of the girls to fetch her a glass of brandy to sip, but it didn't do much good. She still couldn't breathe, so we carried her upstairs."

"What was her daughter doing while all this was going on?"

"She was very upset, weeping and sobbing and kneeling by her mother's chair trying to hold her hand but the old lady wouldn't let her – she kept pushing her off. Mrs Portbury followed us upstairs, still carrying that poker, crying and weeping, but the old lady let us know she wasn't to get into the bedroom, and she herself was so upset one of the maids took her back downstairs and she waited there for the doctor to come."

"Who decided a doctor was needed?"

"Mrs Portbury. She asked me to fetch one and I did. I ran for the man who lives two houses down the road. When he came he said Mrs Ares had had an apoplexy."

"The doctor will give us his testimony later. Please confine yourself to what you witnessed in the house. What did you do after the doctor came?"

"I went into the kitchen and waited. Then Dora, one of the maids, told me that the doctor said that Mrs Portbury wasn't to be allowed into her mother's room because it would upset the patient too much."

"You're presuming what the doctor will tell us again. Please confine yourself to what you actually saw and heard," Abbott reproved.

"All right. After the doctor left, Mrs Portbury called for me and told me to go down to Brixton to fetch that lad Portbury."

"How did she appear to you then?"

"She was still in a terrible state, sobbing and gulping. She said she didn't want to leave the house herself because she hoped her mother would change her mind and let her go into the bedroom. She was desperate to see the old lady."

"So she sent you to fetch Mr Portbury. Was that her husband?"

Bryce's face expressed disapproval. "Yes. She wanted me to go for Portbury," he said.

"You know him?"

"Only too well. He's a damned rogue – sorry, sir. It's him that's been the cause of all this trouble. The old lady would still be alive if it wasn't for him."

"You were fond of Mrs Ares?"

"I'd worked for her for a long time, sir, and she was always good to me, though she did have a fiery temper, that I must admit. But I'm fond of her daughter too, poor soul."

"Why do you say 'poor soul'?"

"Because she's a good lass and because of what's happened to her because of Portbury, though I didn't think much of her first husband, the doctor, either. But the really bad trouble they've had has all come through Portbury."

Abbott paused for a moment to allow this to sink in with the jury and then persisted, "Did you go to Brixton and fetch Mr Portbury then?"

"No, sir, I did not. It wasn't my job to go raking around Brixton looking for a seventeen-year-old lad who'd never addressed a civil word to me and who'd brought shame on Mrs Ares' family."

"How old did you say Mrs Portbury's husband is?"

"He's seventeen."

At this, the eyes of everyone in the courtroom turned to look at Amelia Portbury, sitting white-faced in the dock. There was a rustle of sound and it was easy to hear the whispered words, "Seventeen! But she said she's thirty-five, didn't she?" spoken by a woman in the back row of the courtroom.

Abbott dismissed his witness Bryce at this point for they were now verging on dangerous ground.

One after the other, two scared-looking maids, Dora Mason and Alice Grey, followed Bryce into the witness box. They both confirmed his account of the row between the two women and told how they had found Amelia Portbury holding the poker when they burst into the room the second time. Only Alice remembered that a brass candlestick was lying in the hearth. Dora said she didn't see it. They also confirmed that Mrs Ares told them her daughter had struck her a blow with the poker but neither heard Amelia claim that her mother had attempted to hit her and that she had acted in self-defence.

The more impressive of the two girls was seventeen-year-old Alice, who was only a slip of a thing, barely five feet tall, with pale yellow hair and an ethereal look that made her seem to be in danger of melting away into thin air at any moment. In spite of her apparent fragility, however, she proved to be an excellent witness with a sharp gift of observation.

When Busby asked her how long she'd been working at Victoria Park, she lifted her head and looked him in the eye. "Three and a half years, sir, since I was fourteen, since just before the old doctor died."

"The doctor you refer to was Mrs Portbury's first husband, Dr Joseph Muldona?" asked Busby.

"Yes sir, it was Dr Muldona who got me the position with Mrs Ares after my mother died and I had nowhere to go. My father had been the doctor's coachman but he died too, five years ago, and when I was an orphan the doctor fixed me up with a place with his friend Mrs Ares."

"His friend Mrs Ares? She was his mother-in-law, wasn't she?"

"And his friend, sir. I knew from my father that they were friends before the doctor married Mrs Portbury. He was much the same age, you see. Just a little bit younger. In fact my father used to say that the doctor should have married the mother and not the daughter."

"Really?" drawled Busby, looking across at the accused who dropped her head and did not look up again for a very long time.

"Though you were a comparative newcomer to the household, Alice, were you aware of bad blood between your employer and her daughter?" Busby asked.

Alice glanced at Mrs Portbury before replying. "It was impossible not to know, sir, they didn't hide it. They quarrelled almost every time Mrs Portbury came to the house, especially recently. Both of them wanted the children, you see. I used to think it was hard on Mrs Portbury not to be allowed to keep her own children . . ."

"Hard or not," said Busby suavely, "it's the law. Her husband could appoint anyone he chose as the guardian of his children and he appointed Mrs Ares."

Alice said nothing but her expression showed what she thought of that. Busby then asked her to tell the court what had happened on the morning of February 2nd.

"We heard the mistress and her daughter arguing and then the bell rang so I went upstairs and Mrs Portbury asked me to take the children away because they were upset. I took the poor little things down into the kitchen and closed all the doors so they couldn't hear what was going on. The cook gave them some cake but they were both very scared, especially little Daisy, the lamb, because she didn't know who to side with, her mother or her grandmother. Edward didn't side with either of them, just sat at the kitchen table with his hands over his ears. He's a strange little boy, is Edward.

"Then Dora came down to tell me she'd heard glass and china being smashed in the morning room. The bell was pulled again and we went running up. There was glass and spilled port wine all over the floor."

"A decanter had been broken," prompted Busby.

"More than one decanter. There must have been at least three of them smashed, I think. It looked as if they'd been throwing them at each other. Dora and I cleaned up as well as we could and when we were out of the room again after taking the bits away, we heard a terrible sort of scream. I ran back and saw Mrs Ares stagger across to her chair and fall into it. She looked terrible and she was holding one arm with the other as if it was broken. Mrs Portbury was by the fireplace holding the poker. She didn't seem to know what she was doing."

"What did you do then?"

"I went for Mr Bryce. He was the only person who could calm Mrs Ares down when she got into one of her states."

"So this sort of thing had happened before?"

Alice looked cautious. "They'd fought before – shouted and carried on, I mean. But they hadn't broken things or hit each other. Mrs Ares often threw a temper though. We were used to that."

"How often?"

"Threw a temper?"

"No, how often did Mrs Ares and Mrs Portbury quarrel?"

"Oh I couldn't say, sir, I can only tell you what I heard. Five or six times in the weeks before Mrs Ares died."

"It would be true to say then that there was bad blood between them?"

"I would say they were having difficulties," said the little maid carefully.

"Was it only because Mrs Ares had custody of Mrs Portbury's children?"

"I don't know. It was none of my business, sir."

"Oh come, Miss Grey. You and the other servants must have had an idea what the trouble was about."

"As far as I know, Mrs Ares didn't like Mrs Portbury's new husband and she didn't want the children to live with him and their mother."

"The trouble was about the children, then, and not about a decanter?"

Alice's face went blank. "I don't know sir," she said. Busby tried another tack. "When the doctor came what happened?"

"I helped settle Mrs Ares upstairs and then I went back into the kitchen to sit with the children – I was worried about them. After a bit Mrs Portbury came down to find me and asked me to go to Brixton and fetch Sam Portbury. She said I was to tell him to come at once. She'd already asked Mr Bryce to go but he wouldn't, she said. She was crying fit to burst."

"You knew Mrs Portbury's husband? You knew where to go to find him that day?"

"Oh yes, sir. I've known him since we were little 'uns. His father and my father knew each other. They were both coachmen, you see. They used to work in the same stableyard at one time when my father drove a hansom cab and old Portbury had one too. Sam took after his dad and worked as coachman for Mrs Portbury before she married him."

Another ripple of excitement swept the court.

"As a coachman? So young? How old was he when he went to work for her?"

"He was sixteen, I think. He's nearly the same age as me, you see, but she wasn't taking him on for a big job. It was only a small gig she had after the doctor died. She hired Sam to drive her about because she hadn't been well and her mother said she needed to take the air every day."

"And then she married him? What did you think about that?"

Alice's face went expressionless at this juncture and she looked blankly at Busby.

"She married him, didn't she? What did you think about that?" he repeated.

"Yes, sir, she married him." Her voice was cold and it was obvious she was not going to express any opinion about the marriage.

"You went to Brixton to fetch Mr Portbury though," persisted the prosecuting counsel in a mollifying tone.

"Yes. I went because I was sorry for Mrs Portbury. She was in a terrible state, beside herself really."

"What did Sam Portbury say when you told him what had happened?"

"He laughed. He said the old cow had it coming to her."

"Were those his words: 'the old cow'?"

"Yes, sir," said with a bleak look because she'd been led into saying more than she intended.

"Did he accompany you back to Victoria Park?"

"No, he said I was to tell Em, I mean Amelia – Mrs Portbury – that she knew where to find him when she was ready. He'd been warned away from Mrs Ares' house, you see. She'd put a lawyer onto him, I think."

"But Mrs Portbury had sent you to fetch him, hadn't she? What did she say when you went back without him?"

"She was disappointed. All she said was, 'Did you tell him that I need him badly?' and I said 'Yes.'"

"Did he come to Victoria Park at all during the time before Mrs Portbury was arrested?"

"No, sir, but I think she went down to Brixton to see him. She went out the next night in a cab and came back about an hour later . . . the Wednesday, it was."

"So Mrs Portbury could have left her mother's house at any time if she wanted. She could have run away, evaded arrest, if she'd been in fear of being charged with murder?"

Alice looked at him. "She wasn't a prisoner, sir. She never tried to run away. She just waited there and when her mother died, I heard her say to her cousin, Mrs Downs, 'What should we do now, Isabella?'"

"What was the answer?"

"Mrs Downs said, 'Send for the police, of course. You killed her.' Poor Mrs Portbury just sat down and wept as if her heart was broken."

The next witness, her cousin Isabella Downs, was openly hostile to Amelia Portbury and didn't even attempt to hide her feelings.

They were about the same age, in their mid thirties, but where Mrs Portbury was a handsome woman, Mrs Downs was pinched-looking, severe and malicious-faced with sparse fair hair combed tightly back beneath an unflattering cap of black lace. Her dress too was deepest black, even her jewellery was made of jet for she was in ostentatious mourning for her dead aunt.

As soon as she could she launched into a character assassination of her cousin. In replying to Busby's question about the strained relations between Mrs Ares and Mrs Portbury, she said, "Of course Amelia has always been very rash, very impetuous, quite uncontrolled in some ways. Sometimes we doubted her sanity. Her poor mother spoiled her, gave her everything she wanted ever since she was a baby. My mother, who was Aunt Julia's sister, used to say that Amelia was a classic case of spare the rod and spoil the child.

"Her husband, the doctor, treated her in the same way but I think he had more idea of what she's really like than her mother did. After all, he left that clause in his will saying she'd only receive her annuity provided she didn't remarry, didn't he? He must have known what she was like before he did that. But while he was alive he let her buy the most expensive clothes and fancy jewellery, quite above the station of a doctor's wife. When he died she wasn't a bit upset. I remember remarking on that at his funeral.

"Then, of course, she got herself involved with the coachman, and even her mother turned against her. I mean it was such a scandal! She says she thought he was twenty-one – he told her lies about his age, so she claims – but even if he had been twenty-one, it was still a terrible thing to do – to marry your coachman! And she's the same age as I am, thirty-six next birthday.

"You can imagine what people said. Such a scandal. They talked of nothing else. And now this! Killing her own mother. My husband and I can't hold our heads up in society. We've even had to stop going out – except to church of course. Our faith is our greatest solace."

When she had finished pouring all this out, she

took a deep breath and looked around the court as if expecting applause.

"Mrs Ares shared your feelings about Mrs Portbury's second marriage?" asked Busby when the tirade finally drew to a halt.

"Of course she did. My poor aunt, she was heart-broken. Mrs Ares was a lady, a woman of property. She knew perfectly well what that Portbury was after – the money. Amelia wouldn't listen. When she found out that his mother had been in her house stealing things, she parted with him, but only for a little while. We were all shocked and horrified when she went back to him again.

"Poor Aunt Julia. She was beside herself with worry about those poor children, Edward and Daisy. She kept them away from their mother because she knew Portbury only wanted to get his hands on them because of their money – especially the five hundred pounds a year they had from their mother's annuity that she lost when she remarried. He tried to sneak them away from Victoria Park but Edward had enough sense to make a fuss and Portbury was stopped."

"It seems that money played a big part in the family troubles," Busby said.

Mrs Downs looked surprised at the suggestion that he should think anything else. "Of course it did," she affirmed, and then burst out with her most damning statement. "I never liked her. I never trusted her. I knew she'd come to a bad end. I'm just sorry that it was my poor aunt who paid the price for Amelia's sins," was her final remark.

Dr James Henderson, who treated Mrs Ares at the end of her life, was inclined to agree with Mrs Downs.

After recounting how Bryce had come rushing into his house one day at about noon to tell him Mrs Ares had been taken ill, he went on to describe the scene in Mrs Ares' bedroom when he arrived at her house.

"She was lying fully clothed on top of her bed in a collapsed condition. I knew her already as a patient because she had a weak heart and I'd been called in several times in the past few years. When I examined her this time I found that she had severe contusions on her shoulder and upper right arm. I also suspected she might have a broken rib. She was barely able to talk but she made me understand that her daughter had attacked her and she didn't want the woman to be allowed near her. I passed those orders on to her staff."

"You say she had several contusions and a possible bone breakage, so more than one blow must have been inflicted?" asked Busby.

"Several, I'd say. She was badly bruised down one side and in considerable pain. While I was with her she also suffered an apoplectic fit, brought on by the excitement she had been through."

"So she was not able to tell you exactly what had happened?"

"Apart from saying her daughter had done it, not really. After she had her stroke, she was unable to say more than a few words but the maids told me she and her daughter had been arguing and her daughter had hit her with a brass poker. She must have used considerable force, I'm afraid."

"Could Mrs Ares' injuries have been caused by falling into the fireplace?"

The doctor agreed reluctantly that it was possible. "But unlikely," he added.

"Was Mrs Ares' death caused by the bone breakage and the bruising?" persisted Busby.

"Well, she actually died after suffering a second apoplectic fit on the Friday but she never rallied after being hit by her daughter and the shock of that incident certainly caused her first apoplexy. Following it she became weaker and weaker and in the end died of a blood clot on the brain. Her heart was feeble, as I have already said."

"Was she in very precarious health? Was her death imminent anyway? Would she have died so precipitately even if she had not had the dispute with her daughter?" asked Busby.

"It's impossible to predict how close death is even to the most seriously ill patient," said Henderson. "But I would hazard a guess that if she had lived the sort of life that is normal and to be expected for a woman of her age and her comfortable circumstances, she would probably have lived for several more years."

"So you consider that Mrs Portbury was responsible for her mother's sudden death?" Busby added.

"Yes, I do. When I went to Victoria Park to confirm that the patient was dead, Mrs Downs and her husband asked me what they should do and I said they should call the police and have Mrs Ares' daughter arrested for murder."

"Murder is a strong word," said Busby.

"Not too strong for what Mrs Portbury did to her mother," said the doctor self-righteously.

The last, and most damning, witness against Amelia was her husband, Sam Portbury. The courtroom was packed on the morning he was due to appear and he turned up attended by five members of his family, three men and two women, who clustered round him like a praetorian guard.

He was a strong-looking young man with a pert broad face, hair that stuck up on the crown in a boyish cow's lick, and widely spaced front teeth which gave him the look of a music-hall comedian. To add to the effect he was dressed like a fop in a brightly checked suit, a tight white choker and a pale lemon, round-crowned felt hat with a broad grosgrain ribbon. He looked as if he had just stepped off the stage. Nobody less suited to the elegant Amelia could be imagined and there were people in the audience who tittered because they found the contrast funny.

Not only was Sam showy but he was also unutterably cocky and confident, almost ogling the women in the courtroom.

When asked to identify himself, he grinned and said, "Yes, I'm Samuel Alfred Portbury of Dryden Road, Brixton. I'm nearly eighteen actually – my birthday's in five days' time."

A rustle swept the crowd when he said this because

he looked several years older than his age and acted with the assurance of a man of the world. Sam had been around and it showed.

He was proud to affirm his relationship to the prisoner in the dock. "Yes, I married Mrs Amelia Muldona in May last year," he said, glancing across at her. She did not return his gaze but looked down instead at her twisting hands.

Busby pounced on him when he said this. "How old were you on your wedding day?"

"I was seventeen."

"So why did you give your age on the wedding register as twenty-one?"

"Just to please her, wasn't it? She knew I was seventeen but she didn't care, liked it, in fact," he gave a man of the world grin round the court at this, "but she didn't want other people to know and so I signed the register with the wrong age. Nobody but us would know, she said. Then, when her mother gets at her, she tries to have the marriage annulled because I've given the wrong age. I sweet-talked her out of it though, know what I mean . . ."

Another cheeky grin and a few titters from the body of the court made the prisoner in the dock sink even further down in her seat.

Sam was a voluble witness. When Busby invited him to explain why a boy of seventeen should want to marry a woman of thirty-five, he leaned forward with his thumbs stuck in the armholes of his checked waistcoat and said, "Come on, look at her. She's a good-looking woman, ain't she? Just take a look at her. Tall and handsome like a fine horse. I'd never been close to a woman like that before. And she always smelt so nice – all flowery – and her clothes rustled. It drove me mad when I was driving her out. But I knew my place. I was the coachman and she was the lady. I'd never have laid a hand on her if she hadn't asked me to."

"She asked you? She seduced you?"

"Yes. I'd been with women before, of course, but they were all slags, not like her. She asked me into her house when the old woman was out and she put a hand on me – you know where. It couldn't have been an accident the way she did it. Then she said she was in love with me."

"What did you say?" asked Busby.

"I told her it was impossible." Oh, how righteous he sounded!

"And . . ." prodded Busby.

"She cried and carried on and said men of her age could marry women my age and nobody thought anything wrong about it. Why couldn't she have a bit of happiness for once? That was what she said. I was sorry for her really."

"You married her because you were sorry for her?"

"Yeah, in a way I did. But I wanted her too. I'd never been with a woman like her before, a lady. I wondered what it would be like . . . and she wouldn't let me find out unless I married her – at least not very often, not often enough, if you know what I mean."

A salacious titter swept the court and Amelia Portbury's pale face changed colour to a deep shade of red.

Out of consideration for a distressed woman Busby refrained from pursuing the point. Instead he said, "So you married each other. There must have been opposition to such an unlikely match."

"Yeah. Her mother went mad. Sent a lawyer to Brixton with a hundred pounds in sovs for me if I'd go away. My mother wasn't too pleased either. She didn't like Em. Said she was stuck up and conceited."

"Em?"

"Amelia. That's what I called her – Em."

"You didn't take the hundred sovereigns?"

"No way. You can't buy Sam Portbury, I told him."

"Did you turn down the money because you knew there would be a great deal more than that in it for you if you did get married?" Busby spoke the question with an insinuating smile.

But Sam presented a picture of outraged innocence. "I wasn't interested in her money. She didn't have all that much anyway. When she remarried the money her first husband left her was taken away and given to her children. He'd left something in his will saying she couldn't have it if she married again. Mean old sod."

"But you knew her mother was a rich woman, and she was an only child."

"Like I told you, the old woman hated me. I wouldn't put it past her to leave her money to the Missionary Society or something instead of letting me have any of it. But Amelia was sure she'd get it in the end. She was always saying so."

Busby pounced on that. "Your wife told you she had expectations from her mother?"

Sam looked loftily at him. "Oh, yeah. She used to say her mother was on the way out, bad heart and everything. She used to laugh and talk about the fine times we'd have when the old trout died. We'd travel on the Continong, she said.

"She got me to try to get her children away from the old lady too because she said if we had them, we could use their money to live on, but that fell through. We'd have tried again though. Em said she couldn't live on the money her father left her. She needed a bit more than that and her mother had plenty.

"She often used to say to me that she wished her mother was dead, so it wasn't really a surprise to me when that little maid came down to Brixton to tell me she'd hit her with the poker and seen her off."

"Why didn't you do what she asked and go up to Dulwich to support your wife during her time of trouble?" asked Busby.

Sam cocked a knowing eye. "No way. If she'd seen off the old lady I wasn't going to get involved. It was best for me to stay well away, wasn't it?"

Portbury's evidence swung the court's sympathies against the accused. Not only did he imply that she could have deliberately attacked her mother and caused her death, but the spectators also considered that any woman so ill-advised as to marry such a young ruffian had to be suspect. Their unanimous verdict was that Amelia was guilty of causing the death of her mother.

The judge shared their opinion.

"Mrs Portbury," he told the jury and the shaking, white-faced spectre sitting in the dock before him, "is not only a foolish woman but a wicked one, too. She was plotting to seize her children away from the care of her mother only to get her hands on their money and then, when she was thwarted, she attacked her aged mother and thereby killed her.

"The charge against her is murder and, suspect medical evidence apart, that charge can stand, because if a victim dies within one year and a day of being attacked, they can be said to have been murdered. Her mother died within four days of being attacked by Mrs Portbury."

It was a surprise to everyone when the gentlemen of the jury turned out to be more merciful. When they returned after taking only thirty minutes to reach their verdict, the foreman said that they had found the prisoner guilty of manslaughter rather than murder and they wanted the judge to spare her life.

He seemed almost disappointed as he acceded to this verdict, telling a ghastly-looking Amelia Portbury, "It is fortunate for you that this jury has seen fit to spare your life. Instead of sending you to the gallows, I will commit you to prison for a period of twenty-five years – with hard labour. Take her away."

Chapter Three

Alice Grey's Story
October 30th, 1900

I've never seen a crowd like it, I really haven't. They were packed like herrings in a basket all the way from Paddington Station to the City. The omnibus Dora and I took from the Elephant and Castle got stuck at Westminster so we had to get out and walk.

My feet were aching by the time we reached St Paul's but Dora was so keen to see this special Thanksgiving Parade welcoming the men of the City of London Imperial Volunteers back from South Africa that I didn't let on I was tired. I was surprised that she could bear to watch this sort of parade at all because her husband Tom had been killed last year at Magersfontein while he and his men were fighting alongside the Volunteers.

When I asked Dora if seeing them might not be too upsetting for her, she shook her head.

"Oh no, I want to go because some of the men in the parade would have known Tom. They would remember him. I want to see them come home."

She was really set on it so I went to keep her company because I was pretty sure the sight of the soldiers would disturb her more than she thought. My husband Aaron wouldn't come with us though Tom was his only brother and they were very close. I've never seen him so upset as he was when the news came that Tom was killed. He and Tom were especially fond of each other because their parents had died when Tom was sixteen and Aaron a year younger so they sort of looked after each other till Tom joined up.

Aaron's been against the war from the beginning and he's always telling Dora and me that the government is mismanaging it. The other day he was reading the newspaper and threw it down on the floor in a temper when he read that Lord Roberts had issued a message assuring the British public that the war was over.

"Damned fool," said Aaron, "it's hardly started. The Boers aren't going to give in so easily. There's a lot more than Tom going to lose their lives before this fiasco's over."

When he heard that Dora wanted to go to the parade, he was about to launch into one of his anti-war speeches but I stopped him with a look. If Dora wants to go, let her, I thought. I'm always having to try to stop them arguing because Dora worships the old queen and the royal family and thinks Lord Shaftesbury and the Tories are great men but Aaron is a follower of Keir Hardie who Dora is sure is the devil reborn.

It's been lucky that Tom and Aaron married women who get on well together, for Dora and I have been friends since we were girls and worked as maids in the same household. In fact, it was because we always kept up that I met Aaron. That was a lucky day for me.

By the time we reached the open ground in front of St Paul's my feet were throbbing but I soon forgot the discomfort when the men came marching along behind a big brass band, looking really grand in their khaki uniforms. Then they all stood in line and saluted under the flags and bunting while some clergymen said prayers over them.

At that point poor Dora began to cry, as I knew she would, and I put my arm round her to give her a bit of comfort. I was standing hugging her and whispering "There, there" when I noticed that a woman immediately behind us in the crowd was crying too.

She was a tall thin woman, dressed all in black, but very shabby and poor-looking, and she was alone, just standing there weeping and scrubbing at her eyes with a scrap of hanky. But the funny thing was she had absolutely no expression on her face, none at all. It was like a mask, set and hard, and she was staring straight ahead of her at the soldiers as if there was not another soul around, though people were pressed up against us on every side. She didn't seem to know or care that anybody else in the world even existed. My first thought was to give the poor soul some word of comfort, thinking that, like Dora, she'd lost somebody. It would be her son probably because she wasn't young and her face was all wrinkled and old-looking. But when I opened my mouth to speak, something stopped me. It was if a cold hand gripped my heart and for a moment I found it difficult to breathe.

I know that woman, I thought, and because I know her I don't want to speak to her. In fact I was afraid of her for some reason.

Now that's an odd thing. Normally if I see somebody I know I always want to speak, and if I spot a friend on the street or in a crowd, I'll go out of my way to talk to them. Aaron says I'm too friendly and gabby sometimes: that I could talk the hind legs off a donkey. But something stopped me speaking to this woman and, though I couldn't remember who she was, I instinctively wanted to get away from her. She meant trouble.

Dora had her head on my shoulder sobbing away and I patted her back till she recovered herself. She's a brave person, Dora, and soon she was standing up straight and waving her little flag. She was determined not to let Tom down because he had been a regular soldier and proud of his calling.

The woman behind us still stood there weeping too. She didn't have a flag and she didn't cheer or shout hooray. She just stood like a statue, towering over us because both Dora and I are small women. The top of my head is level with Aaron's heart, he always says, and Dora was the same with her Tom but this woman was taller than Aaron and she could see what was going on without even craning her neck.

When the soldiers had marched away and the parade was over, I held onto Dora's arm because we didn't want to be separated as we were carried along in the press of people. Looking over my shoulder I noticed that the tall woman in black was walking behind us but nobody was pushing her along. People in the crowd separated like a flowing river going round a rock when they passed her. They didn't seem to want even to brush against her.

I put my mouth to Dora's ear and whispered, "Take a look over your shoulder, Dora, and tell me if you know the woman behind us."

She looked back and after a long stare, shook her head but she shook it slowly as if she was thinking the same as me, that she knew her but couldn't place her.

When we got to Blackfriars Bridge we were both too tired to walk another foot and luckily I managed to spot a hansom cab that had just dropped off a passenger. The cabbie agreed to take us to Dulwich and when we were settled in our seats, I looked out of the window and saw the tall woman striding out across the bridge.

"Look, there she is again. I know her. I'm sure I know her," I said to Dora who leaned across and stared out, too.

"My God, you're right, so do I," she cried. "It's her! It's Mrs Portbury!"

I didn't want to believe her. After all, Dora is inclined to get fanciful sometimes. She jumps to conclusions and loves a good story. If it's not exciting enough, she'll add bits to it and when I correct her, she says that I'm too matter-of-fact.

"It can't be her. It's not been long enough. They sent her away for twenty-five years and when she went Daisy was three but she's only twenty-five this year," I said.

Dora was turned in her seat staring through the little

back window of the cab. "Well if it isn't her it's damned like her. Look at that walk, the long stride that she always had. And the way she holds her head, sort of cocked to the side, don't you remember that?"

For some reason I didn't want the crying woman to be Mrs Portbury. "But she was such a beauty, and she wouldn't be walking alone in the crowd like a poor person. That woman looks like a scullery maid or a shop assistant or something. I must have seen her in a shop somewhere. That's why I think I know her."

Dora snorted, "Even Mrs Portbury wouldn't still be a beauty after twenty-odd years in prison."

She was sure the woman we'd seen was Amelia Portbury and all the way home kept on insisting she was right, going on about it so much that I was sorry I'd pointed the woman out.

"She still has the same walk. It's her, I'm sure of it. And that face, that nose. Her mother had the same nose. My God, she looks exactly like her mother. Isn't that the strangest thing!" cried Dora who was enjoying the coincidence. But for some reason I found it horrible.

My dear husband Aaron was working in the window of our clockmender's shop when the cab dropped us at my door. He waved when he saw us and, as usual, my heart filled with love at the sight of him, long and thin with the lock of dark-brown hair flopping down over his right eye. How terrible it would be if I was like Dora, going home to an empty house and an empty bed. Her only daughter, Milly, was away from home, working as a lady's maid at a big house in Sussex, so there was nobody to be with Dora now that Tom was dead.

Because I felt sorry for her, I invited her to come in share our supper but she shook her head.

"No, I'd rather go home. I'm tired. In you go and tell him all about seeing Mrs Portbury," she said.

I opened my mouth to say it wasn't Mrs Portbury but Dora only laughed. "Yes it was her," she told me, "and if it wasn't, it's still a good story, isn't it?"

The funny thing was that though I told Aaron all about the parade, and how Dora cried, and what a big crowd there was and the sort of music the band played, I didn't say anything about the strange woman who Dora insisted was Mrs Portbury. It was as if, by not talking about her, I thought I could hold back the memories and keep her away. Because, as I told myself, there was no certainty that Dora was right.

Certainly Mrs Portbury had been tall like the woman in the crowd but there are a lot of tall women around; she walked with a long stride, and that isn't so unusual either. What would she be doing, standing crying at the army parade anyway if she'd been in prison for the last twenty-two years?

But in my heart I knew the answer to that one. She was crying for Edward.

I suppose it's about time I explained myself and told how it came about that I once knew the infamous Mrs Portbury; the woman who was sent to prison for killing her own mother.

Before I married Aaron Gilland, my name was Alice Grey and I worked as a parlour maid for Mrs

Julia Ares, the mother and victim of Mrs Portbury. Dora worked there too – she was the table maid, and because she's two years older than me she was my senior, but she never ordered me around and we were good friends right from the day I started.

Dora and I were together in the kitchen on the morning that Mrs Ares and Mrs Portbury had their last terrible fight, and we were there too on the day Mrs Ares died and her niece Mrs Downs sent for the police.

I've never seen anyone in such a terrible state as Mrs Portbury when she was taken away after being charged with her mother's murder. She was moaning like a hurt animal, her beautiful dark hair was all tangled as if she'd been trying to pull it out by the roots and her face was stained with tears. It was a bitterly cold day and she went out of the house in only a thin silk dress without a wrapper so I ran after her and put one of her Kashmir shawls, a lovely one with a golden border, over her shoulders to stop her freezing to death. When I next saw her, in the dock at the Crown Court, she was still wearing the shawl so she must have liked it because they had let her send for some other clothes later. I wonder if they allowed her to wear the shawl in prison?

I felt very bad about having to give evidence in court against Mrs Portbury because there was a lot more I would have liked to say but no one gave me the chance. They didn't want to hear how Mrs Ares bullied her daughter and the terrible names she called her in our hearing. They didn't want to know that I liked Mrs Portbury best of the two women and that I sympathised with her, though I knew that what she'd done was very wrong.

Granted, Mrs Portbury had been silly over that villain Sam, but he had a silver tongue if anyone ever did and she was badly in need of someone to love her. Her mother never had and I don't think old Dr Muldona did either, though I have only other people's opinion about that because I rarely saw them together. The doctor was always very civil to my mother and me but Dora says he made her hair rise on the back of her neck for some reason. But, as I have already said, Dora is always very dramatic.

Anyway, when the judge announced that Mrs Portbury was to go to prison for twenty-five years, Dora and I were sitting at the back of the court and we gripped each other's hands so tight that it hurt. I wished I could stand up and shout, "That's not fair! She didn't mean it." But most of all I wished I could go to Mrs Portbury and apologise in case anything I said in my evidence had gone against her. I've thought a lot about it since and it's worried me.

I think the fear that seized me when I first laid eyes on the woman who might have been Mrs Portbury watching the parade was because of the anxiety I've felt all those years about the evidence I gave. I can't really remember what I said because I was so nervous at the time, but I wish I'd said more instead of less.

After the case was over, that mealy-mouthed Mrs Downs, Mrs Portbury's cousin, took charge of the household and the children and was she in her element!

I remember the day about two weeks after Mrs

Portbury went away when she called all the servants into the drawing room and told us the house was to be sold and we were being given notice – one week was all we got.

"And," she added, "I would like it to be known that the children, Edward and Daisy, are no longer to be called by their old name, Muldona. Because of the notoriety of their mother and all that's been written in the newspapers about the family, their name is going to be changed."

She didn't say what to.

When we were filing out of the room, she called out to me and Dora. "Please wait behind. I'd like to speak to you girls," she said.

It turned out she wanted to keep one of us on as nursery maid for little Daisy. Edward, apparently, was going away to school at a place called Harrow.

"Daisy is being very naughty and difficult and my husband and I feel that it would be best if she could be looked after by someone she knows – at least till she settles down," said Mrs Downs. Then she looked at Dora who looked at me.

"You do it, Alice," said Dora. "I've got myself fixed up with a new place already." It turned out she'd anticipated something like this and a friend of her mother's had found her a position as a nursery maid in a big house in Blackheath. Dora's not one to let the grass grow under her feet and I wouldn't be surprised if she didn't find another husband to replace poor Tom before very long.

I didn't like Mrs Downs and wouldn't have chosen

to work for her. But, because she said in that dis-approving voice of hers that little Daisy was being 'difficult' when I knew that the poor little mite was broken-hearted and crying for both her grandmother and her mother and no one was allowed to tell her anything about them, I said I'd take the position. I'd look after Daisy.

They made me sign a contract when they took me on. It said that I was always to call Daisy by the surname of Cavendish, which was Mrs Ares' maiden name apparently. I suspect Mrs Downs – who was a fearful snob – chose it because she thought it sounded well born and distinguished. I was also never to tell Daisy about her mother killing her grandmother or that her mother was serving a jail sentence. Daisy was only to be told that her mother was dead. If I let slip anything else I was to be immediately dismissed.

The Downs wasted no time in moving out of Mrs Ares' house. Mrs Downs said that was because they did not want the children to be reminded of the terrible thing that had happened there.

Victoria Park was a very good house, big but manageable and comfortable with lovely furniture because Mrs Ares' husband had been a wine merchant in the City and very prosperous. There was a lovely garden, Mr Bryce's pride and joy, with fine trees and flowering shrubs. Young Edward said in my hearing that he didn't want to leave the house and he certainly didn't want to go away to school, but no one paid any attention to him because Mr and Mrs Downs had their eye on a much bigger house standing in its own park at Bromley and that was where we went.

"Remember Alice, nobody in this new district knows us or anything about us. Take care not to gossip with other servants. In fact, it would be best if you didn't make any friends here at all," Mrs Downs warned me.

It would have been difficult to make friends because I hardly ever got any time off. But when I could I went over to Blackheath to see Dora and we could talk as freely as we liked because there were no secrets between us.

Dora had found a good place where the family had two little girls, one aged six and the other the same age as my Daisy. You'll notice I call her *my* Daisy because that's what she was as far as I was concerned – my little girl.

I've never had any children of my own but somehow I don't mind too much because, you see, I've got Daisy. All the love I would have given to my own child has been given to her.

I did everything for her, washed her, fed her, took her out for walks, looked after her when she was sick, heard her say her prayers. Poor little scrap, I had to listen her pray to God for Him to look after her dear grandmother and mother in heaven. Her innocence broke my heart.

Sometimes I was allowed to take her with me when I went to visit Dora and the little girls played together. Daisy and Dora's youngest charge, whose name was Emily, were very fond of each other and got on well. They're still friends today as a matter of a fact. The older one, Sybil, was not such a nice child because she was a jealous, scheming little thing who liked to hurt the smaller ones if she could. Dora and I had quite a time watching her. She's married now and living in Brighton.

I was at Bromley with Daisy for fifteen years. After such a long time it wouldn't have been natural for me not to be devoted to her – and she felt the same about me. She says she still does, in fact. She often gives me a hug and says that I'm as good as a mother to her and that she loves me as much as if I really was her mother.

It was Edward who ended it all. It's difficult to describe Edward because nobody really knew him. Even as a little boy he'd been withdrawn and secretive but after the murder, he just shut up like a clam. His eyes looked guarded all the time and he never seemed to drop his defences. He was polite, tidy, never cheeky but you felt that he was not showing what was going on inside him. When Dora and I talked about Edward we used to wonder if he remembered the murder and if he knew about his mother but he never mentioned it or gave any sign that he knew.

Daisy adored him and used to count the days before he came home from school for the holidays but he would shut himself up in his room and read books all day. He never wanted to go out with her or play in the garden like they used to, but mind you, he listened to her when she talked to him. If he was in a good mood, he'd let her into his room and she'd sit on the window seat prattling away while he sat with his books, but he was listening. And sometimes he acted on what she told him.

Like the time when Daisy was about twelve or

thirteen and Mrs Downs decided that she didn't need a nursery maid any longer. What was needed, she said, was a governess – maybe a French one. I was given notice and when I told Daisy I was going, she started to cry and hung onto me saying, "You can't go. You can't leave me. I'll die if you leave me."

Poor little thing. I was the only person in her life that ever gave her a kiss or a cuddle. There were never any visitors from other parts of the family – only that stiff couple, Mr and Mrs Downs, Isabella's in-laws, who thought they were so good because they went to church twice on Sundays and entertained the vicar to dinner once a week.

Anyway, Daisy went to Edward who happened to be at home at the time. He was up at university after leaving Harrow but didn't seem to do much work there and preferred spending time in London with his friends.

Edward put his foot down. He spoke to me first.

"Alice," he said, stopping me in the hall one morning, "are you leaving this position by your own choice?"

It was the nearest to him I'd been, I think, since the day I took him and Daisy out of the morning room when their mother and grandmother were fighting. His eyes were brown like his mother's and he'd soon be a handsome man. He had wavy dark hair and a strong-looking body, broad shoulders and long legs.

I told him I didn't want to leave Daisy but Mrs Downs was her guardian and she had said I was to go.

"We'll see about that," said Edward.

Next morning Mrs Downs called me into her drawing room and told me that I could stay with Daisy 'for the meantime'. A governess would also be hired but I would be in charge of Daisy's clothes. After that, governesses came and went but Daisy and I were as close as ever till she was eighteen and went to 'finish' in Paris. That was Edward's idea too. He decided his sister needed to mix with the fashionable world and just took her away from the Downs.

When that happened, I told them that I wanted to get married. I'd been walking out with Aaron for five years by that time. Dora had married his brother Tom, who was in the army, and that was how I met him. Daisy knew about us and she said I ought to marry him. I think that's why she agreed to go to France because she knew that as long as she stayed in that house with Mrs Downs, I'd not leave her.

She was in France for a year and when she came back I was married and living with Aaron above the shop in Dulwich where we still live. Funnily enough it's not far, only a short walk, from Victoria Park.

Daisy didn't go back to Bromley. Edward bought a little house in Chelsea and they lived there together. She told me that he had been waiting till he was old enough to get rid of the Downs and the moment he could, he took her away from them. His grandmother's will apparently had said that he was to have control of his money when he was twenty-five and on that birthday, he took everything over and found that he and Daisy were very rich, in spite of the fact that the Downs had lived in luxury on their money for years.

Edward hated the Downs – Mrs Downs especially – and took pleasure in giving them *their* notice.

When Daisy told me about it, she laughed and said that Mrs Downs had shouted at Edward. I felt myself chill when she said this because I'd kept my promise not to tell Daisy about the murder and, as far as I knew, she still hadn't the least suspicion that her mother was in prison.

"What did she say?" I asked.

"I don't really know. I just heard her shouting. Edward said he wanted to speak to her in private but she was very angry. He told me that she said she'd given up her life to caring for me. He told her it was you who'd really brought me up and all she and her husband had done was live like a lord and lady on our grandmother's money. Now they've gone back to Camberwell where they were living before our mother died."

As far as I know they're still there. Daisy never sees them but she doesn't see much of me either since she's got involved with her political friends. I don't like the sound of them, but Aaron approves. He says they're radicals, whatever that means, and gets into great discussions with Daisy whenever she comes round. Dora says I'm not to worry and that it'll pass soon and Daisy'll get married and make me a 'grandmother' before very long. I'm not too sure, though. She's a bit of a wild one, is my Daisy, joining clubs and going to political meetings. She's always on about 'women's rights' and the 'slavery of marriage', with that husband of mine urging her on. There won't be any grandchildren while *that* phase lasts.

Chapter Four

Something awful's happened. I've seen that woman
in black again this morning. It gave me quite
a turn, because I think Dora might be right. It
could be Mrs Portbury though she's much older
and poorer-looking. And she looks hard as stone,
not a bit of silliness left in her.

I saw her in Dulwich, walking in the street quite
near her mother's house, or at least the house that
used to belong to her mother. It was raining and she
was going along with her shoulders sort of hunched
and her head down so I didn't get a good look at
her face, but it was the shape of her – tall, broad
shoulders, long neck. And like Dora said, that funny
way of walking that seemed to cover a lot of ground.
I was on the other side of the road and stopped to
watch her coming up the hill and my heart jumped
in my chest when I saw how much she resembled
Edward, and Daisy too come to that, though Daisy's
hair isn't so dark.

When she caught my eye I was going down to the
butcher's to get a bit of mutton to make a stew for
Aaron. She was on the other side of the road, walking
beneath trees that overhang a high garden wall near

the old house. They were dripping raindrops on her but she didn't seem to notice though she had no umbrella and only a thin-looking coat that was no protection against this awful weather.

I could have crossed the road and walked right by her but, again, I was afraid. I'm not sure why. I think it's because I don't really want it to be her; I don't want her to come back because it could mean trouble for Daisy.

What a shock it would be for her to find out about her mother after all this time. Then she'd know that I'd kept a secret from her through all those years. She might be angry that I let her pray for the soul of a mother who wasn't really dead.

After I'd got the mutton, I hurried home and put the parcel on the kitchen table. Then I sat down and tried to think what I should do. I was sitting there still with my hat and coat on when Aaron came through from the shop.

"Hello," he says. "What's up with you? You shouldn't be sitting here in those wet clothes. Come on, love, take your hat off and let me hang up your coat."

I looked up at him, standing there in the doorway. I have never before kept a secret from Aaron and normally take all my worries to him, but till now I haven't told him about seeing Mrs Portbury at the parade two days ago. I thought if I didn't talk about it, it hadn't happened.

"Aaron," I say, "I think Mrs Portbury's come back."

Then I started to cry.

He limped across the floor, dragging his bad leg, and lifted the cat off the other kitchen chair so he could sit down beside me and take my hand. It was very cold and he chafed it gently as he asked, "How do you know that?"

"Because I've seen her."

"Where?"

"The first time I saw her was at the parade at St Paul's – Dora saw her too then. But today it was near Victoria Park; her mother's old house."

His eyes were fixed on my face and I knew he was wondering if I'd been seeing ghosts or something. He was well aware how much the murder in Victoria Park had upset me.

"Are you feeling all right now?" he asked.

I gave him my other hand to warm and nodded my head. "It *was* her, Aaron. I'm pretty sure it was. The first time I saw her I wasn't sure but Dora was, and this time I'm almost certain. Besides she was walking towards Victoria Park."

"If it was Mrs Portbury, I'd think Victoria Park was the last place in the world she'd want to go to," he said. Then he frowned and added, "She was sentenced to twenty-five years wasn't she? In 1878, wasn't it? What month?"

"April. The murder was in February. She was sentenced in April. It was my birthday on the last day of the trial so I remember."

"Then she shouldn't be out till 1903."

"Dora says they let them out early sometimes – for good behaviour she said. I'm pretty sure it's Mrs Portbury I've seen. I wish it wasn't." I let my tears flow. "Oh Aaron. The sight of her makes me go all cold. I'm terrified about what could happen."

He put his arms round me and hugged me tight. "Little duck, little duck," he said, soothingly. "She can't do anything to you. You're only scared of her because of your memories of that murder. It must have been a horrible thing to witness. You were only a child then."

"It's not that. It's not that. I used to dream about the murder but I've not done so for years and years now. I don't really know why I'm scared of her, but I am. It's as if she's a skeleton coming out of a cupboard. What's she come back for? Is it for Daisy?"

"Maybe you should warn Daisy," he said slowly, but I shook my head.

"I can't. That's what I'm afraid of really. I can't tell Daisy after all this time. She'll ask why I didn't tell her before. It's not as if I didn't have the chance lots of times. She used to ask me about her mother – and I told awful lies, Aaron."

"You only told lies because you were forced to, and because you love her. Anyway it *was* probably better for her to grow up thinking her mother was dead rather than knowing she was in prison for murder. But Daisy's not a fool and she's not a child any more. She's an adult and able to face facts, no matter how unpleasant they may be at first."

"Oh, I hope she never has to find out. Why can't Mrs Portbury just stay away? Has she come back to make trouble?"

But Aaron only stared at me. "Maybe she can't

stay away. Maybe she's come back out of penance, or maybe she's looking for her children. Have some pity for her, Alice. It's not like you to condemn the woman out of hand." That made me feel stronger and I began to cheer up a little.

He went back into his workshop, into his seat at the window overlooking the busy road. I set about building up the fire and making the sort of stew he likes best: cutting carrots, turnips and potatoes into chunks, flouring and seasoning the mutton, finally pouring in half a bottle of beer – Aaron will drink the rest with his supper – and setting it all to cook slowly in the little oven at the side of the kitchen fire.

Then I banked up the grate with small coal, put the wire fireguard in front of it, patted the cat, put on my hat and coat again and prepared to go to see Dora. Before I left the house however, I went through to tell Aaron where I'd be.

He had his eyeglass fixed in his right eye and was peering into the works of a little brass carriage clock. On the other side of the window glass it was already growing dark and the street lamps were casting pools of light onto the pavement but there were lots of people going up and down. Every now and again someone would stop and press their face against the glass to watch Aaron working because his work is so precise. He doesn't mind being watched like that but I would hate it.

"I'm off to Dora's for an hour," I told him.

"To tell her about Mrs Portbury," he said, picking up a tiny coil of wire with his tweezers.

"Yes. And Aaron, if you have time, take a look

out of the window every now and again to see if she passes by here."

He laughed. "I've never seen her, Alice. I don't know what she looks like."

"She's tall for a woman and looks like Daisy in her shape but older of course, and she's wearing black – shabby though, poor-looking. Not like the clothes she used to wear. She was so well dressed, so beautiful."

Aaron smiled at me. "I'll look out for her my dear. Now you go off and talk it over with Dora."

"I told you it was her, didn't I?" said Dora triumphantly as she bustled about in her snug little kitchen with a china teapot in her hand while I told my story. I like Dora's kitchen almost as much as my own because there's always a cheery fire burning, the brass is polished so that sparks of light fly off it, and she has a ginger and white cat that is always sprawled along the back of the armchair.

On the wall she has a new photograph of Tom, looking handsome in his uniform, in a carved frame with little crucifixes in the corners. It was taken just before he went off to South Africa because you can see the stripes on his sleeve and the short cane tucked under his elbow which showed how senior and important he had become – a sergeant major by that time.

He was a handsome fellow, but as far as I'm concerned not nearly as handsome as Aaron. I always thought that Tom, with his bristling moustache and roguish eye, looked a bit brutal. Aaron looks like a poet and is the gentlest man alive, though you wouldn't believe it when you hear him talking about politics and the need for the working man to rise against his oppressors. He always gets onto that topic when Daisy comes to call. Then they go at it like a pair of cut-throat Marxists.

Dora saw me looking at the photograph and her eyes filled with tears. "He was a fine-looking fellow, wasn't he?" she said.

I agreed. "Yes, indeed." There was no point saying anything like "you must miss him" because I know she does and talking about it doesn't help much any more.

"Your Aaron would have been as big and strong as Tom if he'd not got that illness when he was little," she said.

"Aaron's lameness doesn't matter a bit to me. I don't even think about it and neither does he except when his leg hurts in the winter sometimes. I think he's the most handsome man in the world,"

"They were a good-looking pair, it's true," Dora said, still all misty eyed, "Remember the day we met them on Blackheath? I'd been trying to bring you two together for ages and the moment you laid eyes on each other, it was love at first sight."

"It was," I agreed.

"But you had to wait five years before you got married because you wouldn't leave Miss Daisy," she said.

"Aaron understood. He said he'd wait for me and he did."

The mention of Daisy brought her back to the

matter that had brought me to see her on a dark winter afternoon.

"I knew it was Mrs P at the parade," she said triumphantly.

"Well I'm still not certain. But when I saw the woman near Victoria Park today I thought you might be right."

"Of course I'm right. And she would come back to Victoria Park, wouldn't she?"

"Why? Aaron says it would be the last place she'd come back to."

Dora stared at me as she poured out the tea. "Because it was her home of course. She'll be looking to see if there's any of them still here."

"Wouldn't she know that the Downs took the children away and changed their names?"

"Who'd tell her? I don't imagine that Isabella Downs would write letters to her cousin in prison, do you? And there wasn't anybody else except the children and they never wrote because they were told she was dead."

"I always wonder how much Edward knew. He was nine when it happened, after all," I said slowly.

"He was a dark horse was Edward. Never let on much, did he? But Daisy didn't know. Doesn't know to this day, does she?"

"That's what's bothering me. She's twenty-five and nobody's ever told her the truth. What'll happen if her mother finds her?"

"I don't think there's much chance of that. The children changed their names and Daisy lives away over in Chelsea – how's she going to find her there? I think it far more likely that she's come back looking for Sam Portbury."

I put my hand over my mouth. "Ooh, I never thought of that."

Dora laid the cup in front of me and poured in more milk because she knows I like it very white. "Well if it was me that'd done more than twenty years in jail, and if I'd been sent there because of the evidence my husband gave against me in the court, I'd be looking for him when I got out, you can bet on that."

"Dora, it wasn't only Portbury that got her sent to jail. She'd hit her mother, she admitted it herself."

"Yes, but Portbury said she wanted the old woman to die, didn't he? He made it look as though she hit her on purpose and wanted to kill her – that it wasn't a terrible accident. I've always thought that Portbury hoped they'd hang her and then he'd have got her children and the money because he was her husband after all, wasn't he? He'd have inherited from her. He took her house and furniture as it was, didn't he? Said it was his because he was married to her. But the old lady had made sure he couldn't get any more by what she'd put in her will, though he wasn't to know that I suppose."

"Heavens Dora, he was never as cunning as that, surely."

"Of course he was. Look at him now. He's as cunning as a bag of weasels."

I hadn't thought about Sam Portbury for years but now I asked, "How do you know all this?"

"Tom once told me everybody round here knows Sam Portbury – especially in Brixton. He owns several public houses and three hansom-cab yards – he's a rich man is our old friend Sam. And he has a new wife, and a family. I wonder if Mrs Portbury Number One knows that? Maybe that's why she's come back here."

I pondered for a bit and then I said, "Why was she going to Victoria Park though? I wonder if she's found anyone from the old days yet. Who's still about apart from Portbury and us?"

Dora frowned. "Well there's Mr and Mrs Downs – they've gone back to Camberwell to where they were before Mrs Ares died. If she goes there she'll find them."

"I don't think she'd be in too much of a hurry to track them down, do you? Who else?"

"The old cook's dead. She died not long after Mrs Ares, and the housekeeper went off to work some place in Scotland, I think, didn't she? She's probably dead now too, because she was quite old when we were all at Victoria Park. But there's Mr Bryce! He's still alive and he's still in the gardener's cottage at Victoria Park. He and his son stayed on when the Downs sold the house, don't you remember? They were the only people from the old staff that stayed."

I clapped my hands. "Clever Dora. There's Mr Bryce. Get your coat on and we'll go over there to ask him if he's seen her hanging about the place."

"Tonight?" asked Dora.

"Of course tonight. It won't take long and it isn't

far – ten minutes at the most. I've got to be home to give Aaron his supper by six o'clock. Come on. Do hurry."

It has to be admitted that I was a little scared when we started to walk to Victoria Park. It was dark by this time and all the gas lights were flaring, but between the lamps there were patches of blackness where you couldn't make out the faces or shapes of people you passed. Any one of them could have been her.

I linked Dora's arm in mine and held it even tighter when we turned into the road where Victoria Park stands. It's still a fine house, standing at the end of a dead-end street with a line of spiked iron railings along the front and an iron gate which always used to stand open to make it easy for carriages to drive to the front door. At the back of the house are the staff cottages and a big stableyard where Mrs Ares kept her carriage and two horses. In one of the cottages Mr Bryce the gardener was still living. I'd seen him in Dulwich from time to time over the years and we always used to say 'good day' but never stopped to gossip because he was a very dignified old chap who didn't like scandal.

He was living with his son who had taken over the gardening post at Victoria Park when his father got too old, but Mr Bryce senior still helped out and gave his son advice. They loved that garden, did the Bryces, almost as if it belonged to them.

It was over twenty years since I'd been in the grounds of Victoria Park and the trees had grown much taller and the bushes lining the drive much thicker. There were no lights in the big house and the whole place looked sinister and haunted – by the angry Mrs Ares perhaps, I thought with a shudder, for when she'd been angry she had been really terrifying.

As we stepped through the gate, I hung back and pulled at Dora's arm. "I don't like it here," I whispered.

But Dora was hot on the trail by this time and not to be diverted. "Don't be silly, Alice," she said hauling me along, "there's nothing to be frightened of. Come on."

"But it's so dark. I can't see where to put my feet. What if she's hanging around in the garden, under one of the trees maybe . . ."

"Don't be stupid. The lights from the lamps on the road will show us the way up the drive. And of course she isn't here. There's two of us to her one anyway. Come on!"

So I went but I have to admit I was shaking and wishing I'd stayed at home with Aaron and our cat.

Once we picked our way round the front of the house it got easier because there was a lamp burning over the gate that led into the stable and other lights shining in the windows of the two cottages. What a relief; everything was normal after all.

Dora prised my hand off her arm and rattled the knocker on the gardener's cottage door. The man who answered was tall and heavily built. He was in his shirt sleeves and had a spotted handkerchief tied round his neck as if he'd been using it as a napkin.

"Is your father in, Mr Bryce?" asked Dora. We always called the gardener 'Mr' because he was superior to us in the Ares' household, just as we called the housekeeper and the cook 'Mrs' though neither of them were married. I never knew their Christian names until they were called as witnesses at the trial.

"He is," said young Bryce – young compared to his father, that is, for he was actually about the same age as us. "Who will I say wants him?"

"Tell him it's Dora Mason and Alice Grey," said Dora.

At that a voice came from inside the house. "Come in Dora Mason and Alice Grey. It's a long time since I've seen the pair of you together."

Old Mr Bryce was sitting in a wooden chair at the side of the fire. He was very white haired now but still upright and healthy-looking with pink cheeks and sharp eyes which were fixed expectantly on the door as we walked through. When he saw us, he laughed.

"Two little maids, eh?" he said to Dora. "How has time treated you?"

She laughed back. "Not too bad . . ." then she remembered that she was a widow, and her face changed, as she said, "except that my poor husband was killed in the war."

Bryce nodded, "I heard that. It's sad. I'm sorry."

Then he looked at me. "And you Alice? Your husband's still alive. He's that clever chap with the clockmending shop near the fishmonger's, isn't he?"

"Yes," I said, glad that he'd heard good reports of Aaron.

"You seem to keep up with the news," said Dora perkily, sitting down in the chair that Mr Bryce's son pushed out for her. He found one for me and I sat down as well. The cottage was clean but sparsely furnished, as if there wasn't a woman's hand involved. I wondered if young Bryce was married.

Old Mr Bryce smiled – fan lines of wrinkles beaming out round his eyes. He had a kind face and I suddenly remembered how gentle he'd been when he carried Mrs Ares upstairs after the terrible fight in the morning room. I shivered suddenly at the memory and Mr Bryce's eyes shot over to me.

"Are you cold, Alice? Come closer to the fire," he said.

I shook my head. "No, I'm not cold. It was just a shudder – you know – a funny feeling."

"A goose walking over your grave," said Dora merrily. She seemed to be enjoying herself.

Then she leaned forward and said, "You must be wondering what's brought us here after all this time, Mr Bryce."

He nodded.

"We've come because Alice thinks she's seen Mrs Portbury recently – twice."

"You've seen her once, Dora," I cried.

Dora ignored me. "The last time she saw her was this morning and Mrs Portbury was walking near Victoria Park so we wondered if she'd been to see you."

Mr Bryce sat back in his chair and sighed. "Why do you want to know?" he asked.

I spoke now. "I want to know because of her daughter Daisy. You see I was given the job of looking after Daisy when her mother . . ."

"Went to prison," said Mr Bryce. "Yes, I know that. You brought the child up and from all accounts you did a good job. She was lucky to have you."

"How do you know that?" I asked.

"I hear things, people talk. What happened in this house kept people talking for a long time."

"Daisy thinks her mother's dead. She's never been told the true story," I blurted out.

The old eyes looked hard at me. "Are you going to tell her now?" he asked.

"I don't know. It depends. I suppose I never really thought that Mrs Portbury would come back . . . I just didn't think about it. I don't know how Daisy'll take it."

Like Aaron, Mr Bryce said, "She's not a child."

"But what a shock! To be told something like that."

"It's a miracle she wasn't told by somebody long ago," said Mr Bryce.

Dora, who was looking first at one and then at the other as we talked, now asked Mr Bryce, "Has she been here then? Was it her we saw?"

He sighed. "She came this morning. The moment I heard you at the door tonight I knew what you'd come for. Poor soul. I was sorry for her when she hit her mother and I'm even sorrier for her now."

I felt my legs shaking when I asked him, "What did she want?"

He shook his head. "That was a bit difficult to find out really. She wanted to talk. I was working in the greenhouse – I help my son Sandy here with some of the light work still – when she suddenly appeared at the door. I thought she was one of those peddlers at first, selling things. Then I took a right look at her and knew her straight away."

"What did she want to know?" I asked again.

"She wanted to know who has the house now and I told her – Sir Granville Morton, MP, I said. Then she asked about the servants and I told her what I knew. She didn't ask about Portbury."

"Did she ask about Edward and Daisy?" Dora and I spoke together.

"She knew about Edward being killed in the war, but she doesn't know where the girl is now. She asked if I did."

"What did you say?" My throat felt tight with fear. Why was I so afraid? Was it some sort of premonition?

He looked gently at me. "I don't know where she is. I couldn't tell her. But I said that you might know and I told her where to find you. Poor soul, why shouldn't she find her daughter if she wants to?"

I didn't go back to Dora's house but made my way home by a shorter road. When I got in, the stew was cooked to perfection and the kitchen was sweet with the smell of it but though I served it up to Aaron, I couldn't eat a bite myself. Then, though Aaron held me in his arms and told me there was nothing to fear, I lay awake all night long wondering when Mrs Portbury would come and find me.

Chapter Five

When I got up next day I was much calmer because I'd made up my mind what I had to do. I was going to Chelsea to see Daisy.

First however Aaron's breakfast had to prepared and something left for his dinner. There was still half of the mutton stew to eat so I put it to keep warm on the hob and told him how angry I'd be if I came home and found that he hadn't finished it.

Then I gave the cat a bit of fish and a saucer of milk before I went up to get dressed in our little bedroom above Aaron's workshop which has a window overlooking the street. All the time I was putting on my stays – not that I need them because I still have the eighteen-inch waist I had as a girl – I couldn't help stopping every now and again to peer out of the window. The road as busy as usual but there was no sign of Mrs Portbury, I was glad to see.

Eventually I picked my way downstairs to the workshop and Aaron grinned when he saw me.

"London dress," he said. "Very smart. You'll not look out of place uptown."

I was pleased and gave a little twirl that made

my long skirt bell out a bit at the hem. The weather had changed and a wintry sun was shining so I'd put on a fine lawn blouse with embroidered spots and a frill round my neck that made me feel very citified. And I was wearing my best boater with a blue and white striped silk ribbon round the brim.

"I'm off to see Daisy," I told Aaron, but he knew that anyway.

"I hope you find her at home," he said.

"I sent her a note by the first post this morning. She should get it by noon so she'll be expecting me," I said.

His eyes were understanding. "Take care, Alice. Don't rush things. You don't know what Mrs Portbury means to do."

"Whatever it is I don't want it to be a surprise to Daisy," I said.

I always love the trip to Chelsea. Daisy's house is beautiful – about a hundred years old, I think, three storeys high and very narrow, with a little garden in front of it and a full view of the Thames. When she and Edward bought it, she told me that the writer Thomas Carlyle used to live along the road. I don't know anything about Thomas Carlyle but Daisy seemed pleased to be living in the same row as him, so I was impressed.

Sitting on the top floor of the horse omnibus, I stared out eagerly and managed to forget for a while about Mrs Portbury as I watched the crowds of people on the streets, the horse-drawn carts, the hansom cabs, the boys on bicycles, and even one or two of those new-fangled motor cars and buses, belching fumes and making peculiar noises. Ugly things. They'll never take over from horses, I tell Aaron, but he only laughs. "They'll take over the world," he says.

I changed buses in Piccadilly and deliberately let a motor bus pass so that I could ride in the horse-drawn one. Better to be safe than sorry.

Chelsea is such a pretty place, almost like a country village I always think, or at least my idea of a country village because I've never really been out of the London area and don't want to go. There are lots of trees, most of them bare now because of the bad weather we've been having lately which has stripped almost all the leaves off the branches, but in the spring and summer it's lovely. Daisy has a magnolia tree in her garden and, in spring, it's covered with great big cream coloured flowers reaching up to the sky. I love that tree and so does Daisy. She says it was what made her and Edward determined to buy their house.

Because I like walking past all the pretty houses, and because the sun was shining, I got off the bus beside the Physic Garden and walked slowly along the embankment till I reached Daisy's gate, which stood ajar. My Daisy was sitting in the bow window of the room on the first floor and when she saw me, she waved her hand and came rushing downstairs to open the door herself.

She does have a maid, a red cheeked girl called Maisie who doesn't know anything about keeping a good house. Daisy does things like opening the door and making the tea herself. She says it's against her principles to have somebody do things for her that she's perfectly capable of doing.

"What do you keep that maid for then?" I ask and she always laughs and says, "So she has a job and isn't forced to go on the street."

Daisy likes to shock me. So does Aaron, and when they're together they pull my leg terribly.

As soon as I stepped into the little vestibule, she gave me a hug and I said, as I always do, "Oh, Daisy, you shouldn't." But I was thrilled really.

"Why shouldn't I?"

"Because I was your *maid*. Ladies don't go about hugging their maids."

"Then they should if the maids were as good to them as you were to me. Anyway, as far as I'm concerned, you're more of a mother than a maid. And you could have been my mother if you'd had me at fourteen."

I was scandalised. "Fourteen! I'd never have had a baby at that age."

"You wouldn't, but lots of people do. It's lovely to see you. I was wondering when you'd pay me another visit. Come upstairs and sit down. You've laced yourself into that awful corset again. It must be killing you."

But as I climbed the stairs I was thinking about what she said about me being a mother to her and my heart chilled with the knowledge of what I'd come to say.

Fortunately she was completely unaware of how I was feeling, thinking my visit was only a social one. As she ran up the narrow stairs in front of me, I suddenly saw what she was wearing – baggy tweed pants that came halfway down her shins and were cinched in at her waist by a broad brown belt. On top she had on a white shirt with full sleeves and a big collar under which she had tied a flowing red bow.

"Oh goodness, Daisy, what have you got on?" I asked her.

She turned, laughing, "I wondered when you'd notice. I put them on specially for you. They're knickerbockers."

"Knickerbockers! Trousers! Oh heavens above! I hope you don't go out in them."

"Of course I do. I ride my bicycle in them. They're all the rage. Women in America are wearing them but they've only just come over here. The ladies of the Rational Dress League are very much in favour of them."

The What Dress League? All I said was, "Daisy, you'll get arrested."

Her face went solemn all of a sudden. "Well, I might, but not for wearing knickerbockers."

When we stepped into her lovely little drawing room, I knew I was looking very disapproving but she put her arm round me and said, "Now come on, cheer up, sit down in the chair at the window and look out over the garden. There's still some Michaelmas daisies flowering and they're a lovely colour – the same blue as your eyes."

"Stop trying to sweet talk me," I told her. "I'm worried about you going out in trousers. It's those friends of yours in that funny dress league that have put the idea into your head, I'm sure."

She laughed again. "I told you that you're like a mother to me. You're scolding me again, aren't you?"

I sat down in the chair she'd pushed forward and sighed. "Maybe, but I know it won't do any good." I wished she'd stop comparing me to her mother for I had no idea how I was going to bring up the subject of Mrs Portbury.

Funnily enough, she did it for me. "Do you think my real mother would have minded me wearing knickerbockers?" she asked.

I remembered Amelia Portbury in her beautiful silks, velvets and furs. How delicious she used to smell when she went wafting through the rooms of Victoria Park. Knickerbockers were definitely not her style. But, on the other hand, she didn't behave in a conventional manner either. Think of Sam Portbury. No ordinary woman would ever have entered into a marriage like that.

"I don't know," I said.

Daisy looked at me and asked, "What sort of clothes did she wear. Do you remember?"

"Lovely things, always very expensive. She had a purple velvet coat with great big sleeves and black fur all round its hem, up the front and round the neck. I once carried it away when she took it off and it felt so lovely."

"Very feminine clothes then," said Daisy.

"Oh yes, very feminine."

In my mind's eye I saw Mrs Portbury as she

is now, wearing that trailing black coat which has definitely seen better days. No furs, no silks, no velvets. Poor thing, oh, poor thing.

"Then I don't think she and I would have much in common," said Daisy firmly.

She went across to the other side of the room and poured something out of a decanter into a narrow little glass which she brought across and put into my hand. "Have a glass of Madeira. It'll do you good," she said.

"Wine?" I asked. "Wine at this time of the day?"

"It's lunchtime, the right time for an aperitif," said Daisy.

"I blame France for doing this to you," I said but I sipped the liquid in the glass and it tasted delicious. In fact it put heart into me.

"Daisy," I said, "do you ever wish you had a real mother?"

She sat down in a chair beside me and frowned. She had a glass of Madeira in her hand too and took a sip at it before she answered.

"I used to. I used to wonder about her a lot. Remember how I pestered you with questions for a while."

I nodded. There had been a time, when she was about twelve, when she was always asking questions. Wanting to know what her mother looked like and where she was buried, things like that. The questions about her grave worried me a lot. I said I thought she was buried somewhere in the country where her family originally came from. I even described the place. Little leaning gravestones, old trees and an ancient church, I said, but I couldn't remember what the village was called.

That had pleased Daisy. "It sounds like Gray's *Elegy*," she said and I agreed. "It might have been there." I'd no idea where Gray's Elegy was – funny name for a place but Dora used to talk about relatives of hers who lived at Bishop's Stortford so it might have been near there. I remember how Daisy had laughed and cheered up when I'd said that. "I'll ask Edward. He might know," she had said.

"Did you ever wonder why I stopped asking questions?" she said suddenly.

I stared at her. "Did you?"

"Yes, I did, because one day Edward told me the truth."

My mouth went dry. "He told you? What did he tell you?"

She was staring out of the window at the little garden below. There were birds pecking around in the bare earth of the flower beds.

"He told me about our mother running away when he was nine and I was three. He said she'd run off with some man after our real father died. She left us with our grandmother but she died, too, and we had nobody . . . only Aunt and Uncle Downs, and you."

Poor Edward, I thought with my heart full of pity for him. But I asked, "Did he remember your mother?"

She nodded. "Yes, he said she didn't care for us

much. He said she was happy to give us to her mother. He didn't like her and said we were better off without her. But he did say the same as you about what she looked like. He remembered her as very beautiful. He told me not to be sorry about her any more."

I felt tears filling my eyes as I said to her, "You must have thought me a terrible liar, Daisy. And a hypocrite too, because I asked you to pray for her each night."

She shook her head. "Oh no, Alice. I knew you were only trying to protect me. Trying to stop me feeling that our mother had left us behind, that she hadn't loved Edward and me."

"But I think she did love you," I protested.

"Well, maybe she did, but not as much as she loved the man she went off with. Edward said he'd heard she went to Italy. A few years ago when we were talking about her, he said he'd heard she'd died there. By that time it didn't seem important to me any more."

I remembered Aaron's advice to be cautious. "Perhaps Edward got it wrong," I suggested but Daisy shook her head.

"I'm sure he didn't. And he never told me a lie in his life. He only told me about her running away because I pestered him for ages. I think he'd have been happier if I'd gone on believing she'd died when I was three. But he told me the truth in the end. He said I shouldn't say anything to you because it would only upset you – and of course I didn't talk to Isabella Downs about it because I never trusted a word she said. It was Edward I trusted and he said he'd got his information from the family lawyer, Mr Singleton."

I remembered Mr Singleton who had been in and out of Victoria Park a great deal both before and after Mrs Ares' death. When Mrs Portbury was sentenced, I remember seeing him in the courtroom and he was grey faced with shock. He'd be an old man now, because he wasn't all that young then.

"Is Mr Singleton still alive?" I asked and Daisy nodded.

"Yes, very much so, though he's well over seventy. He handles all my affairs – Edward's will and that sort of thing. I don't know what I'd do without him."

Edward had been dead for over a year and he'd left everything he possessed to Daisy, who had been comfortably off before but, as a result of her brother's death, was now very rich. Though you wouldn't think it to see her in those knickerbockers, I thought.

"Have you spoken to Mr Singleton about your mother?" I asked her and she nodded again.

"Yes, on one of his last visits he suddenly asked me if Edward had told me about our mother and when I said he had, he seemed very relieved."

"What did he say?"

"Just that's good or something equally soothing. He's not one for emotional scenes is Mr Singleton. He said I wasn't to worry about it because it was all so long ago and quite forgotten. I told him I wasn't worried at all."

"That was all?"

She looked sharply at me. "Yes. Is there anything else?"

Coward that I am I said, "No," but had the grace to add, "I don't think so."

For the first time since I'd known her I did not enjoy my day with Daisy. I could not stop thinking about Amelia Portbury and the confusion that Edward had inadvertently caused. Once or twice I attempted to steer the conversation towards mothers again but Daisy plainly did not want to talk about it.

Instead she was full of the activities of her Women's Suffrage Committee – they were campaigning to get themselves a vote or something, though why they should bother is beyond me. It won't make any difference. Some of the people on that committee with Daisy sound very odd – women who stand at street corners and make speeches, women who smoke cigarettes and dress like men. Oh heavens, is Daisy going to get like them now that she's started wearing knickerbockers?

I also hope she's not giving these women money but I know better than say anything about that because it is Daisy's money and she can do what she chooses with it.

I left Chelsea before three o'clock because I did not want to be walking the streets of Dulwich after dark – in case I came across Mrs Portbury. I knew my fear of her was not sensible but I couldn't help it.

Aaron, of course, was still working away in the

window with the gas light burning above his head when I crossed the road. He seemed to sense I was near and looked up when I was a little way off. Immediately his face lit up with a wonderful smile and my heart was so full of love for him that I felt it might burst.

Even before I'd taken off my hat, I was telling him about the visit to Daisy. He listened carefully, nodding his head from time to time and making little comments. At the end, he said, "You did the right thing not telling her you'd seen her mother. She might never find Daisy. She might not even want to."

"I've been thinking about that," I said. "She must still have an interest in her children or why should she be at the Thanksgiving Parade? Edward died in the war and she was wearing mourning and crying too."

"Maybe it was a coincidence that she was there," said Aaron but I shook my head.

"I don't think so. While I was coming home it struck me that when she came out of prison Mrs Portbury would need money. And who would she get it from? Most likely her lawyer, Mr Singleton."

Aaron nodded. "That's true. But if she did get in touch with him, it's his place to tell Daisy, not yours."

I thought about that for a moment and then said, "I know. What I'd also like to know is whether or not Mr Singleton knows she's out. Do you think I could ask him?"

"It would seem like you were meddling in something that isn't your business," my husband said.

"But it's Daisy's business and that's my only concern. I'm really scared in case her mother confronts her and the whole thing comes out. What a shock it would be for her. I know Mr Singleton is fond of her and he wouldn't want her to be hurt."

"Maybe you could let him know you've seen Mrs Portbury and let him take it from there," suggested Aaron.

"How do I find him?" I asked.

He shrugged. "That's a problem. I've a friend in the chess club who works as a clerk for a law company and he might know Mr Singleton. I'll ask him."

"Tonight, can you ask him tonight?"

"Well, as it happens I am playing chess tonight. Yes, I'll ask."

When he came home at ten o'clock that evening my husband had the name and address of a law firm written on a little scrap of paper.

"Your Mr Singleton wasn't hard to identify. He's very senior in the legal world, very highly respected. His offices are in Leadenhall Street and, according to my friend, although he's nearly eighty, he still goes to work every day."

Dora was really surprised to see me on her doorstep next morning. With her hands on her hips she surveyed me in all my finery. "And where are you going in that hat?" she asked nodding at my ribboned creation.

"To Leadenhall Street and I want you to come with me."

"Oh yes?" She didn't say she wouldn't come. Dora's always ready for an outing. Her hands were busy untying her apron when she thought to ask, "What are we going to Leadenhall Street for?"

"To find Mr Singleton, Mrs Portbury's lawyer."

"I remember him. A nice man. He handled Mrs Ares' affairs. He was very involved in the Portbury business. But is he still alive? He had a big grey beard when we were girls. It must be his son that's the lawyer now."

"As far as I know it's still him, but we'll know when we go to see him," I told her.

She was combing her hair when she asked, "What are we going to see him about?"

"To find out if he knows Mrs Portbury's back. And to ask him what I should do about Miss Daisy."

"Good idea," said Dora.

Mr Singleton's office was on the first floor of a large building in Leadenhall Street. Even Dora was a little subdued when we were shown into the waiting room by a clerk in a very stiff white collar, with a lot of raised pimples on his chin. We had given our names and said our business concerned Miss Daisy Cavendish. We did not have to wait long because Mr Singleton – the same man, but amazingly not looking much older because he had shaved off the grey beard – came into the room and sat down beside us.

He was very easy to talk to and I found my nervousness disappearing as I recounted how we had seen the woman at the Thanksgiving Parade and

I had later seen her again at Dulwich. Our suspicion that it was Mrs Portbury had been confirmed when we went to visit Mr Bryce and learned she had been there asking about Daisy. Then I said that I'd gone to see Daisy the previous day and she told me the story Edward had concocted for her.

At this Mr Singleton's face showed surprise.

"But I thought she knew about her mother being in prison. I asked her once and she said her brother had told her and that she had come to terms with it."

"She thought you were referring to the story about her mother running away with some man and leaving her and Edward," I explained. "As far as I can see she doesn't know about the murder or the prison sentence."

"It wasn't a murder technically," said Mr Singleton mildly. "But never mind. I see there's been a great misunderstanding. Do you think I should go and tell Miss Cavendish the truth?"

I looked at Dora and she looked at the lawyer. "What do you think?" she asked him.

"I think it would be best if things could just stay as they are for the moment," he said. "But . . ."

"I think so too," I put in. "She thinks her brother would never tell her a lie and it would be a shame to stir it up now unless—"

"Unless what?" asked Mr Singleton.

"Unless it is best for the mother and daughter to be reunited," I finished.

"That's what I told Mrs Portbury," said the old man and we stared at him.

"Yes, she's been here. She came to me first

immediately she got out of prison two weeks ago. I had money for her because the annuity left to her by her father has been piling up all those years and I'm the executor.

"I'd already informed her by letter that her son had been killed in the war. She came to ask about her daughter. She wanted to know if Daisy was well and if she'd got all the family money. I said she had. But you have to be careful in matters like that and I didn't tell her that Daisy's name is now Cavendish. To do her justice, she didn't ask. I wanted to see what she had in mind first. I'm afraid that prison changes people. They are often very hardened by the experience."

"And has she been hardened?" I asked.

"She is not the same woman who I knew in the old days but that is to be expected, and in some respects not a bad thing. I'd say she's very angry now but the anger's all inside her and not in the open as it used to be. I'm not quite sure where she's directing her anger though. I asked her what her plans were but she said she hadn't any. When I asked if she wanted to see her daughter she said she didn't know. In fact she suggested that I contact Miss Cavendish first and try to find out how welcome such a meeting would be.

"I'm afraid I haven't done anything about it yet because writing on such a matter is difficult. It really has to be done face to face and I'm a bit chary of broaching the subject, though, as I told you, I thought Daisy knew her mother was in prison. But we have never discussed it between us. It has always seemed to me that both she and Edward deliberately wrote their mother out of their lives. I know for a fact that meeting her would be the last thing her son would ever have wanted. He was quite violent in his detestation of her. I don't know how much of that he passed on to his sister because she is a much less complex character."

I shook my head in confusion. "Oh I don't know what would be the best thing to do. The person I'm worried about is Daisy. What if Mrs Portbury only wants money from her? That would be awful; a mother coming back out of the blue with her hand out."

"Mrs Portbury has sufficient funds of her own for the moment," said the old lawyer. "I'm proud to say I managed to keep Portbury's hands off her money in the years before the Married Women's Property Act was passed. I told him her funds were lost in a bank collapse."

All this made little sense to Dora or me but we looked at him with respect for we could see that he felt pity and sympathy for Mrs Portbury. Perhaps he'd been a little in love with her long ago when she was so very beautiful.

Sensing that he'd given us enough of his time, I stood up to go and thanked him for seeing us. "It was kind of you," I said, "because we have nothing to do with the family really. It's just that I didn't know what to do. I was worried about Daisy. I didn't know who should tell her . . . it's not my place really . . ."

He shook my hand. "Mrs Gilland, Miss Cavendish

and everybody who cares for her has the deepest respect and admiration for you. You have been a tower of strength throughout her life and I can see that you love her very much. Please don't worry. I'm sure everything will work out well and I'll take care of it. If it's best for Miss Cavendish to find out the truth, that will be arranged."

Chapter Six

Amelia Portbury's Story
November, 1900

Sometimes when I think back to the past it seems that I am remembering other women's lives, women I've read about, heard about or imagined. Was I ever Amelia Ares? Was I Mrs Amelia Muldona? Was I Amelia Portbury, wife of Sam Portbury? All of them were so different to each other and even more different to the woman I am today.

What should I call myself now? It's often hard to remember the name I've chosen, especially if I've been thinking about the past as I do a lot these days, now that I'm alone, and because I can change it at will. None of the names that I once had please me any more; none of them have happy memories that I want to cling on to. Especially Portbury. I particularly don't want to call myself Portbury.

Mrs Carey, the woman who rents me this room in Clapham, calls me Mrs Mitchell. I told her that was my name. I picked it because I saw it written along the side of a butcher's delivery cart on the morning, a week ago, when I came out of Brixton Prison. "Thomas Mitchell, Flesher and Poulterer", it said in lovely golden flowing letters on a dark-green background. Very tasteful, I thought, so I decided to call myself Mitchell.

I was sent to Mrs Carey's house by one of the charitable ladies who used to talk to me in prison. Apparently Carey takes in women when they are just out and as confused by the outside world as I am. I had no idea how different everything would be. But then twenty-two years is a long time.

Mrs Carey was not as kind and religious as the woman who sent me to her. She read the note I had with me, nodded and shrugged before she said she might have an empty room. She didn't ask my first name but if she had, I'd have told her it was Gladys. I've always thought Gladys is a particularly ugly name, so that's what I'll call myself – an ugly name for an ugly existence. Gladys Mitchell, born out of a butcher's delivery van.

It really makes me want to laugh sometimes when I remember how I used to count the days, the weeks, and the months when I first went into Brixton as a convicted prisoner. Even when I was tired out from pointless hours on the treadmill, even when I was stinking and my fingers were raw and bleeding after picking oakum, I used to console myself that I had lived through another twenty-four hours and there was one day less left to serve of my sentence.

I marked the days off in a tiny notebook that they didn't know I'd kept hidden. But by the time I got to nine years, they'd beaten me down, broken my spirit, and I stopped caring. The outside world seemed so remote by that time that I never really thought I'd see it again.

In a way I wish I hadn't. Prison was a terrible place but now, outside and looking back, I miss it. I miss the feeling of security; of knowing what was going to happen every day, almost every hour of the day; of never having to take a decision for myself; of risking nothing; of not having to make up my mind what to do next . . . How incredible to remember that I used to look forward to being free.

What would I have said if I could have seen into this bleak future during that time when I was screaming and fighting and refusing to take orders at the start of my sentence. Those years when I sat with my head downbent, forbidden to speak as much as one word to the woman sitting beside me while we separated long strands of fibre from used ropes. I once asked a warder why we had to do that, what use was it? He said the separated flax was used for caulking the seams of leaky ships. Did the sailors know that it was convicts like me who tore apart the oakum that made their ships watertight, I wonder? Would they have cared if they did? Probably not.

Free. Now I'm free after all those years of being beaten, insulted, shut up in solitary for days on end, fed disgusting food, treated like a recalcitrant animal. What a joke. Free. What an empty word. I'll never be free because my mind and my soul are still in prison. Free to lie in my bed at ten o'clock in the morning feeling uneasy because there's been no rattling at the door, no clanking of keys, no shouting voices, no screaming, no fighting – just silence and I'm terrified of that silence. It folds round me like a murderer's arms. It forces me to think, it forces me into deciding what action to take.

This is a foul room, worse than any prison cell. It's right at the top of a shabby-looking house and it's freezing cold. There's a little fireplace on the wall opposite my bed but even when I light a fire in it, the grate is so small that hardly any heat comes out. Ashes are piled up in that grate now and falling out onto the floor. I should clean them up, I suppose, but I can't be bothered. There's a strange satisfaction in being slatternly after having been so regimented in prison. To think that Amelia Portbury – Ares – Muldona – once had maids to do things like clean out grates and polish brass. And if they didn't do it properly how my mother and I used to shout at them!

My mother. I'm not going to think about my mother, not today. Instead I'll think about finding something to eat though I don't really know why I bother. Any discrimination I ever had for food was killed long ago by the prison diet of watery soup and gruel. The best thing for me to do really would be to stay up here till I wasted away and died of hunger. But the pity of it is that I feel hungry and want to eat. My empty stomach is growling away. In spite of everything that's happened, I don't want to die, not yet.

So I put a foot out of the bed and tested the air. The cold gripped me like a vice and I could see that ice stars had formed on the window glass. When I was a child I loved to see ice stars on the windows on winter mornings. They were like diamonds or interlacing ferns and I never wanted them to melt. But in the heat of my nursery they melted away, usually before I was out of bed.

Ice ferns and bed bugs, that's what I have now. It's funny how the cold doesn't seem to affect bed bugs. I once heard that they can live for years in the cracks of a wall waiting for someone to come along so they can feast on them. By the way the bugs in this room bite me they must have been waiting fifty years for a meal. Almost twice as long as I've been away – what an eternity twenty-two years was.

I stood up on the bare boards of the floor, taking care not to get splinters in my feet. It's easy to dress these days because I sleep with most of my clothes on. All I have to do is wash my face – first cracking the ice that's formed over the water in the basin on the floor – then put on my skirt and tie it at the waist.

From beneath the lumpy mattress I brought out the canvas bag with the money Mr Singleton gave me in it and tied that round my waist, too, under the skirt. I never leave it behind and when I go to sleep I wrap one of the strings from its neck round my finger because I don't trust that landlady. Prison teaches you not to trust anybody, especially when they try to be friendly. They're usually after something.

Mrs Carey is not particularly friendly but she is definitely after something. She waits for me going in or out and comes rushing out of her room, rubbing her hands and asking, "Going out, Mrs Mitchell? Coming in, Mrs Mitchell?"

What does she think I'm doing? Turning somersaults? She always calls me 'Mrs' and she manages to get a questioning tone into the way she says it because she doesn't for a moment believe that Mitchell is my real name and she wants to find out who I am. But I won't put her out of her misery. Let her wonder.

Maybe I should say something like, "It's *Lady* Mitchell, actually," in my old Mrs Muldona voice. That would confuse her.

When I was in prison a woman came in who'd been swindling tradesmen by asking for valuable goods to be sent to her on approval at a good hotel and then disappearing without paying for them. She always bought the best – silverware and jewellery were her favourites. Her real name was Maggy Jenkins but she said when she went into shops, she dressed up very smartly and called herself Lady Margaret Jenkins. Apparently, as soon as they heard the title, even the most cautious shopkeepers allowed her to have their best things on approval. She was only caught because she got careless and tried the trick on the same shop twice.

I wouldn't get away with calling myself Lady Mitchell now, though, because I don't have the clothes. What I'm wearing is all I own – a black coat, black skirt, blue cotton blouse, black boots and my hat. It's black felt with a funny high brim and it looks like a pudding bowl. Sometimes I stick a flower or a fallen feather into the ribbon, but not every day. It depends on my mood.

In my bag I've also got an old Kashmir shawl which I was wearing when they first put me in prison. They gave it back to me, along with my old silk gown and flimsy slippers, when they let me out. I told them to burn the clothes but I kept the shawl. The rest of my outfit I got from the charity worker. That and the princely sum of one pound seven shillings and fourpence. How did they arrive at that amount? I have no idea. So much per year perhaps.

I used to love clothes. In fact it would be true to say that what I wore was of paramount importance to me. I spent a great deal of money in the best shops and with the best dressmakers. They all knew me in Bond Street.

I went walking up there, looking into the windows, the other day. The funny thing was that I didn't want anything I saw and it amused me to wonder if any of the women who used to serve me are still there. They wouldn't come rushing to show me their prettiest silks and satins if I went in now. They'd probably wrinkle their noses and shoo me away, especially if they guessed I was just out of prison.

The last few steps of the staircase creak no matter how gently I put my feet on them. Mrs Carey probably keeps them that way so she can hear people going in and out.

When I took the room she looked at me hard and said, "I don't let you bring men back here, you know."

She must have thought I was a convicted prostitute. There were plenty of them in Brixton. "Really?" I said in a surprised sort of voice. I wanted to add that the house looked exactly the sort of place where women would take men and that Mrs Carey looked like a brothel keeper if anyone ever did. She's very short and fat and has her hair dyed jet black and arranged in funny-looking little curls all along her forehead.

"No men," she said very firmly. "I once let a girl bring in a man and he cut her throat. What a mess. It took a week to clean the room."

"Jack the Ripper was it?" I asked without turning a hair. Lots of the girls in prison claimed to have just managed to get away from Jack the Ripper by the skin of their teeth. He was a great topic of conversation among the women there. They didn't know much about what was happening in the outside world but they knew about Jack the Ripper. Some girls said they knew who he was – but they all came up with different names if you asked them.

Mrs Carey drew herself up and hissed, "No it wasn't Jack the Ripper. It was long after his time. Anyway, he only killed loose women and this isn't a house for loose women. I hope you're not a loose woman, Mrs Mitchell or you'll have to find yourself some place else to stay."

"I won't be bringing in any men," I told her. Like fancy clothes, that's something else I've finished with.

I walked to the end of the road and when I reached the junction a wave of terror grabbed me and I wanted to flatten myself against the nearest wall. It's the noise and the traffic – especially when one of those electric omnibuses sweeps past. To me that seems eerie, charging along without horses in front of them. I can't get used to the modern world – gas lights everywhere and even electric in some places. The other day I saw one of those terrible automobiles – such a hustle and bustle. Before I went away I didn't even drive my own carriage and now I can hardly summon up enough courage to cross the road for fear of the onrush of traffic. I sometimes think those omnibuses are out to catch me, to run me down and kill me.

Hunger drove me on though. There's a dairy half-way down the road where I have been buying milk and bread which I usually take into a little park to eat while I think about what to do next.

I'd just got settled when a man came and sat down at the other end of the bench beside me. He was bleary-eyed and unshaven and, as I ate my bread, I knew he was watching me. Eventually I asked him, "Are you hungry?"

"Starving, missus," he said.

I tore the bread in half and passed a piece to him. He wolfed it down and then shifted a little nearer to me on the seat. "You couldn't spare a few coppers, missus, could you?" he whispered.

"No," I said but he wasn't put off.

"Just a penny or tuppence," he wheedled. "I'm an old soldier wounded in the fighting, shot in the leg."

"Where?" I asked him.

"The leg."

"Where in the war?"

"Bloemfontein."

I didn't believe him for some reason. He didn't look like a soldier. I said as much and he nodded. "You're not stupid, missus. I could see that when I sat down. I need the money because I've just come out of prison."

I laughed. It was the first time I'd laughed for ages.

"So have I," I said, got up and walked away, leaving him staring open mouthed after me.

The encounter, the fact that I'd exchanged words with another human being, cheered me up and I suddenly knew what I was going to do. I was going to look for my cousin, Isabella Downs.

There were several reasons why I walked to Camberwell: firstly because I'd nothing else to do; secondly because when I'm walking I can think more clearly; thirdly because I enjoy the exercise, for after twenty-three years with only a prison yard to walk round, it's a delight to see long, preferably empty, streets stretching ahead of me; and finally because I didn't want to spend money on a cab or a bus fare. What I've got in the canvas pouch has to last me for a long time.

I was aware there was a good chance Isabella was still in Camberwell because Mr Singleton, who I went to see yesterday, told me she'd gone back there after my children no longer needed a guardian.

My spirits lifted as I walked along at the thought of what a shock it was going to be for Mrs Downs in Camberwell to see me standing at her front door. I was sure Mr Singleton wouldn't have warned her I was back in the world because I got the impression he didn't like her any more than I do. From what he said I learned that she and her husband had lived off my children's money – and lived very well too, apparently. They'd tried to continue doing so after Edward came of age but he wasn't having any of it, according to Mr Singleton, and he sent them packing and took over the care of his sister himself.

At the thought of Edward, my son, my heart gave a funny little jump and a lump came into my throat. He's dead. Killed in the fighting in South Africa, at Ladysmith, Mr Singleton told me in the letter he had written to me when the news came back to England.

Singleton is a kind old man. Every year he wrote me formal little notes acknowledging that he'd taken payment of the annuity I'd been left by my father and invested it for me, and in a footnote, adding news of my children. Always good news, saying they were well and happy. Then the letter came about Edward.

After that I became ill and they put me in the prison hospital. I was still there when the governor came to tell me that I had been granted a three-year remission of my sentence. "Because of the sad death of your son in action, among other things, Mrs Portbury," he'd said.

I think he was disappointed by my reaction, but I didn't much care if they kept me for another ten years or not by that time. The warders and the other prisoners kept saying how lucky I was. Apparently remissions are quite a new thing – they only began being granted a couple of years ago and I was one of the first long-sentence women to be given a cut in the time I had to serve. It didn't feel lucky though to know that my son had to die in order for me to be regarded as a person worthy of pity. The other things weren't so lucky either but I'm not thinking about them now.

When I try to remember Edward all I can see is his mop of brown hair. It was very curly and he smelt of soap when I put my face down to him. His father had curly brown hair too but it smelt of antiseptic and tobacco and I didn't like putting my face near it at all.

Edward was a withdrawn little boy, not demonstrative like Daisy. I was never very sure what my son was thinking. But he certainly thought, because he was a clever child who spent a lot of time with his head in a book. I'm surprised he didn't study to be a doctor like his father. But Mr Singleton said he didn't do anything very much, apparently wrote poetry and lived on his money until the war broke out, when he suddenly joined the army and went off to fight.

As I walked along I wondered if Isabella Downs had any photographs of Edward and Daisy. I wondered if she'd tell me anything about them. How odd to have to ask your cousin about your own children.

It was a relief to find that Camberwell had hardly changed in the time I've been away. The Downs' house – where Isabella's mother and father used to live and which she and her husband Stanhope took over after they died – stands on a corner. It has a peculiarly blank-faced look. When my mother and I went to call there she used to say that the house reminded her of Isabella – it had the same paralysed-looking stare.

It was nearly noon when I rang the bell and a disorganised-looking little maid answered the door to me.

"Yes'm?" she asked, looking suspicious and I could see her wondering if I should have gone round to the servants' entrance at the back so I put on my upper-class voice – which I'd learned to disguise in prison – and asked, "Is Mr or Mrs Downs at home?"

"Mrs Downs is at home. Mr Downs is dead, deceased I mean."

Mr Singleton hadn't told me that but I couldn't even pretend to surprise or sympathy. "Really," I said. "Would you ask Mrs Downs if she will see me. Tell her it's her cousin Amelia."

Isabella must have been sitting in the downstairs parlour listening because when I said Amelia, she came shooting out and grabbed me by the arm, obviously terrified in case I said my second name.

"Amelia," she gabbled, "come in, come in. It's such a long time since I've seen you."

"Twenty-two years actually," I said as she pulled me into the parlour and closed the door.

Her face and neck were red and mottled as she faced me with her back pressed against the wood of the door. She was dressed in deep mourning but her eyes were sharply alive and glinting with dislike as she hissed in a completely different tone of voice, "What are you doing here? I thought you were still in prison. You shouldn't be out for another three years. Have you escaped?"

"Don't be silly, Isabella. They gave me a remission of my sentence."

"Goodness me, how lucky for you," she managed to say. Then tottered across to a chair into which she sank, keeping her eyes fixed on me as if she was afraid that I'd go berserk with the poker and set about her.

I sat down quite coolly and stared back at her.

"Don't be afraid. I haven't come to kill you. I wouldn't waste my time. I've only come to find out about Edward and Daisy."

There was a gleam of malice in her eyes as she sighed and said, "Your son is dead, I'm afraid."

"I know that. He was killed at Ladysmith."

"So we heard, but I don't know any details. I'm afraid Edward was rather strange when he grew up. Not our sort of person . . ."

I'm glad of that, I thought.

". . . he had very strange friends and as far as I hear so has Daisy. Poor Stanhope and I used to pray for them."

"For Edward's friends?" I asked maliciously and she glared at me.

"Of course not. For Edward and Daisy."

"How is poor Stanhope?" I said, though the maid had told me he was dead. I wanted to hear her saying it and she sighed again, smoothing down the black silk of her skirt with her hand.

"He passed away last year I'm afraid."

I didn't say I was sorry.

Instead I leaned forward in my chair and asked her, "Why did you change my children's names, Isabella?"

She drew herself up in a righteous way and said, "For their own good, surely."

"Why? I went to prison as Amelia Portbury. They were called Muldona. Why change that name?"

Leaning forward she hissed, "I'll tell you why. Everybody in Brixton, Dulwich, even Peckham knew about the case and they knew you as Mrs Muldona.

You were the talk of the district and your children had to be protected from the scandal."

"People would have forgotten in time."

"Nonsense. They haven't forgotten yet. One of your problems was that whichever name you were using it was unusual – Ares, Muldona, Portbury. The moment they heard any of them, people remembered."

"So what did you call my children – Downs? That's ordinary enough."

She shook her head and I persisted, "What?" I hadn't asked Mr Singleton this question because I didn't want him to realise that I didn't know. I thought – apparently mistakenly – that it would be quite easy to find out from other sources.

"I am not going to tell you," she said.

"Why? It's my right to know. They are my children."

"You have no right to anything. You forfeited that when you killed your mother."

I almost hit her then for I felt the old terrible anger that used to seize me from time to time rising up, but I fought against it and sat back breathing deeply. If prison had taught me one thing, it was to keep my temper in check.

"Tell me what you called them," I said slowly.

"If he thinks it right, the lawyer will tell you. He knows. I'm not going to tell you because I don't want you pestering Daisy – Edward's safe enough from you because he's dead. But if he was still alive I know he wouldn't want to have anything to do with you. He once said in my hearing that the only woman he had any liking for was his sister, the rest were evil according to him – especially you."

"I have no intention of pestering Daisy. I only want to see her."

"Daisy is a rich woman. She and Edward inherited their grandmother's fortune as well as what their father left to them – and what he would have left to you if you hadn't forfeited that, as you well know. Now that Edward's dead, she's inherited from him, too. She has to be protected from people who might want to exploit her."

"Is she stupid or something?"

"Oh no, but she's impulsive and impressionable. She's got some strange ideas. Unfortunately she and Edward more or less cut themselves off from my husband and me after Daisy came of age. It was a great grief to us."

I smiled. "And a financial loss, no doubt. Was that when you were forced to move out of the mansion in Bromley and come back here? She can't be too impressionable. She saw through you."

Isabella glared. "She was influenced by Edward who, I'm afraid, liked nobody except her, as I have already said. I brought Daisy up and lavished attention on her—"

"When I spoke to Mr Singleton he said that you left her upbringing to the nursery maid."

She sniffed. "Alice Grey. Nonsense. She was a servant under my control. We took the greatest care of Daisy, even sent her to Paris to be finished."

I was hungry for news of my daughter, hungry for detail, any detail.

"So is she a lady of fashion now? Is she married?"

Isabella laughed, actually laughed. "Daisy a lady of fashion! Certainly not. It would be better if she was really. And she's not married, I can tell you that. At least we haven't heard of any marriage, though you never can tell with those people."

"Those people? What people?"

She folded her hands and reassumed the pious look. "I am not at liberty to tell you any more and I'm certainly not going to tell you her name."

When I left her house, without having asked about photographs and not having been offered as much as a cup of tea, I had the distinct feeling that Isabella felt she had scored a victory. It was certain that I had left her exulting over my careworn and shabby appearance and the terrible change that had come over me.

On the pavement, I stood for a few moments pondering my next move. Finally, I decided I had to find Alice Grey.

Chapter Seven

When I went back to Victoria Park at last it was raining, a cold, grey drizzle which seemed to leach the colour out of everything making the world look like a blurred photograph. It was strange to be walking up the road I once knew so well. In an odd way I felt as if time had turned back and none of the terrible things that have happened to me in the last twenty-odd years were anything but a terrible nightmare.

The road that led to the house was unchanged; the same grim, sour-smelling hedges rimmed the neighbouring gardens, the same potholes full of greasy-looking water marked the carriageway.

My feet faltered and realisation returned when I drew near to the house. Unwanted memories flooded in . . . I paused, trying to drive them away, and stared around. Here was our gate, standing open as always. The stone gateposts were the same, pitted by corrosion and with the usual tufts of grass sprouting up at their base. The drive snaked ahead almost seductively, whispering to me to come on. I followed it. Putting one reluctant foot after another till I rounded the first bend.

Then the house came in sight and I had to stop, filled by a fearful terror. It stared at me implacably, like an old enemy that hadn't forgotten any slight ever dealt to it. Shuttered windows like accusing eyes, the portico over the front door a down-turned, disapproving mouth. For an instance I fancied I saw my mother standing on the step, watching me with that malicious half smile on her face which always prefaced a cutting remark – "Back from prison, my dear. What a delightful outfit."

She was smiling when she told me that there was insanity in my father's family. I'd demurred when told that Joseph wanted to marry me and mother smiled then, too, as she said, "You should accept him. You might never get another chance because everyone knows about your grandmother. He's prepared to overlook it."

"Overlook what?"

"Her being insane. And her mother before her. And your aunt. Raving mad, all of them. That's why I only had one child. As soon as I found out, I decided never to have another."

"You had two children. What about my brother?"

"He was dead by that time. I only had you."

"By what time?"

"When she hanged herself of course."

I reeled and Mother pressed on, still smiling. "Like her mother did . . . and her sister. Keep away from ropes, my dear."

How much she would relish the coincidence if I'd been hanged for her murder.

The house looked shut up, as if there was no

111

one living there, but it was well looked after, the paintwork was perfect and not a single weed marked the flower beds or the sweep of its drive. From one of the chimney pots at the back a thin scrawl of smoke rose to the sky showing there were servants in the kitchen quarters.

I didn't want to present myself at the front door; I didn't want to walk into the imposing hall which I remembered so well; I didn't want to go in at all. Instead, I struck off across the spongy wet grass heading for the gardens where I hoped to find someone who would be able to tell me if anyone from the old days still worked there.

The gardens, as in my mother's time, were immaculate, beds cut into neat patterns, and gravel paths raked to footprint-free expanses of pale grey that made them look like stretches of unruffled water trailing down the sides of the lawn. To avoid marking the path, I walked carefully on the grass till I found myself at the wrought-iron gate which led to the vegetable garden and the greenhouses.

I found him in the geranium house, his gnarled but still careful old hands packing earth into plant pots and pushing tiny green shoots into the middle of each one. They would grow into lovely pot plants with which the maids could decorate the house, I knew. Bryce's pottings-out never failed and were always magnificent.

When he saw me he nodded his head as if we had last met yesterday and murmured something that sounded like "Mmmum . . ." I took it as a respectful greeting but couldn't be sure because I realised what a dilemma I posed for him — his ex-employer's daughter and killer reappearing in such unusual circumstances. In the past I had felt that Bryce's respect and affection was more directed towards my mother than to me, but I wasn't sure.

I didn't waste his time in small talk. He'd never been much of a one for that.

"Do you know who I am, Bryce?"

"Yes, madam, you're Mrs Portbury." He didn't sound a bit surprised or disapproving.

"I've just got out of prison and I'm looking for my daughter. I wondered if there was anyone still here who might know what happened to the children after I was taken away."

"There's only me and my son left from the old staff, madam. Most of them found other jobs, but I stayed on with the new owner, Sir Granville Morton, and my son stayed too. He's head gardener now, and I'm his assistant."

"The maid, Alice Grey, didn't find another job?"

"No, she stayed with Mr and Mrs Downs and she looked after Miss Daisy in Bromley."

"Is she still there?"

He shook his head. "No, they all left Bromley some time ago and Alice got married. She's a fine lass and she did a good job bringing up your little girl."

His hands never stopped automatically funnelling earth into an earthenware pot while he talked and he didn't look at me which was just as well because I was weeping.

"I'd like to talk to her, to thank her," I managed

to say. Then he stopped working and raised his head to stare at me.

"She's married to Aaron Gilland, the man who has the watch and clockmending shop halfway along the main road over there in Dulwich Village," he said, shrugging with his left shoulder to show me where he meant. Then he added, "I hope you're not going to worry her, Miss Amelia."

"I promise you I won't. All I want to do is talk to her about my children. I want to know about them because I missed their growing up and there's no way I'll ever get that back," I said sincerely.

He seemed to appreciate what I said because he nodded gravely. "I know," he said. From the way he bent his head over his work it was obvious he regarded our interview as over.

Why am I crying? I asked myself as I returned through the once familiar garden. I haven't cried for years, not since the first decade of being in prison when I screamed and howled and kicked the walls in frustration. But that didn't do any good. The more I screamed and cried, the more brutal and cruel they were to me. The most horrible wardress used to laugh when she slammed the door of the solitary confinement cell on me.

I think I was probably mad for a long time – how long exactly I don't know – but one day I realised I would have to play the game a different way. Then I became very quiet and docile and hid my anger and my tears. If they were shed at all they were shed in silence, in the darkness of my cell at night when everyone was asleep. But they dried up, like my soul. They disappeared when hope died.

It's difficult to say what I'd been hoping for – to get out? To wake up and find the whole thing was a dream? For the sentence to be overturned? When I accepted that none of those things were going to happen, I hadn't any more tears to shed – till now.

I was almost angry at myself when I felt the tears on my cheeks in the greenhouse while I was tallking to Bryce. I thought I'd got rid of all that stupid nonsense, of feeling things like sorrow, grief, regret or love. Not anger though. I still want anger but I don't want soft feelings of any kind, nothing that reaches into the middle of me and pulls at my guts.

With the back of my hands I rubbed my eyes and after standing for a few moments under the big beech tree near the terrace where we used to take tea on summer afternoons, I headed for the outside world and the present again.

I don't really know why I waited a few days before I went looking for the clockmender's shop. The delay was partly because I was unwell and very nervous after I went back to Clapham from Victoria Park. The pain in my back was almost crippling and I couldn't face another walk to Dulwich. On the fourth day however it cleared, as did the weather, and I rose feeling more cheerful and energetic.

Aaron Gilland's shop had a pretty bay front window which projected into the pavement and there was a green painted door at the side, used both by customers and presumably by the clockmaker and his family, for they seemed to live above the shop. The windows on the first floor had pretty white lace curtains and I saw a cat's face staring down at me when I walked towards the door.

A shirt-sleeved man was sitting at a workbench in the window, in full view of passers-by on the street. He was a handsome lean man with longish dark hair and a narrow intelligent face, bending over some intricate task with one of those jeweller's eyeglasses screwed into his right eye. He was so absorbed that he only looked up when a tinkling little bell told him I'd pushed the door open.

A flicker of recognition seemed to flash in his eye when he looked at me and before I could speak, he asked, "Is it my wife you've come to see?"

"Yes, it is. How did you know?"

"Well, I know most of my customers and I don't know you, and also because she's been expecting you for a few days now. Sit down on the chair and I'll call her. She's in the kitchen at the back."

When he got off his stool and went towards a door behind me, I saw that he was crippled. One leg seemed shorter than the other and as he walked his body swung deeply to the right.

I looked away when I realised this, but he was not embarrassed or inconvenienced by his handicap and pushed past me with a broad smile. "Alice, you have a visitor," he called through the half-open door.

There were sounds of bustle from a back room and then the door was pushed fully open and Alice Grey came into the shop. She had always been a pretty little thing, fair-haired and fair-skinned with china-blue eyes, but she'd been rather too ethereal-looking as a girl. In a way, you expected her to vanish before your eyes like some character from a fairy tale. Now she had firmed up, become more solid, although she was still very slim. She looked healthy and happy, with the poise of a woman who's well loved and possessed of much more confidence than in the past when she had been extremely nervous, especially in front of my mother.

She was drying her hands on a very white cloth and when she saw me she stopped and opened her startlingly coloured eyes very wide. But she didn't seem surprised and she obviously knew who I was.

"Hello, Mrs Portbury," she said. "Has Aaron offered you some tea or perhaps a little glass of port wine? Have you had anything to eat? You look hungry."

All of a sudden I realised that I was tired and hungry. My legs and back were aching again. A pretty painted clock on a shelf behind Aaron Gilland told me it was nearly a quarter to three and I'd last eaten at ten o'clock when I'd had my usual bread and milk.

"That's kind of you," I said in acceptance of her offer.

"Come into the kitchen then," she replied, standing aside and ushering me through the door.

There was a fire blazing in a blackleaded grate with brightly polished brass fire-irons leaning up against the chimneypiece. Two chairs with coloured cushions on their wicker seats stood one on each side of the fire and on the nearest chair the black and white cat I'd seen watching me from the upstairs window lay curled. Pots of plants were ranged along the window ledge; there was a double bookshelf heavy with well-thumbed books; a table with a white cloth spread over it; a rag rug; a carved blanket box on which stood a paraffin lamp with a tall glass funnel and a painted glass shade though there were also glass-globed gas jets on each side of the fireplace.

I looked around for photographs, hoping for some of my children, but all I could see were several coloured prints, mostly views of Venice I think, hanging on the walls. The room looked so warm and welcoming that it filled me with longing to live somewhere exactly the same, not in that miserable hole infested with bed bugs and smelling of stale soot to which I would soon have to return.

"Sit down by the fire," said Alice. "I'll give you some soup. It's still chilly out and you look as if you need filling up."

She sounded as if she was speaking to a child which was funny considering I'm nearly twenty years older than she is. When she gave evidence at my trial she was seventeen and I was thirty-five – now I'm fifty-seven and she must be nearly forty. Sam Portbury must be thirty-nine, with the best years of his life still to come.

The soup was thick and delicious lentil broth with chunks of vegetables floating in it. When I'd cleaned my plate, she cut me a slice of apple pie and pushed that across the table towards me. It was the best food I'd tasted for years. Perhaps an appreciation of real food will return to me in time.

"That was lovely," I told her.

She smiled, pleased that I'd enjoyed it.

"I'm sorry I ate it though," I said, "because it's given me back an appetite. I won't be able to go on existing on bread and milk much longer."

Her face registered concern. "I thought you looked thin and ill when I saw you talking to Aaron. You'll have to eat properly, you know."

"I'll try," I promised like an obedient child.

When she cleared the table, she lifted the cat off the other seat and sat down herself with it on her lap. "Tell me why you've come to see me, Mrs Portbury. Mr Bryce said you'd been to see him a few days ago . . . I've been expecting you ever since."

"He told me that you looked after my children when I went to prison."

She shook her head. "Not Master Edward, only Miss Daisy. Edward went away to school, to Harrow. It was sad because he was very unhappy there. They should have let him stay at home for a bit to get over . . . He was always very angry after that."

I nodded thinking that Edward's anger might have been inherited. My mother was always angry inside and, looking back, I realise now that I was too. It was the eruption of my pent up anger which led to me killing her. I said nothing about what I was thinking, however, to Alice, who was watching me with her frank, innocent eyes, waiting for me to explain the purpose of my visit.

"I came to ask about my daughter. I want to know everything about her and where she is now."

"So you want to see Daisy," said Alice Grey slowly.

"If I can. If she'll see me."

"She thinks you're dead. Mr and Mrs Downs told both the children you were dead when you went to prison. I don't think Edward believed them because hc was old enough to hear and understand the gossip and he used to read the newspapers, but he played the game for Daisy's sake. She believed the story for a long time."

"Poor little thing, has no one ever told her the truth?" I asked.

"Mrs Downs warned me that if I told Daisy about what happened, she would dismiss me at once so I kept quiet because I didn't want to leave the child, she was like my own little girl to me. You see I've never had any children of my own and I was – am – very fond of her. I didn't tell her anything about you but, later, Edward did."

A strange mixture of feelings fought within me – gratitude towards the woman facing me combined with a funny sort of jealousy because she was able to claim an almost maternal love for my child, and because she knew so much more about her than I ever did, or probably ever would.

"Does Daisy still think I'm dead?" I persisted.

"Well, while she was growing up she got into a bit of a state about you. She kept asking questions about what you looked like and where you died, what you died of and where you were buried, things like that. I was worried to death about what to tell her. What I didn't know was that she was pestering Edward the same way and we sometimes told her different things.

"Apparently, one day she challenged Edward about that and he told her you hadn't died after all but that you'd run away with some man and left him and her with their grandmother. He was fond of Mrs Ares, was Edward, and went very strange after she died. I suppose he thought by saying that you'd run away he'd put a stop to Daisy making a sort of saint out of you.

"Then, a while later he told her that he'd heard you really had died in Italy. I think that was where he said you were living. Daisy was shocked that you'd gone off and never contacted them, never sent a message at Christmas or on their birthdays. She stopped bothering me and him about you after that."

"How old was she when he told her those stories?" I asked in a faltering voice.

"Twelve or thirteen when he said you weren't dead, a bit later when he said you were. I don't really know."

"But I did write them letters. I was only allowed to send one a year but I put a letter to the children in with one to Mr Singleton. I thought he'd pass it on."

"If he did they never got it. Maybe he thought he was protecting them."

"But she's a grown woman. If I went to see her now, surely the shock wouldn't kill her. She'd be surprised but pleased, wouldn't she? Or would she be shocked at finding out her mother's an ex-convict? Would I be an embarrassment to her? I hope she's not turned out like Isabella Downs."

Alice drew herself up indignantly. "Miss Daisy's not a bit like Mrs Downs and I don't suppose she'd be too shocked, but she'd be disappointed that she'd been lied to for so long, let down by the people she trusted."

"You mean by her brother, her lawyer and you."

"Exactly," said Alice, firmly.

"But maybe she should be given the opportunity to understand why they did it," I suggested.

"That's what Aaron thinks, but I don't know. She worshipped Edward."

"I don't want to upset her. I don't want to beg from her. I have enough money for anything I need. I only want to see her, to find out about her."

That seemed to touch Alice's heart. "I believe you, Mrs Portbury, but we can't just present you to her. It will have to be handled with care. I'll have to speak to Mr Singleton again about it."

"I've been to see him already," I told her but she nodded.

"I know. I've been to see him too because my sister-in-law Dora – do you remember Dora, the table maid at Victoria Park? – and I saw you at the Thanksgiving Parade and I was worried about it."

"I assure you I won't do anything to hurt or upset Daisy," I repeated, anxious to make her believe that.

"I believe you but I'll have to speak to other

people first. Please leave it at that, Mrs Portbury. I won't just let it drift, I promise."

Before I left I asked her if she had any photographs of Daisy and Edward. She was obviously wondering if she should show them to me and I could read the debate in her eyes, but eventually she said, "Yes. I've got one of Edward taken about four years ago, before he went to South Africa. And I've got a lovely one of Daisy taken when she was going to Paris. I'll fetch them."

She went nimbly up a little flight of stairs which was hidden behind a cupboard door and I heard her pulling out a dresser drawer above my head. In seconds she was back with a black shellac album with magnolia flowers embossed on it in mother-of-pearl. She handled it lovingly, and turned the pages with dainty fingers till she came to the middle and revealed two studio photographs, each one filling a niche in the middle of the page. Around them were paintings of forget-me-nots and bluebirds.

She passed the album over to me. I was almost afraid to look at the photographs in case those inconvenient tears began again, but I managed to control myself and held the heavy book up to the fading light coming through the little window.

"Oh, you need the lamp, I'll light it," she cried and proceeded to do so before bringing it over and setting it down in the middle of the table.

I looked at the left-hand page first and saw Edward, my son. He had changed from the angelic small boy of my memory into a portly, full-faced man with waved hair and deeply pouched eyes.

He must have been in his late twenties when the picture was taken but he had the appearance and air of a man much older. My heart sank when I realised how much he resembled his late father, Joseph Muldona. Looking at him with the eyes of a stranger, I thought he might have been a pompous person and a fop. I struggled to hide my feelings, but Alice was watching me closely as I gazed at him and she said, as if in explanation, "He was very well dressed, Mr Edward, always very smart. He was one of the best dressed men in London."

"He doesn't look like a soldier. What did he do with his time? Had he an occupation?" I replied after a few moments. It was almost a relief to feel dispassionate about this man who had been my son. It was as if I'd faced up to a terrible fear and found it to be much less terrifying than I'd imagined. Would it have been worse for me if I'd been entranced by his photograph?

I looked at him again more closely this time. He had my husband's thick lips and my mother's hooded eyes. I didn't think I would have liked him very much. I wondered if admitting to this made me an unnatural woman. Surely every mother adored her only son?

"He wasn't a soldier. He wrote poetry but I never read any of it, though Daisy said it was published in a magazine that was owned by one of Edward's friends. We were all very surprised when he upped and went to Africa. Daisy said it was because his friend Tilly Dent had to go with his regiment. Edward wanted an adventure so he went too," Alice said.

"Tilly Dent? But Tilly's a girl's name." There was a girl in prison with me called Tilly who'd killed her husband. Stabbed him with a kitchen knife to stop him beating her. They gave her twenty years and told her she was lucky not to be hanged. In the end she hanged herself in her cell. My skin tightened with old fear when I remembered Tilly.

"It was only a nickname. His real name was something like Tilson, I think. He and Edward had been at Harrow together and were friends ever since. I never met him but Daisy told me about him. He was very handsome apparently. I used to wonder if he and Daisy would get married but when I suggested it she only laughed." Alice was smiling as she leaned over and looked at Edward's photograph too. I longed to ask her if she had liked him, but didn't dare because I might be forcing her to tell a lie or examine something she'd never before questioned.

"Was Tilly Dent killed too? In the war, I mean," I asked instead.

"I don't think so. I don't know."

After the disappointment that came when faced with the image of my foppish son, I wondered if I should go away without looking at the one of Daisy but Alice was watching me with such a look of anticipation on her face that I knew there was no way out. She put one of her little fingers on the right-hand page with the same reverence as she would have used as if she was directing my eyes to the Holy Grail.

"The dress was pale green and there were lilies of the valley embroidered all over its bodice," she said. "Edward chose it for her when she was going to Paris. I thought she looked lovely in it."

The girl that stared out of the photograph was standing sideways with one gloved arm resting on the back of a heavily carved chair. Her turned head was crowned with thickly curling dark brown hair and from her ears hung earrings that had once belonged to my mother, long drops of emeralds with tiny diamonds at the clips. I remembered their cold green flash very well for Mother wore them at my wedding – my first wedding, that is. She didn't attend my second.

The face of the girl in the picture was dominated by wide-spaced, honest-looking eyes beneath arching brows. She looked slightly amused, as if she was taking part in a costume drama or playing in a charade.

Alice could not stop herself leaning over my shoulder as I scrutinised my daughter. "She's such a pretty girl. In fact, now that I see you again, Mrs Portbury, she looks very like you, I think."

Did I ever look that that? I wondered. Did I ever look so young, so optimistic, so free and happy as this girl?

"She looks as if she thinks having her photograph taken is a bit of a joke," I said.

Alice laughed. "Yes, she did. It was that dress. It's so grand and Daisy's not a grand sort of person. She's happier in ordinary clothes than ballgowns.

In fact the last time I went to see her she was
wearing things she called knickerbockers. Like
trousers!"

I laughed too. "Trousers!"

"Yes, and when I think how poor Edward kept
trying to make her dress like a woman of fashion.
He wanted her to go into society, but she wasn't
interested. I think she's a bit shy really, and very
fancy clothes embarrass her. After she posed for
the photograph, I don't think she ever wore that
dress again, but it was lovely."

She suddenly took the album out of my hands and
very carefully slid the photograph out of its mount.
"Look at it more closely," she told me and I held
it up in the soft flicker of the lamplight, peering at
the gown because I knew that was what she wanted
me to do.

At one time I was a connoisseur of clothes and I
could see at once that the dress the girl was wearing
was beautifully made and fitted her like another skin;
the satin clinging to her hips and smoothed over her
flat belly. The embroidered flowers on the bodice
stood out as if they were real and I guessed that
the flowerlets were made of seed pearls. It must
have cost a great deal of money. "It is very lovely,"
I agreed.

When I handed the photograph back to Alice Grey,
she said hesitantly, "Would you like to keep it, Mrs
Portbury? Would you like the one of Edward too?"
As she spoke she was taking my son's picture out
of the album as well.

The fact was that I did want them, but I said,

"Oh no, I can't. They're yours, Alice. I can't take them from you."

"They're your children, Mrs Portbury. Please keep the photographs. I can get more from Daisy. She has another one of her in that dress and she'll give it to me if I ask."

I didn't argue but opened my bag and put the photographs into it. Already in the bag was my old Kashmir shawl, the one I have carried everywhere with me since the day I was arrested. As I was tucking the pictures in among its folds, I saw Alice looking at it and the sight of it seemed to make her more gentle towards me.

"If you really want to meet Daisy, I'll do my best to help you," she said. "But, as you know, she thinks you're dead, and we'll have to work out the best way to tell her the truth."

I nodded. "I know. Perhaps she shouldn't be told. Perhaps I'm just being selfish. Perhaps she'd hate me if she knew the facts. Maybe we should let sleeping dogs lie."

Alice's face was very solemn. "Sometimes I think one thing and sometimes I think another. But the fact is that Daisy's a grown woman with her own ideas about things and I know she wouldn't want me making up her mind for her. Please let me write to Mr Singleton, he's got the matter in hand."

I stood up and slipped the handle of the bag containing the pictures over my arm. "I promise you one thing, Alice. I promise that if it is going to hurt or worry Daisy, I won't make myself known to her. And another thing I promise is that I don't want anything from her. I don't want money or support in any way. I too am perfectly capable of looking after myself."

"I can see that," said Alice Grey.

Chapter Eight

The room in Clapham looked even more miserable on my return from my visit to Alice Grey. Though she and her husband were not rich, the domestic comfort and obvious love they shared contrasted painfully with the ugliness and loneliness of my own life.

Until I went to see them, however, I had been drifting, not pursuing any real aim, avoiding direct confrontation. But having started to think about the past, and made direct moves to catch up with the people I had left behind when I went into Brixton Prison, I was imbued with new determination.

When I woke next morning, huddled in the miserable sagging bed, I surveyed my surroundings which looked now even more depressing than they had done the day before. On first leaving prison I had thought only about economy, telling myself it did not matter how I lived for a few weeks. I had things to do . . . things I had brooded over for years . . . and when they were accomplished I planned to buy a passage to America.

In prison I'd heard stories about New York, heard especially how it was possible to hide oneself there, to disappear. Apparently, people going to New York recreated themselves and from the moment they stepped off the boat they had no past. A woman who had been there used to regale us, in whispers, about the wonderful buildings of the city and the prosperity of its people. All you needed to set yourself up in comfort, she said, was a few hundred pounds. Then you could buy a building which you rented out, room by room, because there were always people arriving and looking for a place to live. In time you could become very rich. I didn't expect to become very rich – one must be realistic – but the idea of New York appealed to me because I wanted to be comfortable and, most of all, I wanted to be some place where nobody knew me. Maybe I'd have a future after all.

If I was careful, I had enough money to buy a passage to America and a New York house. Honest and kind Mr Singleton had carefully saved my annuity from my father during my imprisonment. When I got out, he told me I had about two thousand pounds as well as the original annuity coming in each year. He'd had to fight to stop Sam trying to get his hands on my money and told lies in order to fend him off.

"You'll be quite comfortable if you leave your money in the safe securities I found for it," he told me. "But if you require enough to buy a house, for example, I'd be happy to advance it for you."

He was embarrassed that any expectations I had from my mother had, of course, disappeared when I went to prison for causing her death. I have never,

never, never admitted to murdering her, not even to myself, and we did not discuss the subject.

I had not expected to be so well off when I came out of prison, but found it impossible to live like a woman of means. Buying a house in London was the last thing I wanted to do so I only took fifty golden sovereigns from Mr Singleton and put them into the canvas bag round my waist. It makes me secure to feel them there against my skin. They are always the first thing I check when I wake every day.

I checked them as usual on the morning after I saw Alice and then sat up filled with unexpected energy. For the first time since my release I felt capable of doing the task that I most dreaded. I had to find my husband, Sam Portbury. Alice had told me that he was still in Brixton and had apparently prospered through owning public houses and cab yards.

Prospered on my money, I thought with a rush of rage. How strange that I had been shut up behind the walls of Brixton Prison, while probably only yards away, Sam was living the good life. Though I had brooded continously about finding him and wreaking some sort of revenge during my years in prison, I had not been able to make myself look for him since I was free.

That didn't mean I had ceased to think about Sam. He was in my mind continually, and every day I hit on some new way of making him pay for betraying me by his evidence. He'd told lies; he'd demeaned me before the court; he'd been instrumental in having me sent away to that hellish place, the smell of which was still in my nostrils.

Somehow he'd have to pay for that – if I could bring myself to go and find him.

The shock of first emerging from prison, the terror I'd felt on the busy streets of London, the strangeness of everything around me had somehow frozen my fury. It was still there but I couldn't act on it. Perhaps the doctor in the prison hospital had been right when she warned me that it might take some time before I was able to cope after my collapse. She was a kind young woman, recently qualified and very earnest, who told me not to try to do everything at first, to pace myself.

But seeing Alice again brought everything back so vividly that I was imbued with a strange rush of energy; a fierce desire to tidy up all the loose ends. What I had to do after that was meet Daisy, if she agreed to see me, and, finally, set sail for New York. Goodbye Amelia Portbury.

If I took it slowly, I thought, perhaps I could go to Brixton and find out how the land lay with Sam. Seeing me would indeed be a surprise for him.

I was sure that he would not have moved very far – certainly not away from Brixton for it was always part of him. Imagining him any other place is like trying to envisage a fish living without water. Besides, that family of his would have kept him there. Their tentacles spread through the place like the twigs and branches of a tree – cousins, second cousins, aunts, uncles, brothers, sister, parents, nephews and nieces. Such a collection as would make your head dizzy trying to sort them out. They all felt safest ganging up together. For one of them to leave

Brixton would be like the inhabitant of a town under seige stepping out of the main gate and presenting himself to the enemy.

Before I started to dress I took out the photographs given to me by Alice the day before and stuck them up on the narrow shelf above my filthy fireplace. They looked very out of place there – my son in his gentlemanly attire; my daughter in her beautiful ball gown. Never in their lives could they have slept in a room like mine and I hope that Daisy never does.

Again it was ten o'clock when I crept down the stairs; again I bought bread and milk from the dairy but I ate it there and didn't risk another encounter in the park. The young proprietrix, standing white-aproned before a tiled wall painted with a design of a cow and a milkmaid, had got used to my daily visits but still regarded me with curiosity when I patronised her establishment. Today, however, for the first time, she decided to engage me in conversation. "Ain't I seen you some place before?" she asked.

"I can't say," I replied.

"I'm sure I have. Did you used to live round here about ten years ago?"

I shook my head. "No."

"You sure?"

Of course I'm sure. I know exactly where I was ten years ago. I could pinpoint my position to the very cell at any time of the day, I thought. But all I said was, "I'm sure."

"Funny," she said, "I was sure I knew you."

Then I lifted my head to stare her in the face and when I did so, I saw her face change and knew where she'd seen me. She'd been in prison too. I gave a little smile and saw her face go from a healthy pink to deepest crimson.

"Brixton, was it?" I asked. "What were you in for?"

"I didn't do anything. I was innocent but they said I'd stolen ten pound and a gold watch from an old woman I was working for. I didn't, but nobody believed me."

I nodded. More than half of the women I met in prison protested their innocence. Maybe some of them actually weren't guilty, it didn't really matter to me.

The young woman's eyes were fixed on mine, and I could read in them anxiety that I should believe in her innocence combined with regret for having said she knew me. Reaching over I patted her plump arm. "I won't say anything, don't worry."

"It's my children. They don't know. Nor does my mother-in-law. My husband does but he doesn't care."

"When were you in?" I asked.

"Eighteen ninety – three months because I was a first offender. I was only sixteen. I remember you better now. You were a trusty, weren't you?"

By that time I'd stopped screaming and kicking and had decided to play the game. I nodded.

"You weren't as bad as the others. I remember you were kind to me," she said.

Just then a woman's voice came from the back shop, "Megan, Megan, you'd better come through here and cover this butter before that cat gets at it."

135

She rolled terrified eyes at me and said, "My mother-in-law."

I shrugged. "I won't be talking to her."

Either as a thank you or as a sign of solidarity, she pushed back at me the three farthings I'd laid down on the tiled counter for my bread and milk. Thinking it was a good omen for the day to come, I accepted her gesture.

Brixton has always excited me because of the immense energy that seems to surge through its streets and alleys. Even behind the prison walls the pulse of the place reverberated, stirring your blood with longing for the outside world.

On the day I went looking for Sam, the pavements were crowded with people bustling along, intent on some business or errand and not seeing other people in their way. I fought my way through the main street, under the railway bridge that crossed it, and into the wider part of the road that led to the big church. The safest place to walk was on the inside next to the shop windows and walls. I was afraid of being pushed off the pavement into the path of one of those trams or new buses.

In streets leading off the main road, there were a great many new houses and elegant buildings which had not been there when I went away, and I admired them as I walked along. It was obvious that the people of Brixton had prospered in the past twenty-odd years but there was still poverty there too, hidden away in back yards and courts, because every now and again, I was solicited by a hungry-looking woman or child who would sidle up beside me with hand outstretched. I didn't give any of them money, because I was saving everything for New York.

I couldn't remember the name of the road in which the cab yard where Sam worked had been situated, but it was centrally placed and should be easy enough to find. Sure enough, as I forged on into the heart of the community, I began to recognise buildings and knew I was nearing it.

Eventually I found myself beside a big church surrounded by an imposing burying ground. The stables, I remembered, were on the opposite corner of the road. Its big green gate was still there, standing open and giving a glimpse of the immense spread of cobbles that made up the inner yard. It was just the same as it had been when I went there looking for Sam the day after I hit my mother with the poker. For a moment I felt dizzy and reeled a little, not able to collect myself or to remember if it was now or then.

Suddenly weak, I sat down on the low wall which fringed the burying ground. Though the winter sun was glinting down on leafless trees and finely carved marble tombstones, it was cold with a biting wind blowing. Seeing that the church door stood open I climbed a short flight of steps and went inside.

Towards the end of my time in prison, I used to go to chapel on Sundays, sometimes twice. I didn't go because I found any solace in prayer: I went because the chapel was a refuge, away from the din, stink and fury of the main building, and also because a show of piety always went down well with the authorities. It even helped with the remission.

"Amelia Portbury's behaving herself at last. She's had a change of heart," they probably thought and I pretended for them, every week kneeling in the pews with my hands folded, letting my mind range far and near, on anything except religion. The prison chaplain talked to me from time to time and I felt a little ashamed at deceiving him. He was a kindly man but easy to hoodwink because he wanted everyone to find the same consolation from praying as he did himself. When the question of my remission came up he was an advocate for granting it because of my piety and apparent remorse.

In the Brixton church I sat down gratefully in a pew near the back. There was a kneeler on the floor so I bent down to pick it up and shoved it in at the small of my back where that gnawing pain, which I have been trying so hard to ignore, was eating away at me again. The familiar smell of churches – leather-bound hymn books, a faint whiff of incense, dying flowers, candlewax, mouse droppings and dust – somehow soothed me and allowed my mind to range at will just as it had done in the prison chapel.

I closed my eyes and started to think about Sam Portbury. I had to force myself because my thoughts kept dodging away onto something else as they always do when I confront unpleasant memories, and there are plenty of those in my life.

I began by remembering my second wedding.

What possessed me? I must have taken leave of my senses. But when I think back and remember how I felt at the time, everything seemed so possible, so right, every obstacle so surmountable.

We married in a church in Peckham, near where I had lived with my first husband and where I was known to the vicar in charge. In fact he had buried Joseph only two years before he married me to Sam. It was obvious that he was shocked by what I was doing so I told Sam that he must pretend to be twenty-one and not give his actual age – seventeen. I was thirty-five. If the vicar had known the truth about Sam's age, he might have refused to perform the ceremony.

The age difference mattered not a jot to me, however, because I was overwhelmingly, madly, insanely in love. Though I had been a married woman – the wife for fifteen years of a respectable Peckham doctor, and the mother of two children, I had never been in love before. I had never known what it was to be swept away by fierce desire, to live and long and hunger for the sight and touch of a man.

Although he was so young, Sam Portbury was a man of the world, much more of a mature adult than I was, though I was twice his age. When we met he was already a skilled seducer for he began sleeping with women when he was twelve years old. Looking back I suspect that my enthusiastic response to his first blandishments took him by surprise. I had never slept with any man except my husband and that was a cursory and often brutal experience. So when Sam turned his amatory skills on me, I was literally bowled over. I couldn't get enough of him; I wanted him morning, noon and night. Even as I stood at the altar to marry him, all I could think about was what we would do in bed when the ceremony was over. I could hardly wait and the hot desire I felt made me wet between the legs when I looked at him.

But how did it happen? How did I get into that state?

It wasn't as if he was dashingly handsome. The Sam of my memory was a stockily built young man with spiky brown hair and a face that had the look of a cheeky monkey. His teeth were wide spaced, with big gaps between them, and his blue eyes sparkled with impudence. I never knew anyone with as sharp a wit as Sam and his ability to cap a saying, give a sharp retort or outsmart other people, was masterly. He was the epitome of a card.

When he walked he had a little swagger which showed how confident he was in himself for I don't think he ever had a moment of self-doubt in all his born days. Ask Sam to stand up in company and sing a song and he did it; ask Sam to step into the ring with a boxing-booth prize fighter and he'd do that too – and always he ended up bowing, grinning and acknowledging the cheers of those watching him.

As bold and adventurous as he was in company, he was twice as bold in bed. Though by the time I found myself in prison I hated Sam, I still lay on the wooden slats of my bunk at night and longed to have him inside me. He'd wakened a part of me that would have been better to have stayed asleep in a woman condemned to more than twenty years of celibacy.

In fact, it's only since I heard about Edward being killed that I've stopped longing for a man. Some women in prison who suffered as I did substituted their outside lovers with women but that was never an acceptable option for me – it's a man I wanted. I like men's bodies, the hardness of them; I like the difference between them and us. The things they need are not the same as things women need. Those are the things I like and they were taught to me by Sam Portbury.

No wonder I was lingering in the church, afraid to cross the road and try to find him. Hate him as I do, I was afraid to face him because of the turmoil that he might awake in me.

But eventually I got up and left the silent church. When I stood in the porch I saw a smartly trotting little equipage turn in at the stable gate. A man was driving it and a woman, her hat wrapped up in a flowing scarf, was sitting up beside him.

I rushed through the traffic, dodging under the noses of a pair of horses which had been terrified by my sudden running across the road, and hurried through the gate. Busy men, some carrying buckets or bales of hay, forks or driving whips, were trotting here and there. Down one side of the yard stood a line of loose boxes, over the half-doors of which horses' heads poked out, watching everything that was going on with eager curiosity.

The smart trap I had seen was drawn up in the middle of the open space and a full-bellied man, pride of ownership almost visibly oozing from him, was standing with one hand on its gleaming green painted door which he was holding open for the woman. I recognised his gesture. He used to stand just like that waiting for me. He had a thick, brown moustache and was dressed in a light coloured checked suit with a cream bowler hat set slantwise on his head.

I remembered how he had looked when he swaggered into the courtroom at my trial. That day he had carried a light coloured hat in his hand. The man in the yard was definitely Sam.

As I walked slowly across the cobbles, I was aware that people were watching me and wondering what I wanted, but Sam cast only one look in my direction before dismissing me as unimportant and turning away again. One of the young stablemen came hurrying over and asked, "Lookin' for sumfink, mum? If it's a cab you want, you 'ave to pick one up in the street."

I shook my head. "Actually I'm looking for Mr Portbury," I said in my best accent. It was useful being able to turn it off and on at will. My voice carried and made my husband turn again and stare at me.

"Who wants 'im?" he asked.

I didn't say anything as I walked closer, but I kept my eyes on his face and had the satisfaction of seeing him blink. The woman in the trap paused in her descent as Sam's hand dropped away from hers and she noticed his reaction before turning herself round so she could see me too. She was young, only in her twenties to judge by her appearance, and flashily dressed with a pert face and rouged lips.

When I was within touching distance of my quarry I stopped and said, "Hello Sam."

"Christ!" he gasped. "What are you doin' 'ere?"

"I've come to collect," I said. "You owe me, Sam. You owe me a lot."

He lunged forward, nimble on his feet for such a fat man, and grabbed my arm, his fingers pressing cruelly into the flesh.

"I don't owe you nuffin," he hissed. "You'd better get out of 'ere before the boys throw you out." As he spoke he was hurrying me towards the gate and I realised he was terrified of the woman in the trap hearing what I had to say, so I hung back on his hand, making myself a dead weight.

"Is that your wife, Sam?" I asked, looking back over my shoulder. The girl had fully turned in her high seat and was watching us sharp-eyed.

"What's going on, Sammy?" she cried. He didn't reply but kept pulling me along. In spite of my reluctance to be moved we were almost at the gate by this time.

"Yes," he hissed in answer to my question.

"If you don't want her to hear about your other wife – for we're still married, aren't we? – you'd better talk to me."

We were facing each other under the arch of the gate and I could see that though he had aged the old impudence was still in his face. There was something else as well, a slyness and cruelty that I hadn't seen before.

"Where are you living?" he asked in a wheedling

tone. "Tell me where you are and I'll come and see you there. I'll bring you some money tonight."

I laughed. "Sam, I'm not as green as I used to be. If I let you visit me in my rooms I'd probably be found next day with my throat cut. Anyway, it's not only money I want from you. I'll meet you in the open. I'll meet you in that churchyard over there in fifteen minutes."

Prison had taught me a lot and one of the things I learned was to watch my back, so I knew to seat myself on a tombstone that could be easily seen from a part of the road busy with people. The clock on the steeple behind me was striking the hour – noon – when Sam came bustling through the gate and paused, looking left and right for me.

I waved and he came over, the old swagger still there, to say, "Let's go some place quieter, Em, into the church maybe, so we can talk in peace." His voice had the old seducing note. He hadn't lost that but I wasn't falling for it again.

"This is a good place. We can talk here," I said.

He sat down on the carved tombstone beside me and sighed. "Oh Em, fancy meeting you like this after such a long time."

His effrontery amused me. It was the old Sam to the life.

"You could have visited me in prison, Sam. I was only a hundred yards or so up the road," I said.

He didn't reply to that but instead tried to grasp my hand that lay on the stone between us. I drew it away. There was not a scrap of desire for him left in me I was happy to realise. It was like finding you'd wakened up from some sort of fairy enchantment. Now I disliked him intensely and was determined to outwit him.

"You treated me abominably, Sam. Why did you tell lies at my trial?"

He opened his blue eyes – bloodshot now – very wide.

"Lies?" he asked. "I didn't tell no lies, Em."

"Why did you tell the judge that I wanted my mother dead and promised to take you abroad if I could be rid of her?"

"I never said that. You've imagined it."

I shrugged. "Doesn't matter now. I've served my time and that judge would probably have sent me away for all those years anyway. I could tell he didn't like me. He didn't like women, I think."

"And you were very beautiful," said Sam softly.

I glared at him. "Did you want me hanged, Sam? Did you think if you painted me as a wicked woman they'd hang me?"

"Christ Em!" he cried. "I loved you. I married you, didn't I?"

"Yes, and you're still married to me, God help me. If I wanted I could get you had up for bigamy. You are married to that woman over there too, aren't you? Or at least she thinks she's married to you. Have you any children?"

He decided to tell me the truth for some reason. "She's my second wife. The first one died. I've five children – four by the first and one by her."

"You've been busy while I've been away," I said

bitterly. "Did you say anything about me or did you say I'd died?" Like my son did, I thought.

"I said you was dead. I got a certificate from a mate."

What I'd learned in prison made me know that such things were only too easy to arrange. I was probably lucky he hadn't organised my death inside. He looked as if he could have.

"How long after my sentencing did you get married?" I asked him.

He shifted a little on the tombstone which was obviously making him uncomfortable. "A couple of months. She knew we wasn't really married because she knew about you. It didn't matter to her."

"Quick work. Was she some woman you'd been involved with before – before my mother died?"

"I knew her, yes."

I sighed. "Wasn't I the world's biggest fool!"

"It was you that whacked the old girl, Em, it was you that killed her, not me," said Sam.

I glared at him. "But after I went away you made off with my property, didn't you? Was it my money that started you in business? I hear you're very prosperous, running hansom cabs and owning public houses. You're a rich man, Sam. Did my money give you a start? Because you had nothing when I married you."

"I only took what was due to me. I was your husband, wasn't I? I kept the house and what was in it. I was entitled to it. You didn't expect me to walk off and go to live in the street, did you?"

And you tried to get your hands on my annuity

as well, I thought but said aloud, "Did you and your next wife live in my house?"

He shook his head. "I sold it."

"And kept the money."

Silence fell between us, but after a bit he asked, "How much do you want?"

"I don't know. I came here today because I thought you owed me money but now I'm not so sure. I think you owe me my life."

This was lost on him. Pulling a gold watch out of the pocket of his waistcoat, he said, "I 'aven't got all day. I'll give you a couple of hundred. If . . ."

"*If?*"

"If you push off and never come back."

I didn't answer him. Instead I stared out over the churchyard and asked, "Is your mother still alive, Sam?"

"The old lady died last year. The old man died long ago."

"How old was she?"

Irritated, he said, "She was sixty-five. Are you going to take the money and push off? Go away some place."

Sixty-five last year, I thought. She was only a few years older than me but I'd thought she was a different generation. I let her browbeat and bully me. I looked away while she stole things from my house and belittled me to her son because I was afraid of her.

"Actually," I said, "I'm thinking about going to America."

"Good idea," said Sam, "and change your name. Portbury's too . . ."

"Too well known round here for your good. I have changed my name. I call myself Mrs Mitchell now."

He looked relieved and let out a big sigh of relief.

"Look Em, just you sit here for a minute and I'll go across the road and get you some money. You look as if you could use it. You used to turn yourself out real smart and that coat's a disgrace."

"Was that what you liked about me? My fine clothes," I asked.

His eyes glinted. "That, and other things. You were like a snake in bed."

I looked back at him and wondered again at the woman I once was. What passions had driven that woman called Amelia Portbury?

"I'll go across the road and get you some money. I won't be able to get it all but I'll be able to lay my hands on about twenty or thirty pounds and you can get the rest later." He was on his feet and standing in front of me with an ingratiating smile on his face. Hypnotised for a moment, I nodded and he hurried away leaving me sitting there knowing I'd done the wrong thing for some reason.

It wasn't long before he was back. The pale winter sun had disappeared behind a bank of cloud and it was becoming very cold indeed when he counted out thirty-five gold sovereigns onto the tombstone. "There you are, enough for a good feed

and some nice things to wear. Get yourself a fur
and a new hat."

I scooped the money into my hands and poured
the coins into my holdall.

"If you'll go to America I'll make it two fifty,
Em," he said.

"And if I don't?"

"If you don't you'll never sleep easy in your bed
at night. If you threaten me, I'll fix you. I'm not one
to be mucked about with. Think about it. Come back
here tomorrow and tell me what you've decided."

Then he swaggered off through the gravestones
to the gate. As I watched him go, a cold hand of
fear gripped my heart.

Chapter Nine

All the time I was walking home to Clapham through the teeming streets, I worried because I knew that what I had done was wrong. I knew I had made a mistake somewhere but was unable to exactly pinpoint what it was.

When I was in prison I thought I had sorted myself out, become more worldly-wise and perhaps that was true when I was in there. But the outside world was like a jungle to me and I knew that, once again, in my dealings with Sam Portbury I had taken a false step.

Should I have refused his money? Should I never have gone to see him in the first place? Over and over I debated the questions without finding any satisfactory answers. Then, just as I was turning into the street in Clapham where I lived, I realised that I was being followed. Immediately it struck me that my biggest mistake was telling Sam the name I was using now.

A man was tagging on behind me, and he had been there for some time because when I glanced over my shoulder and saw him dodging into an open gateway, I recognised him. It was the man who had first spoken to me when I went into Portbury's yard.

You fool, I told myself. He only went back to get you money so he could tell that man to find out where you lived. You fell for it, hook, line and sinker. You even told him your name, 'I call myself Mrs Mitchell,' I'd said. What would be his next move? I wouldn't put it past him to have me suffer a convenient accident. I'd better move as fast as I could.

If I was going to bolt there was no point trying to conceal where I lodged from my shadow, so I pretended to be unaware of him, stopped at Mrs Carey's house and turned the handle, for the door was always left unlocked during the day. When I was halfway up the stairs, I peered out of the landing window and saw Sam's man standing under a tree on the other side of the road. Then I went upstairs and deliberately let him see me standing in the window of my room. Immediately I did that, he turned and walked away. My hideaway was discovered.

It only took a few moments to throw my possessions into my big carrying bag. The precious photographs went in last, wrapped again in the Kashmir shawl. Then I hurried downstairs and knocked on Mrs Carey's door.

"I'm leaving," I said, and handed her three sovereigns. It was more than I owed and she took them without protest or asking why I was going so precipitately.

What she did say was, "If anyone comes asking for you what do I say?"

"Don't tell anybody anything about me. You don't know where I'm going so you won't be able to help them," was my reply. I didn't know where I was going myself.

Gripping my bag tightly I hurried up to the main road and on impulse turned into the dairy where my new friend Megan was serving a neatly patted pound of bright-yellow butter to a talkative woman. When the transaction was over she turned to me and I asked for a mug of milk thinking, milk's all I seem to live on those days.

As she passed it over she said, "You're looking very peaky. Is that all you ever eat?"

I nodded. "More or less."

"Come through the back and I'll give you a slice of beef. We've plenty of food. My man's a good provider."

The dairy back shop was scrubbed as clean as a hospital operating theatre, and the little parlour which opened off that was almost as clinically clean without any of the signs of cosy domesticity that were to be seen in Alice Grey's home.

Megan gestured to a chair beside the deal table and said, "My mother-in-law's upstairs having her afternoon sleep. She won't be down for another half hour. Sit down and eat in peace. I wanted to thank you for what you did for me when I was in jail. You stopped a gang of them beating me up – and worse maybe."

A fairly common occurrence in that prison, I thought. Though I couldn't remember the particular occasion, I nodded as if I did. The women warders were the worst for picking on vulnerable young women.

Megan was leaning on the table looking at me as she spoke, "I was terrified and you were the only one that was kind to me."

Was I kind? I don't think anyone ever called me that before. "How old were you?" I asked.

"Sixteen and scared to death."

And pretty as a picture, I bet, with round rosy cheeks and curling black hair. Just the sort that attracted trouble from the mannish warders and the coarser prisoners for one reason or another. Usually another. If they didn't agree to share their pursuer's bed, they were beaten up and brutalised. I had suffered unwanted approaches at the beginning of my time but my haughty air and upper-class accent protected me because they were afraid that I might have friends in high places and my complaints would be listened to. I must have used this social superiority to protect Megan, though I couldn't remember anything about it.

"At least you're all right now," I said.

She smiled, one cheek dimpling when she did so. "Yes, so long as my mother-in-law doesn't find out about the past. She'd give me a hard time if she did. This dairy belongs to her, you see, and she might turn us out because she's very religious, against sinners and that sort of thing. My husband has a bit of trouble with the drink and I've two little 'uns . . ." Her voice trailed off and I nodded.

"In my experience husbands always cause trouble one way or another," I told her.

"Did you kill yours or something? Was that why you were inside?" she asked.

"No, I didn't kill him," I replied but I didn't tell her the reason for my sentence. I don't talk about that unless I have to.

She left me to eat while she dashed in and out of the shop to serve her customers and when I'd finished, I tidied away all signs of her hospitality and went through to the front again.

"Thank you, I'm off now," I said.

"Where are you going? You look as if you're moving on judging by the size of that bag you're carrying."

"I don't rightly know. I'm going to look for a place to live in another part of London, as far away as possible."

Her face darkened. "In trouble are you? Where were you staying?"

I nodded across the road and said, "With Mrs Carey."

"I don't blame you for leaving her. She's an old bitch who only buys half a pint of milk a day and waters it down."

Then her face lightened. "I've an idea. Do you remember Rosa Stein who was in prison at the same time as me? A big dark woman who sang like an angel."

I did remember Rosa Stein, whose crystal clear voice used to soar up through the packed floors of the women's block when the cell doors were locked for the night. She sang songs from opera, did Rosa Stein, and when she was in with us, our time was made less horrible. As far as I could remember she had been there for quite a long time, a year or eighteen months at least, but keeping track of time was not always easy in prison. She must have done something worse than steal money and a watch to serve so long but I never knew what. All that interested me about her was her voice.

"I remember her. Why?" I said.

"She and I kept in touch after we got out and she lives in Chelsea now. She rents rooms – but only to people she likes. You could try Rosa's. I'll give you a note."

Chelsea would be perfect because it is a good long way away from Brixton and Sam Portbury. He'd never find me there, I thought. "That's kind of you," I said.

Before I made the trip to Chelsea, however, I went to the public bath house at Stockwell and soaked myself in hot soapy water for a good hour. Then I washed my hair and rubbed it dry with a coarse huckaback towel. When the operation was finished I felt ten years younger, as if I'd sluiced away many of my troubles with the dirty water.

Dressed again, I resolved that tomorrow I'd take Sam's advice and buy myself some new clothes. Not a fur certainly but at least a decent coat and a smarter hat. The clothes I was wearing weren't ragged or dirty but they looked and felt like the charity clothes they were.

Outside the baths an old woman was selling little bunches of violets, all tightly packed together and backed by two overlapping leaves. They were impossible to resist, so I bought myself a bunch and pinned it to the lapel of my coat. While I sat on the train, I kept sniffing at the delicate flowers and they made me feel happy to be alive.

Rosa Stein lived in Sydney Street, in a compact-looking house with a tree leaning across to it from the other side of the road where, once again, there was a graveyard. I seem to be surrounded by graveyards these days

There were soft lights glittering in the house's front windows when I approached it and a lamplighter was walking slowly up the street poking his long pole up at the lamp jets which sprang into life in his wake.

The woman who answered the door when I rattled the knocker was in her late forties and very stout with thick black hair piled on the top of her head into a top knot that looked like a loaf of black bread. The feet and ankles peeping out under the hem of her skirt were swollen and sore-looking so that the straps of her shoes seemed to cut across her insteps making the flesh bulge out on each side of them.

I told her I was looking for Rosa Stein and she said, "In that case you've found her."

"I was sent to you by Megan Davies because I need a room to rent." As I spoke I handed her the note Megan had written.

She held it up to the light coming from a gas jet behind her back so that she could read it. Then she opened the door wider and invited me inside, "Let's have a talk about it then," she said. "Just out, are you?"

"A few weeks ago now. I've been living in

Clapham, in the rooming house of a woman called Carey."

"What's your name?"

"My real name is Amelia Portbury but I call myself Gladys Mitchell now."

She nodded and frowned. "Portbury. I remember that case. I've always read about the big cases in the papers. It was a long time ago, when I was just a young woman though. Killed your mother, right?"

"Right."

"Don't worry, I won't ask questions about that. And you don't ask me any either. This isn't an ex-prisoners' hostel or anything. You don't have to have been inside to get a room here. I just take in people I like or who are sent to me by people I like. If I take you, you'll come into the last category."

She led the way into a room with its window facing out onto the street. The gas lamps were glowing and a cheerful fire was burning. There were colourful pictures in the walls and a treadle sewing machine with scarlet cloth caught under its needle and looping to the ground stood in the middle of the floor.

"I make clothes," she said shortly.

"Do you still sing?"

She stared levelly at me and I saw that her eyes were a pale shade of green. She had outlined the upper and lower lids with black crayon and the effect was to make her look like a gypsy. "Sometimes. I work from time to time in stage productions – operas mostly. But only in the chorus. My voice has gone really."

I nodded. Personal questions were not to be encouraged obviously.

"Why did you want to leave Clapham?" she asked me.

"I got a room there through one of the charity workers at Brixton but there were bed bugs."

She shuddered. "I hope you didn't bring them with you."

"No. I went to the public baths before I came here and really scrubbed myself."

She gave a little smile and her attitude seemed to soften a little. "Sit down," she said, pointing at an upholstered chair by the fire. "You look tired."

I was tired and it was a relief to sit and lay my bag down on the floor by my feet.

Rosa Stein looked at it. "Is that all you have?"

"Yes."

"If I take you in I charge four pounds a month – payable in advance. It's not cheap but that includes two meals a day. The accommodation's good and so's the food, even if I say so myself. My people can be quite fussy, some of them are theatricals."

"I can afford four pounds a month. I have money," I told her.

"As it happens I have a room vacant. Do you want to see it?"

"Yes, please."

The moment she opened the door of a room on the first landing I knew I had found a safe haven. It was fairly large with a window over-looking the back of the house and as Rosa walked across and pulled the velvet curtain closed she

said, "You'll have a view of the garden in day-
light."

There was a wide brass bed with pristine white
covers and high piled pillows, a marble-topped wash-
stand with blue and white china on it, a clothes
cupboard with carved doors like a French armoire,
a table in the window and two chairs, one an
upright wooden one at the table and the other softly
upholstered like the armchair in Rosa's sitting room.
The floor was covered by oilcloth and scattered rugs
and the walls by more colourful pictures, most of
them of flowers.

When she saw me looking at them, Rosa said,
"My father was a painter. Those were his. There's
more pictures in this house than anything else. When
I need money I just sell one."

The fire was laid and she bent down to strike a
Vesta match down the side of the hearth and held a
taper to the kindling sticks which burned up with a
cheerful crackle. The feeling of comfort and felicity
that room gave me took me back through the years
to the comfortable life I'd enjoyed long ago, before
. . . that terrible thing happened.

"I'll take the room," I said and put my hand in my
pocket to pull out my purse that bulged with Sam's
money. Rosa picked four sovereigns off my palm
and shook her head in admonition. "You shouldn't
be walking about with all that money on you. Either
hide it or put it in a bank."

I nodded in agreement and suddenly felt so weary
that I sank into the chair. She walked towards the
door, saying over her shoulder, "Supper's at seven

o'clock. We eat downstairs and I ring a gong. There's six people in the house at the moment, including you and me."

The gong wakened me because I had fallen asleep in the chair by the fire. Jumping up, I tidied my hair and before I went downstairs, stuck the photographs of Edward and Daisy on the mantelpiece where they looked far more at home than they had ever done in Clapham.

Downstairs in the back dining room people were already sitting round a circular table which was covered by a white cloth and loaded with dishes. They barely acknowledged my presence because they were all so busy buttering bread, shaking out napkins and spooning up what smelt like chicken broth to their mouths.

As well as Rosa, there were three men and one woman, ranging in age from very young to middle-aged – the woman and one of the men did not look as if they had yet reached twenty. They laughed and chattered about subjects that I did not understand for it seemed they were both on the stage.

One of the older men, as dark as Rosa, avoided everyone's eyes, ate with his head lowered and did not speak one word during the three-course meal. The other man, brown haired and brown eyed, who said his name was Ramon, was Spanish and spoke English with a strong accent. He was smiling and friendly, sticking out his hand to shake mine.

The food was indeed excellent – a sort of meat stew followed the soup and then came a steaming rice pudding with a crisp brown skin over its surface. To drink we had red wine served from a carafe. I had not tasted wine for so many years that I was almost afraid to take any but Rosa filled a glass and pushed it towards me saying, "Drink it up. It'll do you good."

It did me so much good that when I lay down in bed, I slipped into a dreamless sleep that lasted till ten o'clock next morning. I even slept through the breakfast gong and only woke when a concerned Rosa tapped at the door to find out if I was still alive.

Her tapping woke me and I sat up in bed, totally disoriented, not able at first to remember where I was or how I'd got there.

"What, what?" I called in panic, thinking for a moment that I was back in prison, and she opened the door to look in and reassure me.

"Do you want anything to eat? I'm just clearing up," she said.

Recovering myself, I sat up and said, "Oh, no, nothing. I'm all right . . . just a bit confused."

She laughed. "That was the wine. You'd better come down and have a cup of tea at least." Then her eye fell on my photographs and I saw her give a jump of surprise.

"Who are they?" she asked, pointing at them.

"My children. The boy – the man, I mean – is dead unfortunately. The girl's my daughter Daisy. I've not seen her since she was three and she's twenty-five now."

"Does she know you're out?"

"She doesn't know I was ever inside. She doesn't

know I exist. She thinks I'm dead. Everyone who knows her is worried in case finding out about me is too much of a shock for her."

Rose Stein walked across and looked more closely at Daisy's picture before she said, "She looks quite capable of standing a few shocks if you ask me."

I was climbing out of bed, ashamed that Rosa should see that I slept in my petticoat, but she paid no attention to me for she was still looking at the picture which she now held in her hand. "That's a lovely dress," she said slowly.

"I think so too. Alice Grey, who was nanny to Daisy and who still sees her, told me that Edward, my son, gave it to his sister. He had it specially made for her. It was pale green and the flowers on the bodice were lilies of the valley apparently."

Rosa very carefully placed the picture back in the exact spot on the mantelpiece from which she'd taken it and said, "The flower heads were made of seed pearls and it took two weeks to stitch them all. The material was the very best French slipper satin and it was the most beautiful pale colour, like a tropical sea."

"How do you know that?" I asked.

"Because I made it," said Rosa Stein.

Chapter Ten

I was white faced and shaking when I confronted Rosa in the kitchen downstairs. After she left me in my room, I'd lain for a while on the bed too shocked to move and thinking how terrible it was to have to ask a stranger to tell you your own child's name. Then I collected my wits and went in search of her

She was sitting with a newspaper spread open on the table in front of her and gold-rimmed spectacles on the end of her nose.

I started speaking as soon as I stepped through the door, "I want to know as much as I can about Daisy. It's not as if I'm going to bother her. I'll be very careful. I'll sound the ground out before I break the news to her about who I am and if it's likely to upset her, I won't say anything at all."

Rosa's green eyes were piercing as she stared at me. "Sit down," she said sharply. "We'll talk about that later. You did say you'd been living with a Mrs Carey at Clapham, didn't you?"

"Yes. That's right but—"

"Wait a minute. There's a bit in this newspaper saying she was stabbed by an intruder last night.

She was in an upstairs room, cleaning it out for a new tenant and someone got in and stabbed her."

The breath seemed to be pushed out of my lungs when I heard this. "Is she dead?" I asked.

Rosa looked down at the newspaper again. "Yes. She's dead."

"Oh my God, they must have meant it to be me. She was killed by mistake. I was followed home yesterday afternoon and that's why I cleared out."

"Who followed you?"

My heart was thudding in my chest as I stared at her wondering how much I could trust her. She looked back and nodded as she said, "I won't say anything. I've no more wish to get involved than you do."

"I think it was a man sent by my husband Sam. I think he must have arranged it."

"In that case," said Rosa, folding up the paper, "you'd better lie low. Unless you were especially fond of that Mrs Carey, I don't think you should go to the police either."

I nodded. The last thing I wanted was to attract the interest of the authorities for I dreaded ending up in prison again now that I'd found a safe haven. "I feel bad about it though," I said.

Rosa shrugged. "They'll probably find out who did it on their own, and anyway you might be wrong. Let it be."

I sank down in the chair at Rosa's table feeling very weak indeed while she poured me a cup of tea. When I'd drunk it I felt a little better.

"What about Daisy?" I managed to ask eventually.

"If you tell me where she is I promise I won't pester her." I'd have to meet my daughter as soon as possible and then get on a boat for America.

"That's not really my concern," she said. "I don't want to put restrictions on you."

"Tell me her name," I said. "You see my cousin, who became the children's guardian after I was sent to prison, changed their surname from Muldona, because she said it was too unusual and people would remember the court case so I don't know what Daisy is called now. My cousin won't tell me."

Rose shrugged. "I met your son first and he was introduced to me as Edward Cavendish. He brought his sister to see me and she's called Daisy Cavendish."

Cavendish. My mother's maiden name. A sly jibe by Isabella, I thought.

"Is she still Daisy Cavendish? Is she married now or anything?"

"Not as far as I know."

"Where does she live?"

Rosa was now buttering bread and lifted her head to look at me. "Why does nobody want you to meet her? What are they afraid of?"

I put my head in my hands. "Because I'm a bad person. Because I struck my mother with a poker and she died as a result."

"Did you mean to kill her? If the jury had thought you meant to murder your mother, you'd have been sentenced to hang. You wouldn't be sitting here telling me about it now."

I looked up at her and could barely see her

because tears were streaming down my face. "I don't know if I wanted to kill her. I only know that I was full of rage and hatred. I remember lifting the poker and hitting her. It gave me a queer kind of thrill. I'd been wanting to hurt her for years."

Never before had I admitted as much, even to myself, but I knew that if I had said that in court I'd have been dead long ago.

"Maybe they should have hanged me," I sobbed. "Maybe that would have been easier for everybody concerned. But I've been through hell. I've had time to go over and over what happened. I've had time to repent if I wanted to. That's what they think you ought to do when you're in prison, isn't it? They want you to repent and they want you to suffer. Well I've suffered. I don't know if I've repented but I've certainly suffered.

"One of my children died before I could see him again to ask for his forgiveness because I left him and now I'm afraid to meet my daughter in case she rejects me."

"Did your children mean a lot to you?" asked the dark-haired woman. As she spoke she stuck the kitchen knife by its point into the bread board and leaned her hand on it.

I shook my head again. "I don't know. I didn't realise how much I'd miss them till I lost them. I loved them but I was torn in half – I fell in love with a man who was little more than a child himself and he was their rival for my affections. I never loved their father, you see. He was a very cold and cruel man. It was a relief to me when he died but I couldn't show it of course."

She nodded. "But you played the grieving widow I suppose."

"Yes. In fact I was so confused about what I was feeling that I did seem grief stricken. I kept weeping all the time. Everyone was worried about me. My mother wanted me to go to Baden Baden and take the waters but I was afraid to travel. I wouldn't even go out, so she hired a boy to drive my gig and ordered me to take the air every day. It's ironic that she was the one who brought Sam into my life."

Rosa was still watching me intently. She said softly, "Sam's the one who tried to kill you yesterday?"

"That's what I think, but I may be wrong. I'm still married to him, you see. But he's got another wife and a family. He's a bigamist."

"I remember the newspaper stories about you at the time. Rich widow marries her coachman," she said and there was not a trace of judgementalism in her voice.

The memory of Sam Portbury as he had been, compared to what he was now engulfed me like a wave and I wanted more than anything to unburden myself to this woman. It was almost as if I was in some sort of confessional with a priestess listening to me.

"It was such a thrill for me, being courted by a boy. He coaxed me and flattered me and talked love to me till I lost my senses. When I took him into my bed it was as if I'd entered another world, the world of feeling and sensation that I'd known nothing about before. I couldn't get enough of him, hauling him upstairs three or four times a day. I was shameless. The servants were horrified. The housekeeper eventually told my mother who actually considered having me committed to a mad house – unbridled sexual passion was a mental illness she told me."

"Maybe it is," said Rosa sadly and I knew that she'd once experienced the same kind of headlong passion as had gripped me then. "It would have been better if you'd just slept with him until the first fury wore off. If you were a man that's what you would have done," she added.

"Yes, but I didn't know anything about love except what I'd read in stories and what I'd been taught as a child. I thought I ought to marry him and managed to convince myself that it was a possible thing to do. I thought that people would accept us as a couple in time."

"By people you mean your mother, I presume."

"Yes."

"But she didn't accept it."

"Of course not. She really thought I'd gone mad. We had terrible arguments."

"But you married him anyway."

"In a way her opposition forced me into it. I couldn't admit I was wrong so I married him. I think now, looking back, that maybe I was a little mad at that time. All I wanted was to be in bed with him. Nothing else mattered very much. I didn't worry about how long it would last or anything like that. I was living for the moment."

"And your children? How did they react?"

"My mother wanted to take them away to live with her. She said I was an irresponsible parent. She was going to court to establish her guardianship of them because that was what my first husband had wanted, so I left Sam and went back to live with her in Victoria Park."

"So the magic did wear off?"

"It didn't wear off then, but his family had moved into my house with us, at least his mother did. She was a horrible woman, a real witch."

The memory of Sam's mother made my stomach contract in a tight knot. Even though she is dead, I still loathe her.

Rosa was standing by the table, silent and attentive, so I shook my head and said, "But you don't want to hear about her."

"Yes, I do. I want to understand what happened but if you don't want to tell me, don't go on. I can see you're upset."

"I'm not upset. It's just that thinking about Sam's mother makes me angry. A lot of it was her fault. She moved into my house and treated me as if I was a fool. My mother had warned me, 'They're out to bleed you dry. They're only after your money,' she'd said, and that was exactly what they were after I've realised since. I was so angry when I found out that she was right. Sam's mother was stealing my clothes, my money and my silver – quite blatantly stealing things and selling them."

"You sound as if you were very innocent and trusting."

"I was. I'd never had to think for myself. All my life my parents and my husband did my thinking for me – especially my mother. I don't think she believed I had any sense at all. It wasn't till I was in prison that I began working things out for myself – a bit late, wasn't it?"

"That's the way things are for lots of people who go to prison. They only start thinking when it's too late," said Rosa.

"Was it like that for you?" I asked but she shook her head.

"I haven't got that excuse," she said shortly.

My pent up resentment against Sam's mother would not stay contained. I had to go on talking about her.

"She was a vulgar woman. She drank – gin I think – and it made her smell. Ugh! She wore a lot of cheap jewellery and she had the hardest eyes I've ever seen on anybody, but at first she was so nice to me, always buttering me up, telling me how beautiful I was and how good it was for her son to be working for me. Then, when I married him, she changed so much it was as if she was a different person."

Rosa laughed. "Jealous maybe."

It didn't matter to me – not now. "I don't know. All I do know is that the next thing was she was living in my house, ordering me about. Then I started to realise she was stealing from me, literally bleeding me dry and I was too scared to tell her to stop."

"Didn't you tell your husband?"

"Sam? He was even more scared of her than I was, I thought, but now I realise he was backing her up.

They probably knew I'd come to my senses in time and they were making hay while the sun shone. I was quite a rich woman, you see. At least I seemed like a rich woman though most of what I had was only mine for life – the house, the furniture, even the money."

"Didn't your husband leave you well provided for?"

"For my lifetime, yes, provided I didn't marry again. The children were to have everything when I died. The money was very tightly tied up. I was left five hundred pounds a year for myself – but if I remarried it went to the children and I'd have nothing except an annuity of one hundred a year my father left me. He died when I was just a girl. I expect he thought I'd get all my mother's money anyway and he didn't need to make separate provision for me because I was their only child."

Rosa was moving quietly around the kitchen, gathering ingredients for some dish she planned to make that night. "Money. It causes so much trouble," she said.

"It certainly caused trouble for me. When Sam found out that all I had was one hundred a year – because my mother saw to it that I lost the annuity from my husband the day I married again – he was furious. His mother was even more furious. Sam and she said it was a scandal and I should force my mother to give me more. Eventually I was allowed to sell our big house, the one I'd lived in with my husband in Peckham, and buy a smaller one for me and Sam. That was all my mother would do for me though. She wouldn't even let me take the furniture. She said Sam'd only sell it."

"It was cruel of your first husband to put that restriction about not remarrying on you. You were only a young woman when he died," said Rosa.

"I was more than thirty years younger than him. I didn't realise he might have been jealous of me for he never showed it, but he must have been," I told her.

"Men – money – property – enslavement . . ." she muttered and clattered her pots so angrily that I stopped talking and stared at her.

"Don't worry about me. Go on. Tell me what happened," she said.

"Sam said it was a scandal that my mother had taken away my children and all their money. They got my five hundred, you see, and they already had a good income from their father's estate. He was a successful doctor with a large practice and some very rich patients. My mother was the executor of his estate, along with our solicitor, and she cut me off completely financially when I married Sam – but she'd been generous before."

"Let me guess," said Rosa. "Sam said that you should get custody of your children, because, if you had them, you'd have control of their money."

"Exactly. And that caused terrible trouble with my mother."

"She was probably right to object."

"She probably was but I didn't think so at the time. I was totally under Sam's influence and he was under his mother's. So I agreed to let him try to snatch the children from Victoria Park."

She stared at me. "Did he?"

"He tried. He went there with one of his friends and snatched the children from the garden. My mother's servants, particularly her gardener, Bryce, stopped him though. He raised the alarm when he saw Sam lifting Daisy and the friend grabbing Edward."

"Where were you when this was going on?"

"I was waiting in the gig at the stable-yard gate. I ran in when I heard all the shouting."

"What happened?"

"Sam and his friend ran away but I stayed with the children till my mother came out and she was angrier than I've ever seen her. She stood shouting at me, telling me if it was up to her I'd never see my children again. Edward and Daisy were crying. I remember Edward just turning and walking away, back to the big house, but Daisy had her arms round my legs and she was hanging on to me. She loved her Mama, you see, and my mother wasn't so fond of her as she was of Edward. I loved Daisy too and it broke my heart when they dragged her away from me."

"It must have been a terrible experience for the children," said Rosa softly.

"It was awful for us all. I was crying, my mother was shouting, even Bryce was upset. She threatened to call the police to arrest Sam and me for stealing the children but she calmed down a little and didn't do that. Then, the next day, I went home to her again and said I'd left him."

"Because you couldn't live without your children?"

"Not entirely. That was part of it, but mainly it was because I discovered exactly how much Sam and his mother had been taking from me. So I went home and my mother said I could stay with her. That lasted about six weeks till Sam sent me a letter and asked me to meet him. I did and of course I was lost. The moment I saw him, I wanted him again. I couldn't have stayed with my mother anyway because even after a month we were fighting like cat and dog over the children. She taunted me about Sam and about my first husband not trusting me enough to leave me an income outright. I suppose it was inevitable I'd go back to him."

"We women put up with so much," said Rosa. "One wonders if perhaps the anti-emancipation politicians are right. Maybe we can't think, maybe we are brainless."

Stung, I stopped talking. After a moment I turned and was making my way to the door when her voice stopped me. "Hold on. In my time I've been every bit as stupid as you were. Don't think I'm judging you harshly. I understand. Tell me what happened after you took him back."

"When I went to break the news to my mother that we were back together I thought she was going to die of shock. She shouted, she screamed, she hit me with her fists. She called me terrible things – a bitch on heat was one of them – she swore she'd never let my children see me again. I went back to Sam but returned to see my mother again next day and found her calmer. We managed to talk quite sensibly for a bit till I said something about taking away items of furniture that I wanted for my new house – things that belonged to me, my wedding presents from when I married Muldona – and that started her off again."

"Was that when you hit her?"

"Yes."

"Because she wouldn't let you take away your old wedding presents?"

"That was one of the reasons."

"One of the reasons?"

"The only one I want to talk about."

She nodded. I could see that she noticed how upset I was, how I was shaking and unable to stop my face from twitching uncontrollably. It was almost like the day I hit my mother and I didn't want anything like that to ever happen to me again. I'd spent many hours, weeks, months and years working out what went wrong that terrible day and why I did what I did but the horror of it was still too deeply embedded in me to pour it out to a stranger.

Rosa moved across to the other side of the room, opened a little corner cupboard and took out a small decanter with about two inches of dark liquid in its engraved bulbous base. "You need another drink," she said, unstoppering it and pouring some of the liquid into a thimble-like glass which she handed across to me.

"What is it?"

"Brandy. Drink it. You're in a state and it'll calm you down."

It did. The brandy burned my throat as I swallowed it but it performed some sort of magic on my mind, slowing me down, suffusing me with a peculiar sort of calm.

"You want to know about your children," said Rosa when I'd drained the glass and handed it back to her.

"Yes."

"I don't know a lot, but what I do know I'll tell you. Do you want to talk about it now, or will I wait till you feel better and have got over the shock of the murder at Clapham?"

"If you have time, please tell me now. I've waited a long time and I don't want to wait any longer." The weird coincidence of Megan sending me to lodge with a woman who knew my children seemed so improbable that I had trouble believing I wasn't in a dream – and the brandy I'd drunk added to that illusion.

"Sit down there then and I'll talk while I work. I'm making fish pie for tonight and it has to go into the oven soon if it's to be ready when everyone comes home.

"I met your son first, as I've said, and that was when I was in the opera. He was a keen theatre-goer was your son, you know."

I leaned back in the chair and closed my eyes, feeling like a child that was being told a fairy tale.

"What did he look like?" I asked. "Did he look like that photograph?"

"Not so stolid, but he was tall and imposing. You noticed him. He was rather pompous, I'm afraid. The doorman at the theatre called him Lord Poncebury."

"Poncebury?" I opened my eyes and stared at her.

"He condescended to the working classes, I'm afraid."

"You didn't like him?"

"Not a lot, but I do like his sister."

"But how did you meet him? How did you get to know him well enough to meet his sister?"

Her broad back was turned to me as she stood at the stone sink. She talked as she worked. "When I got out of prison a friend was singing in the opera and she found me a place there."

A sharp feeling of resentment seized me when I reflected that though she knew a lot about my crime, I knew nothing of hers. The newspapers had recorded my case in detail but I would have already been in prison when Rosa Stein came up for sentence and, though I remembered her in prison, the strict code there was not to ask people about their past. I dreaded doing so even now but there were things I wanted to know.

"How long were you in?" I asked.

"Five years," she said shortly.

So I was right, hers had not been a trivial crime. I sat silent, waiting for more but nothing was offered. Rosa Stein was keeping her secrets and I was afraid that if I antagonised her, she might close down entirely so I didn't press the point.

Instead I asked, "Were you singing in the opera before you went in?" Memories of her soaring voice, rising like a bird through the miseries of the cells, came back to me.

"Yes, before but not much afterwards. I was too rusty. My voice had gone. My professional singing days were more or less over. My friend found me a place in the costume department. I'm good at making clothes. That's what I was doing when I met your son."

"Tell me about it, please."

"There were five of us in costumes. One of them became a good friend of mine, a young man called Laurence, very talented. He could make anything and his ideas were wonderful. He had friends in the male chorus and one night he took me with him when he went to a party in a West End hotel. It was given by some army officers and one of them was that friend of your son – the one he called Tilly, the one that also went to fight in Africa.

"Tilly knew Laurence already, but Edward didn't and when they were introduced, I'm afraid he fell for him rather."

I stared at her back. Before prison I wouldn't have had an idea what she was talking about but my time there had been a great education.

"My son was one of those – like Oscar Wilde?"

She turned with a half-peeled potato in her hand and glared at me. "Yes, a homosexual. Does that shock you? Do you think people like that are wicked and should be made to suffer because they love their own sex?"

"Of course not. I just didn't think my son . . ."

"You thought he'd be a happily married man with

a family of children crowding round his knees, did you? Why should he? He didn't have much of a family image to follow."

Confused, I shook my head and said, "I know. I know. I'm surprised, that's all."

She was peeling potatoes again and her voice came over her shoulder, "It's quite common, I assure you. He wasn't the only one. Tilly was the same."

Of course, I thought and then said, "So you went to the party and met Edward?"

"Yes, then he started coming to the theatre to see Laurence. He used to sit in the sewing room when we were working, watching him. I could see he was head over heels in love."

"Was it reciprocated? Did Laurence love him?"

"Is love ever that easy? Laurence loved Tilly who was actually a very nice fellow. His father was a lord or something and insisted that Tilly got married – had to have a son to carry on the line, that sort of thing. He and Laurence had been together for a long time, but eventually Tilly gave in and agreed to marry some girl his father was pushing at him. That devastated Laurence. He understood why Tilly had to do it but it broke his heart. Instead he took up with Edward who didn't ever want a woman anywhere near him, but that didn't last long."

"What happened?"

"Laurence drowned himself in the Thames. Jumped off Blackfriars Bridge one night after the show. The trouble was he left a letter for Tilly in his house but the police found it first."

I felt my face tighten with shocked sympathy. "You were fond of Laurence," I said to her.

She turned. "Yes, I was. He was such a sweet-natured, innocent person. My best friend actually. He left me this house in his will. That's why I'm here. He used to put his arm round me and give me a hug. 'You're like my mum. I'm going to look after you in your old age,' he'd say. It was a joke between us I thought, but he left me his house when he decided to kill himself."

"How long ago did he die?" I whispered because I could see that she had tears in her eyes when she spoke of him.

"Four years. When the police started asking questions, Tilly got himself sent to Africa and Edward went too. Don't ask me how he managed that but some people can buy anything and he had plenty of money and knew people in high places. They were terrified of ending up in Reading prison like Oscar Wilde, you see."

"But Daisy. Where does Daisy fit into this?" I asked after a few moments of reflection.

"She doesn't really. When he came to the theatre, Edward used to talk about his sister sometimes. She really was the only woman in the world he cared about. He didn't even glance at the girls of the troupe though some of them were very pretty, beautiful in fact. He had absolutely no interest in them. I had the idea then, even before you came here and I found out who he was, that he'd had some sort of terrible thing happen to him when he was young, something involving a woman."

"You think it was my fault?"

She glared at me again. "Fault? Why fault? He was happy enough the way he was."

"Daisy . . ." I prompted.

She humphed a bit and shrugged irritably but took up the story again. "Early on in their acquaintance Laurence showed him a gown I was making for one of the prima donnas. It was a lovely thing with a long trailing skirt and an embroidered bodice. Edward was in raptures about it – he was always very interested in clothes, a dandy really – and he asked me to make one like it for his sister because she was being sent off to be finished in France and would be going to grand balls in Paris."

"So you met Daisy."

"And liked her. She's not stiff like her brother was . . . she's very natural, very happy natured."

I stood up and sighed. "But then she was only three when I went away. She won't remember anything about the trouble. Daisy Cavendish. Do you still see her?"

"I haven't seen her much since Laurence died, only now and again. She and Edward came to see me then. He wanted to ask me to say nothing to the police but she sympathised because she knew I'd loved Laurence like a son and was mourning him. She gave me a hug and told me to go to see her any time I wanted."

"Did you go?"

"Yes, a couple of times and she comes here because I make things for her now and again. I made her a pair of knickerbockers last month in fact. I also know people who she knows. They tell me about her sometimes. Don't worry, she's perfectly well."

"Will you tell me where she lives?"

She stared hard at me and then said, "Why not? She's not far away. In Cheyne Walk. In a pretty little house with a magnolia tree in the front garden."

Chapter Eleven

Daisy Cavendish's Story
November, 1900

I love Alice dearly but sometimes it seems to me that she thinks I'm still a child and, to my own annoyance, I find myself acting the part in an effort to be the sort of person that she wants me to be.

"Alice," I long to say, "Alice, I'm twenty-five years old. I'm an independent woman with ideas that would horrify you if I had the courage to discuss them honestly and not skirt round them in your presence. I have friends of whom you would definitely disapprove and I'm planning to do something which make you faint away on the floor if I let you into my secret."

When I waved goodbye to her from my front door two days ago, I watched her neatly waisted departing figure with a mixture of love and exasperation. She'd come to talk about my mother, I'm sure, but there isn't really any point. Edward told me about her long ago. First of all, when I was about twelve, he told me she'd run away and then, when I came back from Paris, he changed his story and said she'd gone to prison for attacking our grandmother and had recently died there.

It was a shock when I heard that, I admit, but I came to terms with it though I've never been able to admit to Alice what I know. True, for years before Edward came clean, I hadn't really completely believed her story about the premature death of our saintly mother but my whole mental picture of her had to be radically changed after Edward's revelations. Since then I've always been reluctant to discuss it with anyone except him – and he hated it when I brought it up and used to become very agitated.

When I did succeed in forcing some information out of him he said that our mother was a selfish, shallow woman who didn't give a fig for either of us or for her mother. He said he could remember her being taken away by the police, all dressed up like an actress. He hated her because there'd been some man involved and Edward hated him too.

But he'd loved our grandmother and treasured a photograph of her. When he went to Africa, he gave it to me. I look at it sometimes, trying very hard to remember the woman who stares out of it at me but I can't, I simply can't. It's as if I have blanked all the early memories out. I asked my friend Emily if she could remember back to being very small and she said she could – she even remembers being wheeled in her perambulator. I have no recollection of anything earlier than playing on a swing in the garden at Bromley with Alice, and I must have been about five then.

Poor dear Alice is acting very oddly, tip-toeing around the subject of my mother. In the past she's tried to bring it up occasionally but this time I was afraid she was going to burst out with some sort of self-condemnation, blaming herself for keeping a secret from me, so I pre-empted her. I said that Edward had told me our mother had run away to Italy with a man and left us with our grandmother. Then she'd died, I said.

Alice looked half relieved and half stunned when I said that – relieved that I didn't know about the murder and prison sentence, and stunned at the idea that I'd kept a secret from her. I hope she leaves it at that. I don't want to go into the whole sordid story again because I've never felt it concerns me. As I said, I've no memory of either of the women involved. That may sound hard to some people, but as far as I'm concerned it is past and should be left like that.

My mother and my grandmother are both dead now and the best thing to do is to put the whole thing out of my mind and live my own life. What's past is past. The dead are buried in their graves and they should stay there.

I'm Daisy Cavendish – not Daisy Ares, Daisy Muldona, which Edward said was our real name, or anything else equally outlandish. When Edward showed me the newspaper cuttings about our mother and I found out that our real name was Muldona, I was relieved it had been changed because I think Muldona sounds very odd and foreign, though Edward said he thought it was Irish. Cavendish is better, much more anonymous.

It made me sad though to see how twitchy Alice was on this last visit to me. I don't want her to be unhappy so I'll have to admit to knowing the whole story eventually. I'll go to see her when the project I have on hand is completed but I don't want to be distracted right now.

At the moment I'm busy with my plans. It's a strange coincidence that our target, Sir Granville Morton MP, lives in my grandmother's old house. Some years ago, when I saw an engraving of him in the print shop, standing up straight and righteous-looking with one hand stuck in the front of his frock coat, I thought he looked like a pompous fool and then I read his speeches and knew he was exactly that. He's the very worst of the Shaftesbury crowd, a dyed in the wool Tory.

Some of the others in our group are against the idea of attacking him. They think it's dangerous and too radical; they say that it will only give a bad name to our movement but, from my point of view, you've got to be radical if you want to be taken seriously. The time has come for us to make an impact and the more shocking the better. It's the only way we'll be listened to. We've crept around far too long, being reasonable and well-behaved, in fact being ladylike – what an awful word. Sir Granville Morton would like it. It's time we turned into viragos. That's the only way to wake them up. Especially since Morton is the spearhead of the anti-feminine movement and says such awful things about women in the House of Commons. A few months ago he actually said that it was dangerous to educate women because too much learning overloaded our brains and we are then in danger of going mad! We'll show him how mad a woman can be. He needs a good shock and I'm planning to give him one.

I read in *The Times* the other day that he had spent the last three months on the continent as his wife is an invalid, but he's back again and spouting his usual nonsense. Margaret knows people who know him and she found out he lives in Victoria Park during the time the House is sitting. His wife never comes to town and lives in the country when she isn't in the south of France. I'm glad she won't be there when we put our plan into action because I wouldn't want to hurt her. Being married to Sir Granville must be punishment enough for any woman.

This afternoon when I was working on the new plan, I looked out of the window and saw a woman in a black coat and hat loitering about on the pavement beside my gate. She was just standing there, staring up at my windows, and she didn't seem to be sure whether she ought to come into the garden or not. I stood behind the curtain and watched her for quite a bit, trying to make up my mind about her.

I don't think the police could have sent her because none of us are under surveillance as far as I know. We haven't done anything to attract police attention apart from attending a few meetings. But when we go, we're very careful and don't stand up and shout slogans or ask questions because we know there are spies planted in the crowd, just watching. To all intents and purposes the three of us are very respectable, reasonable women – on the outside.

Margaret's friend Ramon, who is as suspicious and distrustful as me, continually harps on about not trusting anybody, even your closest friend, your husband or your wife – if you have them. But that's because he's friendly with those Irish anarchists who think that every road sweeper or hansom-cab driver has been sent to spy on them.

Working on the Ramon principle I've warned Margaret against telling even him about our plan. There's only the three of us who know the details and we're keeping them to ourselves. It'll be such a shock for the others when we pull it off – and I'm determined that we will. Absolutely determined.

When I went back and looked out of the window, the woman in black was still there, but not making any attempt to hide herself. This time I really studied her. She was carrying a parcel wrapped in brown paper under her arm. She was tall and very thin, but quite distinguished-looking, actually, though her clothes were poor quality and faded. Her face was very pale and when she stared at the house I saw that there were enormous dark smudges of weariness under her eyes. She looked ill. I wondered if she was a beggar or a lunatic but she seemed too clean and tidy for begging and too under control to be mad.

It was about two o'clock when I first saw her but fifteen minutes later, she was still there, pacing up and down, looking at the house every now and again as if she was waiting for something. Could one of the others have sent her? I wondered. But if that was the case, why did she not knock at the door? Why wait on the pavement drawing attention to herself?

I remembered Emily saying that she had met some Russian woman whose husband had been sent to Siberia by the Tsar and who'd fled to England. According to Emily she might be of some use to us because she claims to have knowledge of explosives. When Emily said she'd sound her out some more I told her not to be so stupid because we don't know anything about the woman and she might go around talking about us. Just to show interest in explosives could be dangerous, especially afterwards if we are successful in our project. Surely Emily hadn't been so silly as to tell the woman to come and see me to persuade me to change my mind about her.

When that thought struck me, I didn't ring for my maid but ran downstairs and opened the front door myself. The woman was standing beside the stone gatepost but not making any effort to hide from me. I went up the path and opened the gate which squealed horribly as it always does in the winter time. A bitter wind was coming off the river and I saw the woman's lips were blue with cold.

"Are you looking for me?" I asked.

She stepped forward and stared hard at me out of those exhausted eyes, which, I saw, were dark brown with long luxuriant lashes. Though she was quite old and very worn-looking, she must once have been beautiful.

"Is your name Daisy Cavendish?" she asked. Her voice was well-modulated and very English. No trace of a foreign accent there.

"Yes. I am Daisy Cavendish."

"Then I am looking for you. Rosa Stein sent me

189

round with this parcel for you." She shoved the paper-wrapped bundle into my arms. It felt spongy, like a roll of cloth.

"In that case you'd better come in and not hang about in the street any longer. You've been out here a long time. Weren't you ever going to knock on the door?"

"I was trying to make up my mind whether to or not."

This surprised me. "If Rosa sent you, she'd have been annoyed if you went back without delivering the parcel surely?" I asked. "What is it anyway?" I hadn't any dressmaking commissions outstanding with Rosa as far as I could remember.

"It's the cloth left over from your knickerbockers. She thought you might be able to use it for something . . ." Her voice trailed off and I laughed.

"Rosa doesn't usually bother about sending me the off-cuts," I said.

This woman didn't seem to know what she was doing at my house. I'd certainly never seen her before but somehow I didn't dislike or distrust her.

"Come in. You look freezing cold. Rosa might have put a note in with the cloth," I said, leading the way and ushering her quickly in front of me because the wind really was cutting and I only had on a thin blouse. I didn't entirely believe the Rosa Stein story and Rosa knows Emily. When we were inside and the door closed I asked her, "Did Emily send you?"

She furrowed her brow, shook her head and said, "Who?"

"Emily Pemberton."

"I don't know any Emily Pemberton I'm afraid."

"Then who told you about me?"

"Rosa Stein."

So it was really Rosa but it still didn't make sense, I thought, as I unwrapped the parcel and found the knickerbocker cloth all neatly folded. In the middle of it was a slip of paper. "This is delivered by my friend Gladys Mitchell," it said.

I read it, shook my head and stared at the stranger. "How odd," I said. "Does she want to be paid for it?"

"No," replied the woman and then she shuddered as if in the grip of an ague. Suddenly I felt very sorry for her.

"Come upstairs. There's a fire burning and you can warm up before you go back to Sydney Street."

I led the way upstairs to my sitting room and watched as she huddled over the fire, holding long-fingered hands out to it. At first her thin shoulders were shaking beneath the thin cloth of her coat but that gradually stopped as the heat from the flames gave her comfort. A feeling of pity that I couldn't quite explain swept over me so I told her to take off her coat and asked if she would like some tea.

"That would be kind," she said without protests about not wanting to trouble me or anything of that sort. When I walked past her to reach the bell pull, I saw with embarrassment that there were tears on her cheeks. My first thought then was, What have I done bringing this odd woman into my house? If she asks for money I'll give her a sovereign and get rid of her as quickly as possible.

She must have sensed my switch of mood because we made very stiff conversation about the bitterness of the weather while Maisie, my maid, came clattering upstairs with the tea tray and then went back to the kitchen to bring up the spirit kettle which she put on the table in the window. Then, curious about the stranger, she began lighting the gas jets and wanted to brew the tea for us but I sent her away.

When the door was firmly closed, I decided to call her bluff and said to the woman by the fire, "What exactly do you want? The cloth from Rosa was only a ruse, wasn't it?"

"It's about your mother," she said.

Not about the plan! Not because Emily or Margaret have been talking out of line! Thank heavens, I thought and let out a breath of pure relief which I hoped she didn't notice. "My mother? Good heavens, what about her?"

As I looked at the woman it struck me that she could be an ex-prisoner. She had a strange hunted look about her, animal and furtive, as if she was long used to making every effort to avoid being noticed.

"Did you know my mother in prison?" I asked suddenly.

A look of unfeigned surprise crossed her face. "So you know she went to prison!" she exclaimed.

"Oh yes, I know. And I know what she went there for in spite of my relatives and my lawyer doing their level best to keep the knowledge from me. My brother told me long ago when he heard she'd died."

"When she died," sighed the stranger, looking back into the heart of the fire.

"Was that what you came to tell me, that she'd died?"

"Yes, that was what I came for."

"It was kind of you but there's no need to worry about it. I never knew my mother and have no memory of her at all. It might sound harsh to you but when you've never known anyone, and only heard bad things about them from people who did know them, it would be false sentiment to get weepy about my mother."

"I don't think it's harsh. I think you're very sensible. I'm glad you know about your mother. Did your brother feel the same as you do?"

"Edward was much more violent against her than I am. He remembered quite a lot about her, you see, and told me that she didn't care a fig about us. He said we were better off without her. He was fond of our grandmother, and it infuriated him that our mother had murdered her."

The woman by the fire visibly winced. "She told me your grandmother died because she had heart trouble. That it wasn't really murder," she said.

"Probably she did suffer from heart disease but she wouldn't have died when she did if our mother hadn't hit her. She wanted her mother to die, Edward said, because she wanted her money."

The stranger shook her head. "That's awful, awful," she whispered. "How terrible for her children to grow up believing that. I'm so sorry for you."

I walked across to her and took the empty teacup

out of her hands. "Let me give you some more tea," I said, "And please don't worry about me. I never give my mother a thought. I've too many other things to concern me. And Edward didn't worry about her either. As he said, we're better off without her. If she wasn't dead I wouldn't know what to do or say if I ever met her. It would be so embarrassing! Imagine meeting your own mother under circumstances like that."

She looked up at me and said with great sincerity, "I can assure you that the last thing your mother would want would be to embarrass or hurt you. She was very fond of you and she told me that when you were small you were fond of her too."

I felt my face harden and said, "I was only a baby when she was sent to prison. I don't remember anything about her and I suppose that all babies are fond of their mothers, aren't they?"

Suddenly I wished this woman would go away. I began fiddling irritably with some little pieces of china on the tea table in an effort to make her realise that she should soon take her leave. But the warmth of the fire had her in its thrall and she didn't seem to be capable of keeping her eyes away from its glowing heart. She stared into it as if she was mesmerised. A strange silence fell over us both till I asked, "You met my mother in prison?"

"Yes, I got to know her in Brixton."

"Why were you there?"

She took her eyes off the fire to answer that though I knew it was something that in courtesy I shouldn't have asked.

"For being a fool. For being very, very foolish.
Not for being dishonest. You needn't worry about
me stealing anything from you or wanting help or
money. I've learned my lesson and it was a hard one.
I'll never be so foolish again."

Suddenly shamed, I asked her, "Did my mother
ask you to contact her children? Edward's dead,
you know. He was killed in the war – no, actually he wasn't, he died of some sort of fever.
He wasn't shot or anything. I don't think he ever
saw any fighting which is just as well because he'd
have hated it. He wasn't the fighting type, my poor
brother."

"When I got out I heard your brother was dead
but I came to see you because your mother wanted
you to know how sorry she was that she had to
leave you. How much she wished and wished she
could have turned back time and done everything
differently."

My heart was touched in spite of my determination to steel myself against sentimentality. "Did
she say that? That she wanted to turn back time?
Poor thing. But I read the newspaper accounts of
the court case and she sounds rather stupid and
impulsive – running away with that young boy and
attacking her mother."

"She regretted all that, she regretted it very much.
You can have no idea how she regretted it."

"What did she die of? And when did she die?
Edward didn't seem to know. He just said he'd
been informed by our lawyer that she was dead,"
I told her.

She hesitated and then said, "She died of consumption seven years ago. There was a lot of sickness in prison."

I sat quiet for a few moments thinking about my mother wasting away in misery and remorse. "How tragic," I said, "but I suppose it was the right way for her story to end. What would she have done if she'd come out?"

The woman by the fire shook her head. "What indeed?" she agreed. "If anything, coming out is worse than being inside. I'm finding it very hard."

Suddenly she stood up and reached for her skimpy coat.

"I'm sorry to have taken up so much of your time, Miss Cavendish, you've been very kind," she said.

"It's you who were kind, coming here to tell me about my mother. You must have liked her," I said, sorry for my suspicions of her motives.

She shook her head. "Liking doesn't come into it really. The main thing is that she wanted you to know she was sorry."

"Have you some place to stay?" I asked.

"I'm at Rosa Stein's."

"Of course," I exclaimed. "Rosa was in prison once too. Did you meet her there? I remember hearing that she was sent away for five years I think but I don't know what for. She's not my idea of a criminal though – she's a remarkable person."

"I knew her then but I don't know anything about the reason for her being there either. Prisoners don't talk about why they're inside unless they're trying to convince you that they're innocent and when they start that you're always suspicious of them."

As we walked downstairs I was struck again by the meagreness of her clothes and by the way the wind was howling off the river. "Do you need money? How are you managing now that you're back in the world?" I asked.

She turned and gave me a most magnificent, beguiling smile that conveyed a glimpse of what she must have looked like when she was young. For a moment I thought she was going to embrace me but she stopped herself when she saw me stiffen.

"It's very kind of you to ask but I've plenty of money for what I need and I'm managing perfectly well. It's the company I miss more than anything really. You're never alone in prison," she said.

Chapter Twelve

The visit of the mysterious Mrs Mitchell left me troubled in a way that I could not entirely understand and during the two days that followed I found my thoughts returning to her – worrying about how she looked and what she said – very frequently. Most of all I was haunted by the air of imprisonment that still seemed to hang about her and the feeling that once she had been a beautiful woman who was reduced to a nullity by the time she had spent shut away from other human beings.

What if the project Emily, Margaret and I are about to undertake fails and we too have to sacrifice our lives or end up serving prison sentences? The thought terrified me, but I had to drive it away and take care not to show misgivings to my friends as we finalised our plans. We'd gone too far to back out now and I knew that if I showed weakness, the others' confidence would evaporate too.

On the second day after Mrs Mitchell's visit, I took a cab to Alice's and surprised her and Aaron who were finishing off their midday meal by drinking a cup of tea in the window of their shop with their cat sitting watching them like a fond parent. When I saw them from across the street I paused to take in the scene. They are such a delightful pair – Alice who overflows with affection for the whole world and is entranced by Aaron, who not only loves her back but is an acutely intelligent man and kind as well, a real rarity. I love them both and Alice has been dearer to me than any mother could be. Remembering Mrs Mitchell and the strange news she brought me, I suddenly decided that I must not go on acting a lie with dear Alice any longer. I'd tell her that I knew about my mother being in prison for the murder of my grandmother.

When she saw me crossing the road, she got up and went rushing about flapping her hands. "Daisy, dear Daisy, come in. I've just made tea. Come in and sit down," she cried holding open their front door with one hand and reaching to draw me in with the other.

Then she sat me down and practically tucked a napkin under my chin in her anxiety to feed me, while Aaron looked on with a smile on his face because I know he can see that I'm no longer the innocent little girl Alice imagines me to be.

"Alice," I said, suddenly brave, "there's two reasons I've come to see you and the first one is that I want to tell you that I've known about my mother going to prison for killing her mother for at least six years."

She stopped dead in the middle of the floor and stared at me. "You've known that! But you told me you thought she'd run away with a man to Italy."

"Edward told me that first when I was little but

later he told me the truth – that was after he heard she was dead. I suppose he thought it was all right then."

"He told you after she was dead," said Alice staring first at me and then at Aaron.

"Yes, when I came back from Paris, he said she'd died when I was away."

"Why have you waited so long to tell me this?" asked Alice.

"I don't know. I didn't want to upset you I suppose but the reason I'm telling you the truth now is because a very strange woman came to see me two days ago."

Alice's face looked stricken as she stared at me. "A woman, a strange woman. Who was she?" she asked in a faltering voice.

"She told me she knew my mother in prison. It was when she told me about her that I realised how stupid it was for all of us to be telling lies to each other."

"What did she say?" Alice's legs seemed to have collapsed under her and she sank down into her chair looking very strange.

"She said my mother asked her to go to see her children when she got out and explain how sorry she was for what she'd done. She said to tell us that if she could turn back time she'd do everything differently."

"Was that all she said?"

"She said my mother died in the prison hospital of consumption."

Alice looked at Aaron as if she wanted help

from him and he asked me, "Did she tell you her name?"

"She said it was Gladys Mitchell. She was a strange woman, but interesting-looking. I think she's quite ill – not mad, I don't mean that, but physically ill. I tried asking her why she was in prison but she wouldn't tell me."

"No reason she should if she's served her sentence," said Aaron and I nodded in agreement.

"She made me wonder about my mother though. She made me think there might be more to the story than Edward and the newspapers said. It's all very tantalising and I want you to tell me everything you know, because now I'm interested. I wasn't really before. Do you have any photographs of my mother, Alice?"

She reeled. "Photographs! Me! No, dear, oh no."

"But you have one of my grandmother, the same one as Edward had. I've seen it."

"I kept that when Mrs Downs was clearing out the big house. I thought you'd like to see it when you grew up."

"Didn't you take one of my mother too? There must have been some about."

But Alice shook her head. "No, dear I didn't."

Why didn't I believe her?

"How did this Gladys Mitchell find you, Daisy?" asked Aaron suddenly.

"She's lodging in the house of an acquaintance of mine, a woman called Rosa Stein. Rosa makes clothes for me sometimes but she was once in prison too and they met then."

201

Alice gave a small cry, "Jailbirds!" she exclaimed, but Aaron interrupted her by asking me, "But how did she know your name? It was changed after your mother began her sentence. Does this Rosa Stein know who you really are?"

"I suspect she does. She was much more friendly with Edward than with me once and he used to talk about things when he'd had too much to drink. He might have told her about our background."

"Oh dear me," moaned Alice. She was really very upset and I felt sorry for causing her such trouble so I jumped up and put my arms round her. "Don't take on so, Alice. I'm not a bit upset about it. In fact it tidied up a lot of loose ends and worries I've always had about our family and I was very pleased to hear our mother was sorry for what she did. She seems more human to me now and it's made me want to know more about her. That's why I was asking about the photograph. Come on, put on your coat and hat and come for a walk with me so we can talk about this.

"The second reason I came today is to persuade you to take me up to Victoria Park and walk round the garden with me. I've always avoided it in the past because Edward hated the place so much."

"There's a Member of Parliament living there now. We won't be able to wander about his garden as if we owned it," she said doubtfully.

"He'll never see us. You know the gardener there, don't you? It's still the man who worked for my grandmother, you said. Let's go to see him and ask him to show us round the garden, just so I can see it again. I wonder if I'll remember anything about it," I told her in reassurance.

"You were only three when you left. This is all because of that woman telling you about your mother, isn't it!" she exclaimed angrily.

But I looked at her so pleadingly that she did what I wanted as I knew she would, and went like a lamb to put on her coat.

We walked slowly along the street and up the hill to where Victoria Park stood behind a deep fringe of interlacing trees and a high stone wall. Alice hung back when we stopped at the gate but I determinedly pulled her on and, with her looking nervously over her shoulder, we walked up the drive, skirting it as if Alice was ready to dash into the shrubbery the moment anyone appeared.

"Do calm down, Alice,' I said to her. "They must get people making deliveries and that sort of thing all the time."

"I'll not be happy till we're round the back. We should have come in by the stable gate," she said. My heart gave a little jump when she said that. So there was another entrance. That was handy.

"We'll go out by it then if it'll make you feel happier," I told her.

The drive was quite long. You couldn't see the road from the house and when we reached it, we might as well have been in the middle of the country. When it eventually came into sight it proved to be large but not enormous, just a sort of overgrown country farmhouse really, white painted and with a long frontage that looked as if bits and pieces had been added higgledy piggledy over the years. There was a sort of colonnade along the middle section with a porticoed front door in its centre. From the house's appearance, I guessed it was built at the turn of last century but it didn't belong to our family then because Isabella Downs used to tell me my grandfather only bought it about 1850 after he'd made a fortune selling wine to city merchants.

She despised him for his low-born origins but on the other hand was very proud of how rich he was – though he doesn't seem to have left any of his money to her. Her consolation was that her father's family were far better born – but poor, of course.

When we reached the wide expanse of grass and gravel that fronted the house, we saw that most of the windows were shuttered which meant the proprietor was probably not at home, but Alice wouldn't go up the front steps. Showing her first signs of serious rebellion, she stuck in her toes and said, "We must go round the back, Daisy. We must."

"But my grandmother owned this," I protested.

"She doesn't own it now," said Alice, pulling at my arm.

She was happier when she found herself in the service yard at the back. "There's the kitchen door," she said pointing at a smaller pillared portico with a green painted door and an enormous shining knocker in the middle of it. She nipped smartly up two pipe-clayed steps and rattled the knocker. It was answered by a cook, a fat woman with floury hands wearing a white apron, who glared at us and said, "Yes?"

"We're looking for Mr Bryce," said Alice.

"Junior or senior?"

"Senior."

"He's in here having his tea. Who will I say wants him?"

"I thought it might be his teatime about now. Will you please tell him Alice Grey has brought Mrs Ares' granddaughter to see him."

The old man who came to the kitchen door looked oddly familiar though I would not have recognised him in the street. His eyes were very sad and slightly puzzled as he stared at me. Then he said, "My word, you look just like your mother."

That was a shock. I had never thought of myself as looking like anybody and never held any image of my mother in my head. Somehow I didn't want to be compared with her.

Alice saw my face change and hurriedly said to him, "Daisy – Miss Cavendish – Miss Muldona – asked me to bring her to her grandmother's old house so she could see it. She wonders if she can remember anything about it."

Bryce just shook his head slightly and looked again at me. "Is this because of your mother? Do you remember it at all?"

I shook my head. "Not really, but coming up the drive I felt as if I was in a sort of a dream. I knew I'd been here before. It's oddly familiar though I don't remember it exactly."

"Can we have a look round the garden, Mr Bryce?" asked Alice hurriedly.

"Certainly. Hold on a minute while I get my coat,"

he said and disappeared back into the dark labyrinth behind him. I stared into it with longing. That was where I really wanted to be.

The gods must have been with me because when Bryce came back he was accompanied by a tall, thin woman in a high-necked black dress. She smiled at me in a surprisingly cordial way and said, "When you've seen the garden, Miss Cavendish, perhaps you'd like to have a look at the inside of the house. Our employer, Sir Granville Morton, is away from home at the moment but only until tomorrow, then he'll be in residence for several weeks while the House is sitting – he's a Member of Parliament, as you may know. In his absence however I'm sure he wouldn't mind if I showed you the principal rooms of the house." She had a precise way of speaking that made her sound like a sharp-tongued schoolmistress but I gave her my brightest smile and said fulsomely, "Oh thank you so much, how very kind."

Alice and I followed a fairly taciturn Mr Bryce round the gardens which were vast and most impressive. There was a terrace fringed by empty flower beds that must have bloomed in jewel colours all summer; impenetrable shrubberies; a walled garden, empty too, now, except for withered vegetable stalks and bare fruit canes; a vast tropical wonder of a greenhouse full of ferns, palms, and exotic but somehow sinister flowers. Adjoining it were other greenhouses where grape vines and the bare branches of peach trees were trained along red brick walls. That garden was capable of producing enough food to satisfy hundreds of Roman banquets every year.

"Was the garden as big as this when my grand-mother lived here?" I asked Bryce.

"The same size and growing the same things," he said solemnly.

"But she was a widow. There was only her – and my mother, me and Edward. We couldn't have eaten all the things you grow."

"Mrs Ares was very generous to her friends, as is the present owner," said the gardener solemnly but I thought they could have fed a village and never noticed the difference.

Though our garden tour was impressive, I had trouble suppressing my eagerness to get inside the house and fretted silently while we solemnly trod from rockery to geranium house, from leek beds to apple orchard. Eventually we turned back to the house where the intrigued housekeeper was waiting for us with teacups arranged on a long refectory table in the servant's dining room. She was obviously eager to speak to me, to show round the granddaughter of the woman who was slain in the downstairs parlour by her own daughter! That was almost as good as seeing the ghost of my grandmother as far as she was concerned and she'd talk about it to her friends for weeks to come.

I played the game, telling her again how I felt the house to be familiar but had no definite memories of it – and definitely no memories of the murder I implied, though no one actually brought up the unspoken question.

At last my guide, whose name was Mrs Speed, stood up and said, "Follow me, Miss Cavendish.

207

I'm afraid I can't show you the bedrooms – they're private of course – but I can let you see the reception rooms. There's been no structural alterations since your grandmother – left. And I believe from Mr Bryce that a lot of the furniture was hers too. Apparently when the house was sold to my employer, he bought most of the big pieces in it. He has another house in Wiltshire, you understand, and one in Menton. This is only his London residence, the one he uses when the House is sitting."

Sweeping me in front of her, she led me away. Alice was not invited to accompany us and neither was the gardener so they sat meekly saying nothing with their teacups in front of them.

The house was palatial but strangely chilly and unwelcoming inside, not as homely as its exterior promised it could be. There was a vast drawing room furnished by fragile-looking pieces with spindly legs and much ormolu decoration; there was a library with row upon row of leather-bound books, a huge desk, a deep leather sofa and leather chairs; there was a dining room with a gleaming table bearing curving branched silver candelabras and a sideboard groaning with salvers and covered tureens; there was an entrance hall behind the front door with a black and white marbled floor and high-backed chairs arranged along the side walls; there was a ballroom with a curving ceiling encrusted with decorative plaster like a wedding cake and with its walls bearing plaster-outlined painted panels showing cupids and crinolined women on swings. Off the dining room opened a conservatory in which there was a fountain and a grotto of artfully piled stones surrounded by fleshy-looking green-leafed plants which soared towards the sky from deep earthenware pots.

In every room except the ballroom and the conservatory vast oil paintings hung, many of them so dark that it was difficult to make out what they represented. I eventually worked out that the house's owner had a liking for biblical or classical subjects: Samson having his curling locks shorn; Caesar lying bleeding on the steps of the Capitol; the infant Moses being discovered among the bullrushes.

Mrs Steel saved the parlour – she called it the morning room – till last and when she flung open the heavy door and showed me in, I felt a strange surge of terror. For a moment I considered backing away and telling her I didn't want to see it, but she was looking at me with such eager expectancy that I could only do what she wanted and step inside, feeling my feet sink into the plush pile of the turkey-red carpet.

"This," she said softly, "was your grandmother's favourite room. The one she always sat in . . ."

And the one she was killed in, I silently finished for her.

It should have been a pleasant room. There was a deep bow window looking out into the garden with a cushioned window seat running round the base of the window sashes. Somewhere, from the depths of my memory, came the knowledge of what it felt like to sit on those soft window cushions with your face pressed against the window and your breath misting the glass with a pearly screen. I could almost see my infant self in the window, hiding behind the curtains.

A vast black marble fireplace was set in the middle of the wall facing the door. Though sticks and paper were arranged in the fire basket, they were not lit. Brass fire-irons were ranged in the proper order at each side of the dark void.

She saw me looking at them and told me, "I'll light the fire later to warm the room. The master of the house sits here when he returns from Westminster."

The floor was covered with a vast red carpet and the furniture was much more comfortable-looking, and certainly more battered, than in any other of the rooms we had toured. The pictures here were less terrifying and portentous, this time mainly watercolour landscapes and flower still lives. There were books and magazines fanned out on a side table and a pot of purple violets on another. They were, I realised, the only flowers I had seen in the whole house. Poor Bryce was labouring away, tending his lovely greenhouse plants in vain.

"Does the present owner of the house have a wife?" I asked for I was surprised at the lack of any feminine touch in the house.

Mrs Steel nodded her head. "On yes, but the poor ladyship very rarely comes here. She's not at all well and prefers the country. In fact, at the moment, she's in Egypt because she suffers with her lungs and she won't be back till spring when she'll go straight to Wiltshire. I've only met her three times in all the eighteen years I've looked after this house, as a matter of fact."

"Do they have children?" I enquired, wondering about who lived in the vast place with Sir Granville.

"A son and a daughter but they're both grown up and married. They don't come here much either and never did. Our employer lives alone when he is here. It's a lonely life for him but he's always very busy when the House is sitting, always out at meetings and that sort of thing. But he'll be in the country with his children and their families for Christmas and not come back till mid January."

I walked around, looking at everything. "The house seems rather lonely. Was the room like this in my grandmother's time do you know?" I asked.

She smiled. "As a matter of fact Mr Bryce says that it has hardly changed. The furniture you see now was all here – except a chair that was thrown out . . ."

"And the pictures?"

She looked at them indifferently. Pictures obviously did not mean much to her. "I suppose so. They've been here all my time and the master never buys that sort of thing."

I didn't ask about the fire-irons but they seemed to glitter and gleam at me like terrible beacons. They couldn't be the same ones, surely?

As we crossed the hall again, she waved a hand at the curving staircase and said unctuously, "I do hope you understand why I can't show you the bedrooms. It wouldn't be right, would it? But as far as I'm led to believe your grandmother slept in the big room facing the front, the one above the drawing room. That's where Sir Granville Morton sleeps too."

When we returned to the kitchen Alice and Bryce were still sitting side by side like obedient children. Their faces were expectant when they looked at me. I nodded to reassure them that I wasn't upset, and said to Mrs Steel, "Thank you so much for taking me round the house. It means so much to me to see everything."

"Do you remember any of it now?" she asked eagerly.

"Not really but I don't feel as if I'm seeing it for the first time. It's difficult to explain. There's a great sadness about it for me though."

Mrs Steel didn't mind this at all and was too tactful to suggest that my impression might be affected by a memory of my parent and grandparent having their last terrible quarrel, but I knew that was what she was thinking.

"At the moment it's a house of sadness because her Ladyship is so ill. She's not expected ever to get better, you see . . . That might be why you think it still feels sad," she said.

Telling her I understood exactly, I pressed two sovereigns into her hand. It was an over-generous tip but I wanted her to know that, as a lady, I knew what was expected of me. She accepted the money with great solemnity, and we parted on good terms.

When we went back into the yard, Alice said, "What did you really think about the house?"

"I thought it was a cold, cruel place. It made me

shudder," I told her with a vehemence that surprised even me, though it was true.

"It always had that effect on me, too," she said. "Even in the summer it felt cold. It seemed as if bad things were always waiting to happen in that house."

"But I'm glad I saw it. Very very glad," I told her in total sincerity.

It was growing dark and though there was no longer any fear of being seen from the house by outraged eyes, I said, "We'll do what you want. We'll go out by the back way. Show me where the gate is."

"That's a good idea," she said and took my arm. Oh Alice, how terrible and traitorous I felt then.

Chapter Thirteen

When Gladys Mitchell brought the parcel of cloth from Rosa Stein, it gave me an idea.

It is necessary for Emily, Margaret and I to go in disguise on our fire-raising expedition to Victoria Park and we thought the best thing to do would be to dress up as young working men. But how to buy the suits without arousing interest in people who might remember us later was a major problem. Also, I knew no man except Ramon who I could ask to buy them for us and I am never too sure about how safe it is to tell him anything.

Rosa was the perfect solution because she works a lot for theatrical companies and is very inventive, but best of all she is also extremely discreet and not given to gossiping. Even if she thought the commission puzzling, she wouldn't go around talking about it. However, she did raise her dark eyebrows in an expressive way when Emily and I went round to see her the day after I'd been to Victoria Park and told her what we wanted her to make for me this time.

"Last time it was a pair of knickerbockers and now it's men's suits," she said. "For both of you?

Trousers and jackets like the sort men wear? Why not just go out and buy them?"

"Yes, we want men's suits but we don't want to buy them because it might be embarrassing – people would think it odd that women are buying men's suits. They needn't be perfectly finished or anything. They just have to look like working-men's clothes – you know, trousers with belts and short jackets, the kind with collars that we can turn up against our throats. And they have to be dark coloured, black perhaps," I said.

She looked puzzled. "A masquerade perhaps? It sounds more as if you want complete cover-ups."

I gave a little laugh, but with an effort. "Yes, a masquerade. That's right. Working-men's clothes, perfectly ordinary clothes so no one will pay any attention to us – and so we can't be seen in the dark."

"You'll look like a pair of black ghosts."

That's exactly what we want to look like, I thought, but I said, "Not just two. We want three suits. Margaret Campbell should have one as well."

Rosa's mouth pursed and I guessed that, like many people of my acquaintance, she doesn't care for my friend Margaret who tends to be loud and argumentative. She is also courageous and loyal and exactly the sort of person I need for this project. In fact, the whole thing was originally her idea but I'm the one who's organising the practicalities because Margaret's good on theory but not on practice and Emily wouldn't have come along if Margaret had

215

been the one in charge because she thinks she's too rash.

Another drawback about Margaret is that, if anything, she's too enthusiastic. She even says she's quite prepared to go to prison if necessary, but Emily and I don't agree with her there. Emily is particularly against that because she's recently fallen in love with a young man who works for the Indian Civil Service and is going back there soon. As for me, since meeting Gladys Mitchell the idea of spending time in prison chills me to the bone.

What I do agree with, however, is Margaret's desire and determination to make a dramatic gesture. I'm tired of the wishy-washiness of the Fabians and the other women's organisations who are always having meetings and debating endlessly but never actually doing anything. It's action that counts now. If we can't persuade men to take women's claims seriously, we'll have to force them.

"I hope you know what you're doing and I hope it's not dangerous," said Rosa who seemed to be able to sense my mental turmoil. "But don't tell me what it is. I don't want to know. Just bring Miss Campbell here so I can take her measurements."

"We need the suits quickly, Rosa," I told her.

"How quickly?"

"Two days?" I ventured. From my reading of the newspapers I see that Sir Granville Morton is currently taking a big part in political debates about the franchise and women's rights. He's always against them, of course, and rabidly so. We have to strike while he's drawing attention to himself and winning headlines in the newspapers. Then people will realise without being told why his house has been targetted and set on fire.

"Two days. That's not long," demurred Rosa.

"Please try. Take our measurements now and I'll bring Margaret along this afternoon."

"I could probably manage it if I had some help. There's all the material to buy, you know, before I can even start cutting."

"Get Mrs Mitchell to help you," I suggested. "We'll pay."

Emily and I stood with pleading expressions on our faces, urging her on. Eventually she nodded and said, "All right but it'll cost you two guineas each – plus the material."

Exorbitant, I knew. It wasn't as if we wanted superbly finished clothes – we'll never wear the suits again after the first time, so they could just be cobbled together as I said to Rosa. But cobbling together was against her working practice and she pulled a face at the very idea. Even if we'd been having them made by West End couturiers we wouldn't have had to pay that sort of money, but we needed to get them quickly and we needed to get them from someone who wouldn't talk afterwards. So, of course, we agreed to two guineas each. After all, none of us is poor and Rosa knows that.

While we stripped down to our petticoats, Rosa opened the door of her sitting room and called up the stairs, "Are you there, Gladys? Come and lend me a hand for a minute, will you?"

Almost immediately footsteps clattered on the

stairs and the woman who came to tell me about my mother stood in the doorway. When she saw me, her pale face flushed and for a moment it looked as if she was about to go back upstairs again, but Rosa handed her a piece of paper and a pencil and said, "When I measure this pair, you take down the figures for me."

"These suits don't have to be perfect fits," I told her again as I stood ramrod straight and let her thread the tape round my waist.

"They've still got to be big enough for you to get into them and move around, I presume. You're both tall and that Campbell girl is huge. When you're all done up in the suits I make you, you'll look like three men," said Rosa.

"That's exactly how we want it to be," Emily told her.

Before we left, Rosa asked Mrs Mitchell to go to a large cloth shop in Chelsea and buy ten yards of black serge material.

"I think it's best that Gladys goes because they know me there. Give her the money, Miss Cavendish, I'm not putting this on my account," she said turning to me.

Wise woman. Even without asking questions she knew it was best to dissociate herself as much as possible from our enterprise, and to muddy the trail for anyone trying to find out about us afterwards.

Later that afternoon we went back with Margaret to find that Rosa already had my suit cut out and pinned together. When I stepped into it and folded the collar up against my neck, I looked like a long

black fish and was delighted with my reflection in
the dressmaker's pier glass.

"All you need now are black capes and you could
be the Three Horsemen of the Apocalypse," said
Rosa grimly sticking pins into the hems of my
trouser legs.

I laughed but said nothing though I noticed that
Mrs Mitchell, who was acting as Rosa's assistant,
handing her the tailor's chalk and pins, was staring
at me with a peculiarly fixed expression. When she
saw me looking at her, she turned her head away.

"We'll need hats," I said next.

"What sort of hats?" asked Rosa, speaking with
difficulty because her mouth was full of pins.

"Something to hide our hair. Let's have cloth
caps," suggested Margaret, "the kind working men
wear. Dark coloured ones with peaks that we can
pull down over our faces and hide them to—"

"This enterprise of yours sounds highly suspicious," said Rosa as she measured our heads with
the tape and said to Mrs Mitchell, "Go out again and
buy three men's caps. There's the sizes. You heard
them say what sort. Buy them in different shops too.
Give her the money, Miss Cavendish."

She was back within half an hour with three
cloth caps wrapped up in brown paper and string
– separate parcels, I noticed, so I knew she'd taken
Rosa's advice. The caps she'd chosen were dark grey
with capacious crowns made of soft, cheap material.
When we stuffed our hair into them we looked like
schoolboys and laughed at the sight of each other.

I was exhilarated at the thought of what we were

going to do and could barely contain my excitement. It would be a complete success, I was sure.

When we left Rosa's, we went back to my house and sat around the fire with the plans I'd made of Victoria Park after my visit there, spread out on the floor between us.

"We'll go in by the back way because there's less chance of being spotted from the main road," I said, pointing out the stable-yard gate with a pencil. "We'll wear our suits and try to walk like men – we'll have to practise that. But it'll be late when we're about so there shouldn't be many people around to watch us. Make sure you don't take anything with you that can be identified – not even a handkerchief with an initial or a laundry mark. It could be dangerous if we lost anything and were traced through it.

"We'll have to arrive at Victoria Park separately, too, and walk from the station if we go by train. Though I think it would be best if each of us chose a different means of transport. Whatever you do, don't hire a cab. Cabbies talk and they always pay close attention to their passengers.

"We'll time our arrivals, but we'll have to hide in the garden for quite a while till it's late enough to go into the house. Morton won't get home till after midnight for the House sits late usually, and I'd like him to be there when it happens."

Emily was bending over the plan. "Where does he sleep?" she asked.

I pointed to the drawing room. "The housekeeper said he sleeps in the room above this one, a big bedroom with windows overlooking the lawn and the main gardens."

"I think we should just blow the house up and not bother trying to set fire to it," said Margaret suddenly.

"But people might be killed then," protested Emily who was the most gentle minded of us.

"It wouldn't matter if he was killed. In fact it would be a great lesson to people like him. We could warn the others – the servants and his family or anyone else in the house," said Margaret boldly.

"There's only the servants there according to the housekeeper and we're going to warn them anyway," I told her. "We're not going to endanger innocent people. We've no fight with them and I don't want their deaths on my conscience. That's why I don't like the idea of explosives, they're too difficult to handle, too volatile. We might even kill ourselves and I'm not for that at all. It would be best if we just burn down the house and make sure he gets out safely."

"I don't care a fig about him. I'd rather he went up with it," persisted Margaret who seemed to have rejected all ideas of moderation. "He's a monster. I went to hear him talk at a women's rally in Westminster last week and I couldn't believe what he was saying. He said women shouldn't have the vote because they didn't want it, only rabble rousers and men haters want it, according to him. He also said that a woman's place is in the home, ministering to her husband and children, and that if they are denied that, they are in danger of becoming deranged.

"Apparently he believes that women's brains are

smaller than men's and mustn't be too agitated. Isn't that nonsense? What was almost as bad was all those stupid women sitting nodding their heads and agreeing with him. My mother was there clapping in approval, believe it or not."

Her face was flushed and angry when she poured this out. Poor Margaret is so violent because her parents are both strong anti-reformers. Her father, who is a Cambridge don, treats her as if she was an imbecile and refuses to allow her to be educated because she is a woman, though she is twice as clever as either of her brothers, both of whom have received the best educations.

"Margaret, listen to me, we mustn't kill him or we could be hung for murder," I told her in a firm but soothing voice, trying to calm her down.

"If we were hung, we'd be martyrs to the cause." She was almost shouting now and I looked anxiously across the room to make sure the door was closed and my maid couldn't hear what was going on.

"I'm not all that keen on martyrdom," drawled Emily, standing up and drawing on her gloves. She is on the verge of marrying Philip, that fellow in the ICS, and I'm quite sure that if she'd met him before she got involved with us, she wouldn't be here now. Fortunately she's loyal and the sort of person who, when she commits herself to something, follows it through. I suspect that this last gesture of Emily's will be her swan song as far as political activity is concerned.

"Neither am I," I agreed. "Let's concentrate on burning his house down and telling him why."

Margaret stood up too. "But I want to blow it up and with any luck, he'll go with it."

I glared at her, angry now. "Do be sensible. That's much more dangerous and difficult to arrange. I've worked out exactly how we can burn it down with the least danger to ourselves or anybody else and that is what we're going to do whether you like it or not."

Margaret was furious. "We should blow it up!" she repeated. "I've banked on blowing it up. I know a man who could make a bomb for us. He's been working in Paris with an anarchist group and learned how to do it there."

I could feel my face flushing and my temper rising but Emily, quiet sensible Emily who I've known and loved since I was a little girl, stepped between us and took control of the situation.

"Calm down both of you. We are not getting mixed up with any anarchist groups, Margaret. They're riddled with informers and internecine squabbling. The moment they hear what we plan to do, they'll spread it all over London. And besides, those anarchists are always blowing themselves up with their home-made bombs. I absolutely refuse to have anything to do with them. If you continue as you are doing, Daisy and I will leave you out of our plans altogether. We might even abandon the whole thing."

Temporarily quelled, because Emily so rarely showed her temper, Margaret glared at me and saw that I, too, was in favour of leaving her out of the plan.

"All right then," she said grudgingly. "I just hope

it comes off. So how do you plan to do it? How are you going to burn down the house?"

I told her. "It won't be difficult. There's masses of straw in the stable yard and we can hide fuel oil in the garden or the shrubbery beforehand. Then we'll pile straw in the main rooms, soak it with the fuel, set it alight and raise the alarm so everyone gets clear. Each of us must know what we have to do and do it properly. That's all."

Margaret sat down heavily, giving in with ill grace. "Let's make plans then," she said.

Next day I went back to Rosa's and found her alone.

"Where's Mrs Mitchell?" I asked.

"Out somewhere. I didn't ask her where she was going."

"What do you know about her? She's an odd one I think. Did you know she came to my house and told me she knew my mother. She said my mother, who's dead, wanted me to know how sorry she was about what happened – Edward told you the story I presume," I said, watching Rosa as she worked away on the sewing machine finishing one of our suits.

Rosa nodded without looking me in the eye, continuing to bend over her work as she spoke. "He did tell me a long time ago. He said you didn't know though, and I wasn't to mention it to you. As far as Mrs Mitchell's concerned, I don't know anything about her apart from the fact that she was sent to me by a friend I have called Megan who lives in Clapham and that she and I were in prison at the same time, though I didn't know her well then either. I took her in because she's a friend of Megan's and because I could see she needs help. I don't think she's very well. She looks exhausted half the time. But she's a quiet woman, pays her way and gives no trouble. I wish they were all like that."

I nodded. "I noticed how ill she looks too. That was the first thing I saw about her. You don't think she'll tell anyone about Emily, Margaret and me having those suits made, do you?"

"Why should she? But I might as well warn you, Miss Cavendish, to tell your friend Margaret Campbell to watch out what she says and how she says it, both here and outside. She's been meeting Ramon and his peculiar friends, you know. They're a dangerous rabble, I'm afraid, and I happen to know that the police have their eye on Ramon."

"How do you know she's seeing them?"

"Ramon told me. I think even he's a bit worried about the way she's carrying on. He said if she doesn't calm down she'll get herself killed. I'm not asking what you three are up to, but I wouldn't like to see you or Miss Emily getting into trouble. So be careful."

I assured her we would, but I was even more uneasy about Margaret than I had been before and that was bad enough.

The following day, the suits were delivered to my house, and it was Mrs Mitchell who brought them. She untied the string that bound the parcel with careful hands and spread the costumes along the back of my sofa.

"Splendid," I exclaimed clasping my hands. "They're exactly what I wanted."

She looked at me from her dark-circled eyes and said, "If you're going out in disguise at night, remember to blacken your faces."

I looked at her in surprise. "What makes you think we're going out in disguise?"

"Ramon said something about it at supper last night. Just remember to blacken your faces, that's all and don't speak to anyone who might recognise your voice," she said quietly. "You've got a very distinctive voice and you wouldn't want to be picked out and identified afterwards."

The weariness of her attitude touched my heart and I said, "Please don't worry about me. I'll be all right. Can I give you something to eat? You look tired."

She shook her head. "Rosa gives me more food than I want. I'm just worried about your safety . . ." There was a pause during which she obviously wondered if she should go on, but then, in a sort of a rush, she continued, "You see, I was fond of your mother and when I met you I felt that I wanted to help you somehow . . . I don't think you realise how dangerous life is. It's only when you're older you find out things like that. Don't throw your life away like your mother did. Please don't."

I stared at her aghast by her vehemence. "You mustn't worry about me. I'll be all right," I told her again, suddenly afraid that her anxiety might make her report us to the police in an effort to stop us. I wasn't sure how much she knew or had guessed.

She must have sensed my misgivings because

she shook her head gently. "Don't worry, I won't betray you or do anything to stop your plans. I just want you to be careful, very careful, and not risk anything. Above all don't trust people who might act impulsively."

I knew she meant Margaret but I didn't say anything, reluctant to discuss my friend with a stranger.

"Please don't worry," I repeated but more firmly this time, and she stood up to go.

"I'm sorry," she said, "perhaps I'm being over-anxious. You see I feel as if the fates are conspiring against me at the moment. As if it's an unlucky time for me just now. The woman I used to lodge with was murdered in what was my old room a couple of days ago."

This came tumbling out as if she'd been bottling it up, eager to talk about it to someone. I was aghast that she'd chosen me. "Oh, how terrible. I can imagine how that must have upset you. But you weren't there, were you? It's lucky that it wasn't you in the room." I couldn't think what to say that didn't sound uncaring but I didn't really want to hear about the dark shadows that filled this woman's life.

She gave a wry smile. "Perhaps it would have been better if it had been me. I don't know what I'm staying alive for. But every day there seems to be something new to worry about that's happening tomorrow . . . and I feel I've something still to do."

I didn't ask her what that was.

Though it was not far to Sydney Street, my guilt at having rejected her efforts at making some sort of contact with me meant that I insisted on calling a cab to take her back there. She looked as if the walk might be too much for her.

There was such a lot to do the following day that I hadn't time to worry about her, though the memory of the ravaged, anxious face came back into my mind every now and again. For most of the time I was worrying about the dangerously indiscreet Margaret, who, though she appeared to have acquiesced with Emily and me over the matter of burning the house down, was acting strangely – too acquiescent and pleasant, I thought.

Emily noticed it too. Later that afternoon, when we were alone together she suddenly said to me, "There's something up with Margaret. What do you think we ought to do about her? Should we drop her from the plan or perhaps put it off till she calms down a little?"

"Blast Margaret. Why does she have to do this to us now? We can't put it off," I said, angrily. "We'll never get so good a chance again. Morton is making a great spectacle of himself in parliamentary debates at the moment, popping up everywhere denouncing the women's movement. There's no one but him in residence in Victoria Park just now, so there's no danger of us hurting innocent people. It's the perfect time. There might never be another as good for our purpose."

Abashed by my vehemence Emily looked defeated. "All right, don't worry. I'm not trying to back out. What do we still have to do? Just tell me and I'll do it."

"You go home and rest. We'll need all our energy for tomorrow. When it's really dark, I'm going to hide a can of gasolene in the garden at Victoria Park so it's ready for us when we get there."

It was after ten o'clock when I reached Dulwich. A terrible tiredness and depression swept over me as I tramped up the hill, lugging the heavy fuel can that I'd bought earlier from a dry goods store, telling the man that I needed it for my gasolene stove. Ever since leaving home, I felt as if I was being followed. When I stopped and looked back there was never anyone to be seen. It's your imagination, I told myself, but the feeling persisted, a strange prickling between my shoulder blades as if hidden eyes were fixed on my back. I could almost hear the pursuer breathing behind me.

Victoria Park's drive was a narrow tunnel of blackness, like a sinister road into the underworld. When I had walked about a quarter of the way up it, and turned the bend I saw that tonight there were lights in the house. Two of the lower windows, one of them my grandmother's parlour, were glowing.

Full of fear that I might be seen I hurriedly dodged off the driveway into the shrubbery, which was dense at that point. Ignoring the wicked thorns of blackberry twigs which had entwined their way through the bushes and tore cruelly at my clothes, I fought my way into the undergrowth and hid my burden at the bottom of a low-branched yew tree. Then I piled dead leaves over it so that it would not be seen. There was little fear of gardeners poking about there at this time of the year because the

229

weather had turned bitterly cold and what garden work that was being done was in the greenhouses.

When I made my way back to the drive, my heart suddenly jumped because I thought I saw a dark figure standing behind a tree on the other side. When I looked a second time there was nothing and nobody there, only shadows. My nerves were playing tricks on me. For the first time since we embarked on our plan, I began to have second thoughts about the whole idea. Someone will give us away, I suddenly thought. It's going to end in tragedy, I just know it. Then I rallied and told myself not to be weak and stupid. We'd come so far, it had to be finished. So I took courage in remembering what Margaret had often said, if we succeeded, as she was sure we would, our standing would be greatly enhanced. We'd have struck a huge blow for the rights of women. We'd be heroines.

But trudging back to the train station I wondered if acclaim and heroism would be worth the trouble we were taking. What was even more disquieting was my worry that burning down Victoria Park would achieve nothing for our cause. That I would not permit myself to think about.

To my surprise I found Emily in my little sitting room when I reached home and she stood up to meet me at the door when I walked in.

"I came back and waited for you. I was worried about you. You seemed so desperate this afternoon. Thank heavens you're all right," she said.

She had a kettle steaming on the hob and a glass of whisky with sugar and lemon waiting on the hearth.

Pouring hot water into the glass, she handed it to me and I gulped it down gratefully.

Then I collapsed into a chair and said, "I hope this is all going to be worth it."

My oldest friend leaned forward with her hands clasped before her and said, "I hope so too. You see there was another reason I've come back. Margaret came to see me after I went home. She wanted to talk me round to her point of view. She still wants to blow the house up. She's got a bomb apparently."

I groaned and put my hands over my eyes. "That's awful, that's terrible. She's far too aggressive. She's dangerous. I wish I'd never got involved with her in the first place."

"Daisy," said Emily very earnestly, "I've been seriously thinking that we should call this whole thing off."

I glared at her. "We certainly won't call it off. We've gone too far for that. If we don't do it now, we'll never do it. If Margaret's a liability, we'll tell her she can't come with us. We'll do it alone."

"Just the two of us? Is that possible?" Emily looked scared and I realised then how much her enthusiasm for the project had dwindled as her involvement with Philip had progressed.

"Why not? You're not going to back out on me now, are you? Two of us can do it. I'll set fire to the house, you raise the alarm and then we'll both disappear."

"But Margaret won't let us go without her. You know what a strong character she is and how forceful."

"She won't know. We'll do it earlier than we've planned. She thinks we're going to start the fire tomorrow but we'll do it earlier. In fact," I said sitting up and feeling better as the whisky began surging through my veins, "we could do it tonight instead of tomorrow. Everything's ready. We'll just have to go up there together and do it now."

Chapter Fourteen

We went to Victoria Park that night.

The exhilaration I felt when I first saw the reflection of myself wearing the black suit was replaced by nervous disquiet the second time I donned it. Fortunately Emily's suit was still in my house, so she dressed too. There was solemn apprehension on both our faces when we looked at each other standing face to face in my sitting room.

"Do you think it'll be all right?" Emily asked me and I stretched out my hand to shake hers.

"Of course it will. Good luck friend," I said.

She took my hand and replied, "Good luck Daisy."

When we stealthily let ourselves out of my front door, I heard the little chiming carriage clock which sits on my sitting room bookshelves strike one o'clock.

With our hands in our pockets, we strode like young Jack o' lads along Cheyne Walk, taking longer, freer strides than usual. If I hadn't known it was Emily walking beside me, I'd have thought it was a man. Without speaking we walked to Vauxhall Bridge, passing only one solitary man on the way.

233

He glanced sideways at us and muttered some sort of greeting which we both ignored.

Crossing the bridge we headed in the direction of Waterloo but when I saw the lighted face of Big Ben with the hands of the clock standing at twenty-five past one, I suddenly stopped and stuck my arm up to attract the attention of a hansom cab that was clip-clopping along the road in the opposite direction.

The cabbie leaned down from his box and peered suspiciously at us. "Where to lads?" he asked.

"Herne Hill," I said gruffly. If I pretended to be drunk, he might not engage us in conversation, I thought. I was unsure of being able to sustain a sufficiently deep voice for more than a couple of words. Emily saw what I was about and reeled as she stood by my side, pretending to be drunk too.

"Ger'off. Herne Hill at this time of night?" scoffed the cabbie.

"Herne Hill – fast," I repeated and stuck my hand in my pocket to pull out some coins which I held towards him in my cupped palm. There was a couple of golden half-sovereigns among them and he spotted them immediately.

"Get in," he said, reaching behind him to open the cab door.

Fortunately there was almost no traffic as we rattled along Kennington Road and into Brixton. All the carts, trams, bicyclists and pushing people that normally crammed the thoroughfare had gone, leaving just a long expanse of empty road that looked strangely eerie when deserted. When we reached the foot of Half Moon Lane, I leaned forward and thumped the driver on the shoulder. "Drop us 'ere," I said.

There would still be a bit of a walk to Victoria Park, which lay bowered in its trees in the green land beyond Dulwich village, but I wasn't prepared to leave a trail that could be traced afterwards.

It was nearly half-past two when we stood on the pavement, pretending to prop each other up, while I held out my handful of money to pay the cabbie. He took the half-sovereigns as well as four florins, I noticed, but said nothing, just nodded blearily as if I was too drunk to care. Emily and I waited till he had driven off before we started to walk with speed and determination towards our destination. The night was very dark for a swirl of cloud obscured the fading moon.

There wasn't a soul apart from us on the street as we went without speaking through Dulwich Village, past Alice and Aaron's darkened shop, and turned into the road that led to my grandmother's old house. It was bitterly cold and the skeleton shapes of trees rising over garden walls looked like threatening spectres, reaching out to grab us as we walked beneath them. Somewhere in the distance a dog howled. The sound chilled my blood.

At the front gate of Victoria Park, I said to Emily, "We'll go round the back, to the stable-yard gate, but I'll have to come back here because I hid the gasolene drum halfway along the drive."

"Do you want me to wait here for you?" the reluctant Emily asked.

"No, come round to the stables where there's bales of hay and straw that we'll have to pile against the front door and set fire to. I really meant to get inside the house and make fires in all the downstairs rooms but we haven't got time for that now – lighting bales at the front door will have to be enough. With any luck the whole house will go up before the fire's discovered."

Emily shuddered and hunched her shoulders against the bitter wind. "I wish I was home in my bed," she muttered. "I hope this is all worth it."

I grinned at her because my own spirits were beginning to return now we had got so near to our objective,

"*Courage mon brave!*" I said. "Just think about the tale you'll be able to tell your grandchildren when you're an old lady."

"If I live long enough to *have* any children," grumbled Emily, but she did seem to cheer up a little.

"Come on, it'll soon be over. Let's go," I said briskly and set off round the edge of the property by the path that Alice had shown me.

For a man so sedulous in seeking the public eye and courting controversy, Sir Granville Morton was not security conscious. The stable-yard gate wasn't locked and neither were any of the service buildings. When we creaked the hay shed door open, a horse in one of the loose boxes gave a soft nicker but no one except us seemed to hear it. Silence hung over the whole place like a shroud.

It was easy for us to drag out a straw bale each and carry them round the gable end of the house. When we laid them down on the top doorstep, however, they were dwarfed by the vast breadth of the door and didn't look big enough to do any damage, so I whispered to Emily, "We'll have to go back and get some more."

We were pulling another two bales out of the shed, when there was a sharp, loud noise from behind us that stopped us both in our tracks. It was like a cannon burst and it came from a projecting side wing of the house overlooking the yard where we stood. Emily and I stared at each other with terror on our faces. Then we grabbed hold of each other as a tremendous explosion shook the ground beneath our feet. This noise also came from the main house behind us and, jumping round to face it, I saw a long jet of orange flame erupt like the tongue of a ravenous dragon from one of the upper windows.

We were still clinging to each other, gasping and sobbing in terror, not knowing what to do when, in the same instant one idea struck us both . . . "Margaret!" we shouted at the same time.

"Come on, come on, there's people in the house," cried Emily sprinting towards the kitchen door and I followed her yelling at the top of my voice, "Fire, Fire, Fire!"

We were both screaming hysterically, our disguise as men forgotten, while we thumped on the knocker and used our fists to hammer on the wooden panels of the door. My one thought was to get the people in the house out before the fire, which was already beginning to swallow up the side wing, engulfed them.

Behind us, people came running out of the gardener's and groom's cottages. They were shouting, pointing and pulling on their clothes as they ran about looking for water buckets.

Old Bryce appeared at the kitchen door and pushed me aside as he thrust a key he was carrying in his hand into the huge old lock. It swung open and he disappeared inside, shouting, "Fire, fire," as he went.

Emily and I stood helplessly in the middle of cobbled yard, staring up at the roof of the side wing where flames were already racing along the tiles like evil demons. As we watched there was first a sigh from the house, then a fearful crack followed by a tremendous whoosh, as the old, dry wood of the burning roof subsided revealing charred and broken rafters jutting out from the fiery inferno which was the centre of the house.

At the same time a group of frightened women came running out of the main building, all of them in long white nightdresses, clutching coats over their shoulders. Their hair was streaming down and their faces strained with fear and horror as they huddled together to watch the house burn.

I saw the housekeeper, the fat cook and a couple of maids but there was no sign of anyone who looked like the house's owner.

At that point a man who could have been the

groom came running over towards us yelling, "Give us a hand you fellows. Don't just stand there. Come and fill water buckets."

Water buckets will do no good against that inferno, I thought, but I asked, "Is everybody out?"

"Only the master is still inside. He sleeps in the front. The Bryces have gone in to get him."

Now that I was watching the house burning down I realised, a little too late perhaps, that I did not want anyone – even our *bête noire* Morton – to be killed or injured. But what about Margaret? Where was she? No one but us knew she might still be in there.

Grabbing Emily by the arm, I pulled her along with me to the front of the house, running, stumbling and panting across the flower beds and carefully raked paths to the neatly trimmed spread of grass before the main door. When we reached it, we stood staring up at the front windows, scanning each one for signs of life. Emily sobbed brokenly with tears streaking her smoke stained cheeks.

"What about Margaret? Poor Margaret. Oh, what are we going to do about Margaret?"

I followed her eyes to the ravaged wing at the back of which the fire had started. The windows were only empty holes now, like the eyes in a skull, and most of the roof had gone. Anyone in there had to be dead.

"She'll have got out before the bomb went off – if it was a bomb," I whispered but how could I sound as if I meant it when I was as doubtful as Emily? If Margaret had got out, we would surely have seen her. But would she have waited to see the results of her handiwork? Perhaps she was hiding in the shrubbery or between the closely growing trees along the drive where my tin of gasolene was still hidden.

Not knowing exactly what to do, I went across to a line of men who were passing buckets of water along in a vain attempt to staunch the flames that were already licking eagerly at the colonnaded columns around the door. Our bales of straw were still there on the step, I noticed, leaning drunkenly against each other. In a few seconds they'd be a heap of ash, the evidence of our intention destroyed completely.

As I was about to grab a bucket too, one of the men in the front of the line gave a shout. He pointed up at a window high above the door where a tall figure could be seen silhouetted like a black cut-out against a hellish background of yellow and orange flames.

"Jump, jump," some of the men began to shout, but the window was high and the drop to the ground would be at least twenty-five feet and the landing would have to be onto the flagstones of the terrace. The black figure – a man in a long nightshirt – smashed the glass by hitting it with a chair, but hesitated when he saw the distance he would have to fall.

"Jump, jump," came the call from the watchers again but I yelled out, "No, wait," and ran forward to pull out the already smouldering bales and line them up beneath the window. Then I called up to him, "Jump, jump! It's safer now."

The watching men realised my idea at the same time. "Yes, jump, sir, jump," they yelled, louder than me. Some of them threw the water from their buckets onto the straw turning its small flames to pungent smoke.

Trusting us, the trapped man climbed over the window sash and launched himself into the air. There was total silence from us all as he fell right in the middle of the smoking straw bales and lay still for what seemed like an age. Then he gave a groan and, at that, everyone in the crowd rushed towards him. Though he was writhing in pain, for one of his legs was twisted beneath him in an unnatural way, he was alive and safe. The bales had broken his fall.

I was among the crowd of people that pressed around him and when I saw he was going to survive his ordeal, I stepped back and leaned weakly against a stone statue on the terrace. I was staring at the big front door wondering about Margaret when it suddenly swung open and a man carrying another body in his arms came staggering out, collapsing on the ground as soon as he was clear of the crashing debris which was beginning to fall from the building.

"It's Sandy Bryce," yelled a man on my right and ran towards the rescuer. The person he had been carrying was his father.

People crowded round them, helping them to their feet. Miraculously both were unhurt. Old Bryce, it transpired, had been on the verge of being overcome by smoke when his son carried him out of the flames.

I could not stop myself staring over their heads at the dark hole of the hall and the open front door. As I was looking into it I suddenly heard a voice screaming – a woman's terrified and piercing scream that chilled my blood. As if impelled by some force that was beyond my control, I began to run, shouting over my shoulder to Emily, "Margaret's still in there. I'm going to find Margaret."

She reached out to stop me, saying, "No, no, don't go! You'll be killed."

But I was out of her reach and nothing was going to stop me as I ran up the front steps into the marble-floored hall. Wreaths of smoke and tongues of flame were coming down the curving stairs and I could hear the crackling of a greedy fire somewhere very near. It was pitch dark and I paused, but only for a second to get my bearings and to work out where the room the explosion had started in would have been. Then I pulled my jacket over my head and charged up the stairs onto the first landing.

Coughing and spluttering, I headed along a corridor to the heart of the fire but I didn't get very far before I heard the scream again, this time fainter and more despairing. Throwing open a door at my side, I was met by a blast of heat which nearly threw me off my feet. The moon had come out from behind the clouds and gave enough light for me to stare into the empty room and there, lying in the middle of the floor, I saw a huddled body.

"Margaret, Margaret!" I shouted and ran towards her. When I bent down and turned her over, however, I saw it wasn't Margaret. Even though the face that

242

looked up at me was blacked and burned, I knew it was Gladys Mitchell.

She was horribly injured, her skin was yellow and crinkled like charred leather and what remained of her hair was in wisps. But her brown eyes were open and I could see she knew what was happening. She stared at me, gasping, tried to smile and in a faint voice croaked, "Oh Daisy. My Daisy. Don't stay here. Get out, get out."

I was trying to pick her up but she thrust me off, so anxious was she to make me go. She was a tall woman, as big as me, and I was afraid I would hurt her if I pulled at her too much.

"You must let me help you Mrs Mitchell. There's still time to get out if you let me lift you," I said urgently, but she pushed with surprising strength at my shoulder.

"Go away. Get out. I don't want to be saved," she groaned.

"Don't be silly," I shouted at her. "I must get you out."

She tried to raise herself on one elbow but couldn't do it. Her glare was fierce, though her voice was weak and faltering as she said, "Go away. I'm your mother. I'm very ill. I want to die here and not wait any longer. Go away and leave me."

I couldn't really take in what she was saying but ran to the window and yelled out to the men on the grass, "Help, help, there's a woman here. Please help me get her out."

Two of them managed to get up the now flaming staircase which collapsed behind them as they ran.

They lowered her out of the window, dropping her
into the arms of others waiting below. Then, because
the elevation of the house was lower here than it was
at the front, the men and I jumped after her into soft,
recently dug flower beds, scrambling to safety only
minutes before the whole roof caved in.

They laid her on the grass in a bed of straw and
as I knelt beside her holding her hand, she died very
quietly in seconds, never speaking again but keeping
her eyes on my weeping face. I was still sitting with
her blackened, claw-like hand in mine when old Mr
Bryce came along and bent down beside me.

"Ah poor thing, poor thing," he said softly, putting
his hand on her face and closing her eyes as gently
as if she was his most delicate plant.

"Who is she?" I whispered. He hadn't recognised
me in my men's clothes and cap and because I was
so black with smoke.

"She's Mrs Muldona – Mrs Portbury. The daughter
of Mrs Ares who used to own this house. Ah poor,
poor woman. She had a terrible life."

I bent my head and started to weep as Emily, who
had been silently watching, bent down beside me.
Putting her arms round me she gently pulled me
to my feet. "Come on, my dear. Come on. We'll
have to go home. There's nothing we can do here,"
she said.

I leaned on her and sobbed. "We'll go to Alice's.
Alice will look after us."

Alice and Aaron were in bed but awake, for they
had been roused from sleep by the clanging of the

bells of the fire engine as it galloped through the Village.

It was Aaron who came down when I yanked on the bell at his front door.

I couldn't speak, just stared at him and sobbed. He didn't recognise me at first but, being a kindly man, he saw we needed help when he realised the smoke blackened, shocked and tattered state of us.

"Come in, come in," he said holding open the door and ushering us into the warm kitchen where the cat sat in the armchair with its eyes wide and staring in fright.

We sat down and both of us started to cry. Then Aaron saw who it was he had taken in. "Heavens above, Miss Daisy! What are you doing? Where have you been? I'll get Alice," he cried.

She came in her long flannel wrapper, knelt by the chair where I sat and hushed me as if I was a baby again. "Now, now, now, just you cry and get it out. Now, now, now, you're all right. Don't try to talk. Aaron's making tea – put a drop of brandy in it for these poor girls, Aaron. Now, now, now."

Aaron handed a cup of brandy-laced tea to Emily and another to me. Emily drank silently. She had stopped sobbing by this time but seemed to have lost the power of speech. When I drank mine, however, I was able to tell them where we'd been and what had happened, though I didn't explain what Emily and I had been doing at Victoria Park at that time of night and they were so amazed at the rest that they didn't ask.

When I told them about Gladys Mitchell dying

on the lawn after she'd said she was my mother, I started to weep again. "I think she was out of her mind," I sobbed.

Alice stood up and said firmly, "I'm sorry, but I think she was your mother, Daisy," she said. "If the woman who died up there at Victoria Park was the one who came here saying she called herself Gladys Mitchell, she was Amelia Portbury, your mother."

Aaron was limping up the stairs. "I'll put on my clothes and go up there to find out what I can," he called back over his shoulder.

"And you two," said Alice to Emily and me, "will lie down in my bed and go to sleep. You won't be able to do anything until you've had a rest."

Before she went upstairs Emily found her tongue. She looked across at me and said, "Oh dear I wonder what happened to Margaret?"

When I woke it was noon and Emily was sitting up in the bed beside me with her fair hair all tousled and a bemused expression on her face. Alice, I noticed, had washed our hands and faces and taken the black suits off us before she let us lie down to sleep on her pristine bed.

"I've got to send a note to Philip," Emily was muttering. "I've got to see Philip."

I sat up too but had to lie down again quickly because my head was swimming. It was difficult to remember what had happened at first but then, in a terrible wave, it all came back. I shuddered as I remembered the dying woman on the grass with her claw-like hand in mine – the woman who said she was my mother.

Alice popped her head around the door and when she saw we were awake, came across to the bed and handed me a cardboard-framed studio photograph.

It showed a tall, slim, dark-haired woman in a full-skirted gown with a cascade of what looked like roses looping up the skirt. She was standing sideways on to the camera with a large fan in one hand and her head turned towards the camera. It was unmistakably the woman I had known as Gladys Mitchell – much younger but still recognisable.

"I did have a picture of her. It was taken the year your grandmother died," said Alice, "but I didn't want you to see it in case you recognised her from it. I thought if she was going to tell you, she'd do it in her own time."

"Mr Bryce said I look like her," I replied, staring intensely at the woman in the picture. "Do I?"

"Yes, very. She was lovely when she was young and even though prison brought a terrible change in her, both Dora and I recognised her when we saw her again. She had those sort of good looks, the kind that never leave you," said Alice sadly, staring at the photograph.

I said, "You told me she was dead. Even Edward told me she was dead."

Alice nodded. "I suppose we all thought it was the best thing to say. We didn't think she'd ever come back, you see."

I sat up more slowly this time and said, "If I'd known it was her, I could have asked her so many questions. There's such a lot of things I want to know and to say to her."

"She probably wouldn't have known the answers herself, poor soul," said Alice. Then she added more briskly, "Aaron's back. He says Victoria Park is completely destroyed. There's nothing left but a pile of ruins. The police are up there and they told him that they think Mrs Portbury must have got in last night before the owner got back from the Houses of Parliament, waited till everyone was in bed and then set off a bomb or a big fire in the empty west wing. It hasn't been used for years. Even your grandmother never used it. They think she did it because the house had such bad memories for her – murdering her mother there and everything. They're saying she'd lost her mind. The prison doctor has told them that she was very ill, dying in fact, and it was amazing she lived this long. She had a growth in her stomach, apparently."

I laid the photograph down on the bed clothes and said, "She told me she was dying . . . I don't think she wanted to live any longer."

"Were any more bodies found?" asked Emily in a shaky voice.

Alice shook her head. "They haven't found anybody else and everyone who was in the house was saved. But they're looking for two young men who were up there at the time – probably trying to break into the stable tackroom according to the police. They turned into the heroes of the hour because one of them brought Mrs Portbury out. They've disappeared and the police aren't too surprised about that. I think they should stay disappeared, don't you? I'll go out and buy you a couple of new skirts and two new hats and then you pair can go home."

Emily lay back against the pillows and her face was almost as white as they were. "But what about Margaret?" she whispered to me.

Chapter Fifteen

It was afternoon by the time we rode home in a hansom cab, sitting each in opposite corners, staring out of the windows and not speaking. Emily was dropped off first at her parents' home in Blackheath and I rode on alone to Cheyne Walk.

Wearily I climbed the stairs to my sitting room, ignoring the curious looks of my servant, and threw myself into an armchair.

I didn't know what to do. I didn't know what to think. I was in total confusion. Should I go to the police and tell them that I feared Margaret Campbell had been killed in the fire at Victoria Park, and that the woman they were blaming for it was not responsible at all? That would involve Emily and me, of course, and Emily wanted to marry her Philip and go with him to India . . . I didn't want to go to prison either.

But what had Mrs Mitchell – I could not yet think of her as my mother or refer to her as that even in my head – been doing in the house? How had she got in, and why was she so horribly burned when the fire was only just beginning to take hold in the room where I had found her?

250

I leaned back in the chair with my eyes closed and my head throbbing and might have fallen asleep again from sheer exhaustion if there had not been a sudden pealing of the front door bell. Whoever was out there was in a great hurry because before the maid had time to answer, the bell was rung again and a voice shouted, "Let me in!" Then feet came thundering up my stairs and Margaret burst through the door with an evening newspaper in her hand.

Waving it at me, she said, "Have you seen this? Here in the Stop Press. Victoria Park was burned down last night!"

I ran behind her, closed the door and put my fingers to my lips to warn her to be quieter. Then I threw my arms round her, hugged her tight and started to cry. I was surprised at the vehemence of my grief. I couldn't stop the tears flowing, and Margaret hugged me back saying, "What's wrong? What's wrong? Please stop crying Daisy. Come and sit down and tell me what's wrong."

She guided me to my chair and knelt on the floor in front of me, asking anxiously, "What on earth is wrong? Are you ill or something?"

"No, no. It's because Emily and I thought you'd been killed at Victoria Park last night. We were sure you were dead."

For a moment she looked scared but then she sat back on her heels and smiled. "Look, feel me. I'm not a ghost. You can see that I'm perfectly well. I've had a good night's sleep and I'm as fit as a fiddle. Why should I have been killed at Victoria Park?"

"We thought you'd try to go there a night early like

251

we did. We thought you were so keen on blowing the place up, you'd do it by yourself. It was completely destroyed, you know. I saw the ruins."

"My God! Who would do a thing like that?" gasped Margaret. That might have made me smile if I hadn't been so distressed and I snapped, "You were going to do it, remember? Perhaps someone else had the same idea."

"But who? And why? And what were you doing there when it was destroyed?" Her face changed and she said in a regretful tone, "I never thought about going a day early. I wish I had."

I said sarcastically, "I'm sorry about cheating you out of that, Margaret, but we were afraid that someone would get killed if you blew the place up, so we decided to burn it down first ourselves . . ."

"You and Emily?" asked Margaret.

"Yes."

"Hmm, I didn't think she had that much courage. I'm not surprised at you though. But why haven't you sent a letter to the papers saying you burned it down as a gesture on behalf of women's liberation? That's what we were going to do, wasn't it?"

"Because we didn't burn it down. We didn't even strike one match. I told you, someone else beat us to it."

Then I told Margaret the whole story – even the bit about my mother. She listened silently, astonished and absorbed.

Finally she said, "What an amazing tale. Did she burn it down because it was the place where the most terrible things in her life happened, do you think?"

"I don't know. I can't understand it."

Margaret stood up. "Well, the first thing we should do is go to Rosa Stein's and ask her what she knows. That's where your mother was living, wasn't it? Rosa probably doesn't even realise yet that your mother – Mrs Mitchell I mean – is dead. Come on, perk up. I'll send that useless maid of yours out to bring us a cab."

Rosa was alone, for once not working. It seemed as if she was expecting us for when she let us in, she only nodded at me and said, "The police have been here about Gladys. She was identified by the gardener apparently, and she had this address in her pocket. I'm glad you're safe, Miss Cavendish. I've been very worried about you. And you, Miss Campbell. How's the other one?"

"Emily's all right, but she's very shaken."

"You'd better sit down then and tell me the whole story. I know you've been up to no good so there's no point trying to wriggle out of it."

When we'd finished a short account of our ill-fated venture Rosa looked from one to the other and said sharply, "You should be ashamed. It was a very stupid plan. It probably wouldn't have worked and even if it did, it wouldn't have achieved any-thing, only hardened the prejudices of people against women's rights. And you shouldn't have involved me in it. I didn't tell the police about anything I knew though – and certainly not about making you the men's suits." She was obviously angry and upset.

Margaret and I stood together in her sitting room

like chastened children and I humbly asked, "How much did you know before today, Rosa?"

She turned and lifted a newspaper off the table. "I can put two and two together. I've read this and I've spoken to the police and Gladys told me some things before she went out last night. But I didn't tell the police about that.

"Believe me, I don't like the police and I try to avoid them as much as possible. A few years ago I served time in prison because I performed an abortion for a friend and she talked about it afterwards. That experience was enough to put me off helping anyone ever again."

She brandished the paper under my face. "I suppose you've read what this says, 'Victoria Park, home of Sir Granville Morton, MP, was burned down in a mystery arson attack last night. The body of a woman identified as Mrs Amelia Portbury was found at the scene of the fire and it is thought she was responsible for the outrage.' Then it goes on about your mother being recently released from prison where she had served a twenty-two-year sentence for killing her mother at the very house destroyed by the fire.

"She told me she'd been watching you, Daisy, and when the police came here to tell me what had happened to her I knew that you three were involved as well but, mercifully, here you are, safe and sound after all. I don't suppose you realised she was going to Victoria Park last night?"

At first I couldn't speak, only shake my head wordlessly. Then I found my voice and said, "I went there earlier in the evening myself – to hide some gasolene. I thought at the time someone was following me but I never dreamed for a minute it was her. I was afraid it was the police – or you, Margaret."

Rosa sat down heavily in her chair and said, "I was worried when she didn't come back but I thought she might have gone to Clapham to see Megan and hear more details of the murder that was committed in the house she used to live in – she was sure she was meant to be the victim.

"I should have guessed there was something odd going on though because yesterday afternoon she gave me a letter to deliver to you, Miss Cavendish, if anything happened to her. She said she was afraid that her husband, Portbury, would get her eventually. She told me he'd had her followed to that Clapham rooming house and when he found the wrong woman was dead, he'd start looking for her again."

In anguish I put my hands over my face and shuddered as the memory of my mother's burnt face came back to me. "She didn't seem to care that she was dying," I said.

"Did she tell you she was your mother? I didn't think she was going to do that," said Rosa.

"She told me when I tried to drag her out of the house. She wanted me to leave her there."

"You didn't know before then?"

"I had no idea. I thought she'd been dead for years. When she came to see me, she said my mother was dead but had wanted me to know how sorry she was about what happened with my grandmother."

Then I started to cry and Margaret put an arm round my shoulders as she asked Rosa, "Have you any idea why she would want to burn down Victoria Park, Miss Stein?"

Rosa looked hard at her and said, "I think it was because you talk too much, Miss Campbell. Ramon told us about you asking him for a bomb, and he told us what you were going to do with it. You wouldn't make a good plotter, I'm afraid. Gladys was horrified when she heard what you three were going to do. I think she must have decided to pre-empt you, to save you from yourselves."

My head was swimming but I heard myself say, "Can I have the letter she gave you for me, please?"

Rosa got up and walked over to the crowded mantelpiece. From behind a china vase painted with a seaside scene, she drew an envelope and handed it over. Judging by her expression as she did so, I felt sure that she despised Emily, Margaret and me for the way we had behaved.

There was nothing I wanted more than to get out of that house but she had something else to say before she let us go. "Your mother killed her mother by hitting her with a poker, Miss Cavendish. I'm afraid you've killed yours because she died trying to save you from your own folly."

Margaret wanted to stay with me while I read the letter but I was adamant that I wanted to be alone, and sent her away. Then I sat down in my own chair, by my own fire, and slit open the envelope.

It was a long letter, three closely covered pages

with writing on both sides and a fourth tattered scrap that had writing only on one side. Judging by the different colours of the ink, and the variation in the style of writing, it had been composed over several days.

'Dear Daughter,

I have just met you for the first time since you were three years old and I am delighted at your beauty and sweet nature. You've turned out so well and I am very grateful that you are happy and have enough money to live a comfortable life. My biggest regret is that I didn't meet my son Edward again, but from what I have heard I doubt if he would have wanted to see me.

I have already told you about the remorse of your mother for bringing notoriety and tragedy on her children. What I didn't say was that she was sorry for bringing about the death of her mother, your grandmother Julia Ares, because that would have been a lie. I'm not sorry that my mother died, but I have always believed that I did not murder her. She died from heart disease. I only hurried that death along. She deserved it, though, because she was a wicked woman.

If that shocks you, let me add that your grandmother Ares only pretended to the outside world that she was a good person. She was a bully and a liar; she was a snob and a bigot. You would not have liked her and she probably would have bullied you too if she had lived long enough to blight your life as she blighted mine.

From as early as I can remember my mother criticised me and ridiculed my opinions. If I said I liked something or someone, she would set about making me look stupid or deceived. She told my father lies about me, saying I had said nasty things about him, or that I had stolen money from his purse or done things he expressly ordered me not to do. He always believed her and if I protested that I was innocent, that was another proof of how wicked I was.

Now I realise that my mother was intensely jealous of me. In fact she was jealous of all women and had no real female friends – only men friends or sycophantic women who hung around her for what they could get . . . women like Isabella Downs and her mother who was, if anything, worse than Isabella.

The trouble was that my mother had been very beautiful when she was young. She was also a superb actress and put on a wonderful act for the outside world. It never fails to surprise me how people judge by appearances. If a woman is beautiful and pretends to be virtuous, they take her at face value. Even some of my mother's servants – but not all – thought she was a good person who had to put up with a deceitful daughter and an overbearing husband.

If you grow up being told over and over again that you are stupid and wicked and ugly, you begin to believe it. There was nothing I wanted more in the world than to please my mother, to make her love me, to ingratiate myself with her, but nothing I ever did really pleased her.

When I was young I had a few suitors but none of them pleased my mother. She said one was only after her money, another was too weedy and feeble-looking to provide me with healthy children, and another, the one I liked best, was too impudent. In fact he saw through her, I think, and wouldn't have played her game.

Anyway, she had her own plans for me. Just before my father died, she married me off to her doctor, Joseph Muldona. He was fifty-three to my eighteen on the day we married. The next morning I knew I had made the most terrible mistake of my life.

Less than a year later, when I was nineteen, my father died. He hadn't played a big part in my life because he was absorbed in business, and I hardly missed him. In his will he left me only a small annuity. He said that my husband was a man with a good medical practice and well able to provide for me. My mother had convinced him about my inability to handle money and he was content to leave things so I would have what was left of her considerable fortune after she was dead. That gave my mother and my husband even greater power over me.

From the very first day of our marriage I hated Joseph. He repelled me physically and because I showed my repulsion, he was a brutal lover. I had no idea that there were men like that and dreaded having to share a bed with him. Then one day, when I shrank away from him, he laughed and said that my mother wasn't like me. She was much more adventurous in bed. Apparently they had been lovers for years, even when my father was alive. I think arranging a marriage between her lover and her despised daughter gave my mother some sort of illicit thrill. It also provided him with my money and gave my mother grandchildren.

I asked my mother if it was true and she screamed at me that I was a liar and had a wicked imagination. She said I was mad with evil sexual fantasies and that she and Joseph could have me confined to an insane asylum. She said she would have my children removed from my care – you were newly born at that time – and put into her guardianship. That was what she wanted, she wanted my children.

My marriage lasted for fifteen miserable years but one day when you were still tiny, Joseph died of a heart attack. The relief I felt was so strong that it made me intensely guilty, so guilty that I almost collapsed with remorse. I wept and howled and carried on like a mad woman. But I wasn't mourning him, I was mourning everything that had happened in my life.

My mother was in charge of my affairs. Joseph had made her the executor of his estate and only left me five hundred a year providing I didn't remarry. She said I should take more exercise, but I refused even to go out, so she hired a young boy to drive my gig and ordered him to take me out every day.

He was such a cheerful funny young fellow that he made me feel like a girl again. His name was Samuel Portbury and he was only sixteen years old. Because I'd never had a real girlhood, it was easy for me to become young again with him. I fell in love, head over heels, hopelessly, dreadfully in love. It was a feeling I'd never had before and it obsessed me. I couldn't contemplate life without him.

When my mother guessed what was going on, she dismissed Sam. The only way I could keep him with me was by marrying him and that was what I did.

I thought he loved me as much as I loved him, but when he found out that marrying meant I lost my five hundred a year from my husband, he was very angry. He said I'd tricked him and then he suggested that we try taking you, my children, away from my mother, who had been caring for you since I became ill with grief, and who refused to give you back when I married Sam. If we could get the children, Sam said, we'd get their income as well, for Joseph had left you well provided for financially.

I think I must have been mad at that time because I let him try to snatch you out of my mother's garden but Bryce, the gardener, saw him and stopped him. That made my mother even more determined to hang on to you.

When I discovered that Sam and his mother

were stealing things out of my house, I left
him and went back to Victoria Park. The house
I'd lived in with Joseph in Peckham had been
sold. But Sam won me back, sweet-talked me,
seduced me and got me back to our little house
to live with him again.

Can you imagine how my mother reacted to
that? Like a mad woman, I assure you. She
screamed and shouted and accused me of all
sorts of things, called me all sorts of names. We
were having our last row, over a trivial decanter
that I said was mine and she said was hers, when
I hit her . . . she died three days later.'

The final part of the letter was written on the tattered
scrap that looked as if it had been hurriedly ripped
out of an exercise book. The writing was only a
scrawl but the urgency of the message seemed to
cry out from the trailing script . . .

'Ramon, one of the lodgers here in Rosa Stein's
house, told me tonight that you and your friends
are going to blow up Victoria Park with a home-
made bomb tomorrow as some sort of political
gesture. That is madness. Even if you succeed
you will ruin your life and end up in prison
like your mother. I must stop you. Ramon has
sold me the bomb that your friend Margaret
Campbell wants to buy from him and I am
going to blow up the house before you ever
get there.

That house is a place of ill-omen to our

family. It is best destroyed and perhaps all the old evil will go with it.

Please remember me. I am your mother and I love you. Everything I did that was wrong was done out of stupidity and because I wasn't loved until it was too late and then by the wrong person.

Goodbye,

Amelia Ares.'

Chapter Sixteen

January, 1901

By a weird coincidence, the inquiry into the death of Amelia Portbury and the fire at Victoria Park were held on the twenty-third anniversary of her fatally hitting her mother, and in the same Lambeth courtroom where she was committed to prison for her crime. The public benches were again crowded because the fire and the notorious woman blamed for causing it had aroused a great deal of interest.

The most illustrious witness was Sir Granville Morton, MP, who hobbled into the court on a silver-topped walking stick, for his left leg had been broken by jumping from the window.

"I have absolutely no idea why this woman Porbury – of course, Port-bury," (in response to prompting about the name from the court clerk) "why she should want to burn down my house and endanger my life. I have never laid eyes on her.

"When I bought the house in 1878 I was told about the unfortunate incident that had taken place there but I didn't give it a thought. I certainly never met any of the people involved and the whole matter was handled through lawyers."

He went on to describe the events of the night of the fire.

"I returned from the House about midnight. No, I didn't notice anyone in the grounds. I ate the supper left out for me in the downstairs parlour, had a glass or two of brandy, cast my eye over the newspaper and retired to bed about one a.m.

"The next thing I knew was a hellish commotion which woke me from a deep sleep. People were shouting and running about in my grounds. When I got up and opened my bedroom door, I saw flames at the far end of the corridor. I ran out onto the landing and along to the window above the front door. I jumped from there onto bales of hay my servants piled on the stone flags of the terrace. They broke my fall but, unfortunately, my leg was broken in two places and I fainted so I don't know anything about what happened after that."

Asked if he thought the fire-raising had some sort of political motive in view of his strong stand against the campaign for women's rights, Sir Granville scoffed and said firmly, "I do not think so, not for a moment. Even the most rabid of the women barracking for the vote would have no reason for burning down my house. If any of them were so foolish as to think of such a thing, I would advocate confining the culprit in prison for a very long time. Such behaviour would do their cause no good – even if it had any chance of success, which it hasn't."

Sitting side by side and watching him from the middle of the court were Margaret Campbell and Daisy Cavendish. Emily was not with them because two days before the inquiry opened she had sailed for Bombay with her new husband Philip Knight.

Feeling Margaret shift in her seat as Sir Granville gave forth his vehement assertion, Daisy put a hand on her friend's arm and made a soothing noise. Margaret looked round at her and shook her head, conveying the message that although she deplored Sir Granville's sentiments she was not going to make any public protest against them. Margaret was going to work for her cause through more conventional means in future, but she wasn't going to stop. Neither was Daisy, but her crusading zeal was temporarily overshadowed by confusion and sorrow about the death of her mother.

During the investigation into the fire, she had been interviewed at her house in Cheyne Walk by a tall, blond-haired detective who asked her about the visit the woman who had called herself Gladys Mitchell had paid on her.

"Who told you she came here?" asked Daisy defensively.

"Miss Stein from Sydney Street. Mrs Mitchell was a lodger in her house and she said she told her that you lived here. She did come to see you, didn't she?"

"Yes, she did. She came to tell me that my mother wanted me to know how sorry she was about everything that had happened – about her killing my grandmother and her sorrow at having to leave her children when she was sent to prison."

"Was that a surprise to you?"

"No. My brother, who was older than me, had already told me the story. My mother's cousin and my nursemaid had tried to prevent me knowing about the

murder and the prison sentence because they thought
it would upset me."

"It didn't?" He had very blue eyes, pale china blue
which seemed capable of boring into her brain, she
noticed.

"At first I suppose it did but I had no memory of
my mother, none at all and it's hard to grieve about
someone you can't remember."

"So you didn't recognise the woman who called
herself Mitchell as your mother?"

"No. I believed her when she said she'd befriended
my mother in prison."

"What did you think of her?"

"I thought she was very sad and very ill. I was sorry
for her."

"How did you find out that she was actually your
mother?"

"When the police went to Miss Stein's where she'd
been lodging to say she'd been killed at Victoria Park,
Miss Stein gave me a letter my mother had written for
me. Do you want to see it?"

How much she wished she could unburden herself
to this man, to tell him how she had felt when she
had held her dying mother in her arms on the grass
outside the blazing house. She'd never forget the
terrible noise when the roof collapsed and the strange,
almost pleasant smell of the burning wood. She knew it
would be a very long time before she could rid herself
of the memory of that night and she would probably
always feel terrible guilt because she feared Rosa Stein
was right. Had she, Daisy, caused the death of her
mother Amelia just as surely as her mother had killed

her grandmother Julia? Were the three generations of women in her family linked together by guilt?

How ironic, she thought, that the police did not consider her sufficiently involved to be a witness at the inquiry. Even the official identification of the body had been done by a doctor from Brixton Prison who testified that it was indeed that of the convict she had known as Amelia Portbury.

That witness, Dr Mary Milton, a straight-backed young woman in a neat dark-grey coat and skirt worn with a high-collared blouse, told the court that she had been called in to examine convict Portbury after she collapsed in her cell one morning during the summer of 1899.

"She was extremely debilitated and low in her spirits because she had recently received news that her only son had been killed in South Africa. She told me she had last seen him when he was nine years old and had longed through all the years of her imprisonment to meet him again.

"When I examined her, however, I discovered she was suffering from more than grief. She had an advanced cancer of the stomach and did not have long to live. I think she knew how ill she was because she insisted that I tell her the truth about her chances of recovery and when I did, accepted my diagnosis with dignity. Her only regret, she said, that she would die in prison without seeing her other child, a girl, who had been three years old when she was sent away.

"Because I felt such pity for her I suggested to the prison governor that she might be considered as a candidate for sentence remission which had recently been introduced. She had behaved very well for several years and we eventually succeeded in having three years cut off her sentence. I said goodbye to her the day before she was released at the end of last year. The next time I saw her was when I was called in by the police to identify her body at the morgue."

The coroner leaned forward in his seat and asked Dr Milton, "So you were responsible for turning this dangerous woman loose on the public?"

She fixed him with an unafraid eye. "There was nothing to indicate that Mrs Portbury had any intention of doing anybody any harm. As I have told you, she was gravely ill and would not have lived much beyond this month, if she managed to see that out, which was doubtful. Her illness was very advanced. I was treating her with Christian mercy by recommending her release."

"Are you suggesting that by setting fire to her old home she might have been committing some sort of bizarre suicide?" said the coroner.

"No. I'm not suggesting anything of the sort. I have no idea why Mrs Portbury's body was found at Victoria Park. The reason why I am in this court is to testify to her identity and to tell what I knew of her medical history, that's all," said the young woman firmly.

In her, both Daisy and Margaret recognised one of their own kind, and watched her with admiration when she returned to her seat.

The two Bryces, father and son, gave evidence after the doctor. Old Mr Bryce described the visit Mrs Portbury paid to him a couple of days before she was found in the burning house.

"Why do you think she went to see you, Mr Bryce?" he was asked.

He shrugged. "Who knows. I thought it was just to look round the place. She spent most of her young life there and she loved the garden."

Daisy, holding herself tense in her seat, wondered why he did not tell the court of her own visit but he did not mention it, perhaps he thought it insignificant. Mrs Speed, the housekeeper at Victoria Park, who might have returned to it, was not called as a witness at the inquiry and did not appear to be in the audience either. In fact, she had been sent to work in Sir Granville Morton's Wiltshire home to help her recover from the shock of the fire. The cook had gone too, and only the outdoor servants remained on the property in Dulwich.

When he stepped down from the box, however, Bryce looked across in Daisy's direction. From a flash that came into his eye then she could have sworn that he knew she had been the one holding her mother's hand when she died. His silence had been deliberate.

He was followed by his son who told of rousing the servants when two young strangers gave the fire alarm.

"I heard them shouting in the yard. I think they'd come in to steal from the tack room. The groom used to leave the stable-yard gate unlocked most nights though he'd been told not to," said Bryce junior.

"What did you do when you heard the men shouting about the fire?" asked the coroner.

"My father and I roused the servants in the house and then my father took off up the stairs to get the master out. I went after him. The whole of the upper floor was in flames . . .”

“And?” came the prompt.

“And my father tried to get to the master’s bedroom but I saw it wasn’t possible, so I hit him.”

“You hit your father?”

“Yes sir. I knocked him out. It was the only way to stop him killing himself. Then I carried him out of the front door. I didn’t see why he should make himself a hero at his age . . .”

His voice trailed off and what might have followed was swallowed up by the coroner’s voice as he said, “When you carried your father out what did you see?”

“I saw a crowd of people in front of the house. They were helping the master who’d jumped out of the window. There were two strangers among them, young chaps, rough looking lads I’d never seen before. I reckon they were the thieves. But they weren’t such bad lads because one of them heard the woman, Mrs Portbury, shouting, and went in to get her, though the house was well ablaze by that time. He got her out in the nick of time, just before the roof fell in. It was a very brave thing to do, but a bit mad if you ask me.”

“When did you see that young man again?”

“Never. I was taking care of my father. I laid him on the grass and he came round quite quickly. I hadn’t hit him too hard. Then I went over to help with the master, trying to get him onto a gate stretcher and when I was away my father saw the woman on the grass and recognised her as Mrs Portbury. When he was kneeling down beside her, she died and the young man who’d saved her just got up and walked away, melted into thin air, like, Dad said. None of us saw either of them again after that."

When he went back to his seat, Alice, who was sitting on the opposite side of Daisy to Margaret Campbell, noticed that her sister-in-law was sitting between him and his father in one of the front benches. Dora was wearing a new hat with a bunch of yellow flowers stuck in the brim – certainly not a mourning hat.

Ah ha, thought as much. Dora won't be a widow much longer, she said to herself with a little smile, pleased for her friend.

The blond-haired police officer who'd interviewed Daisy next testified that extensive enquiries had failed to reveal the identities of the two young strangers who were at Victoria Park that night.

"We have no reason to believe they had anything to do with the arson attempt because it was started by some sort of amateur bomb in a deserted wing of the house while they were in the stables," he told the court.

Wide-eyed and with hearts beating very fast, Daisy and Margaret watched him giving evidence.

What a nice-looking man he is, thought Daisy, surprising herself by such an unexpected reaction. Alice, sitting on her left, slid a gloved hand along the bench to grip her fingers when the police officer stood down. This, Daisy knew, was meant to convey the assurance that even if they pulled out her teeth one by one Alice would never tell about the two hysterical young men in dark suits who had turned up at her house on the night Victoria Park went on fire.

The next important witness was Rosa Stein, described as a dressmaker and lodging-house keeper, who stood dark and monumental in the box like an avenging fury. She explained how the woman who called herself Gladys Mitchell was sent to her by a friend in Clapham who knew she rented out rooms.

"Did you know she was the notorious Amelia Portbury?" asked the coroner.

"Yes, I did. She said she'd been let out of prison early and was trying to find her daughter. As it happened I was acquainted with her late son and also knew her daughter, Daisy Cavendish, who is one of my dressmaking clients. I told her where Miss Cavendish lived and gave her a parcel to deliver there. I thought it would give her a chance to at least see her daughter, even if she didn't make herself known to the girl, which she didn't."

"How do you know that?"

"She told me."

The coroner fixed her with an eye as steely as her own and asked, "Did you have any idea that she was preparing to burn down her old home?"

"None at all. On the last day of her life, she gave me a letter asking that I should give it to her daughter in case anything happened to her. She was afraid that someone was planning to kill or injure her for some reason. And of course she was very ill. She knew that and so did I. You only had to look at her to tell she hadn't long to live."

"Someone was trying to kill her? Did she say who?"

Rosa Stein cast her black eyes over the assembled faces of the court room but selected no one in particular before she turned back to the bench and said, "She didn't name any names, sir."

"And the letter? What happened to it?"

"I gave it to her daughter after she was dead."

"Had you read it? Did she tell you what was in it?"

Rosa glared. "No I hadn't read it and no, she didn't tell me what was in it. That was none of my business."

"Where is this letter? It may be significant," said the coroner addressing the police contingent in the court and the blond officer stood up to say, "When I went to interview Miss Daisy Cavendish she showed me the letter. It was a long account of the events that led up to Mrs Portbury murdering her mother twenty-three years ago. Her explanation for what she did then. Nothing in it gave any indication that she harboured ill feelings towards Victoria Park or its present owner. I have the letter here if you want to see it, sir."

From a folder he drew out a sheaf of papers. What he did not know was that before she gave him the letter, Daisy had removed one crucial page, the last one.

There were two more witnesses. First came Isabella Downs, as whey-faced and vindictive-looking as always, but triumphant too as if all her most fervent wishes had come to pass.

"My cousin Amelia called on me unexpectedly one morning at the end of November. She'd recently been released from prison, she said, and wanted to know where she could find her daughter. I refused to tell her because I thought she was either going to beg money off Daisy or bother her in some other way, move in with her perhaps. My husband and I went to great lengths to prevent the child knowing the truth about her mother and finding out by that woman turning up on her doorstep would have been a terrible shock."

"You didn't offer to put the girl in contact with her mother if she chose to do so?" asked the coroner.

Isabella shook her head. "Daisy has rather gone her own way, I'm afraid. I don't think she really appreciates what was done for her by us."

"What impression did you receive of Mrs Portbury's frame of mind when she called on you?" was the coroner's next question.

"I thought she was insane, quite mad. Her expression was most odd and her conversation disjoined. I was anxious to get her out of my house before she did something dangerous. She was well capable of it, I knew. It didn't surprise me a bit when I read in the newspaper that she'd burned down Victoria Park. That's just exactly the sort of crazy thing she'd do. She was always very impulsive."

Sam Portbury, the last witness, tended to agree.

"She turned up at my yard on a Tuesday morning at the beginning of December. Just walked in as cool as you like and says 'Hello Sam!' Gave me quite a turn I can tell you because I'd been told she was dead – I've even got a paper saying so – otherwise I'd never have got married again, would I?

"'Oh Em,' I says to her, 'What do you want coming 'ere?'

"'I want money,' she says, 'I want enough to set me

up in America. If you don't give it to me I'll report you to the police as a bigamist.'"

Conscious of the eyes of the court on him, he blossomed as he had done when he was seventeen, straightened up, rolled his eyes and became Sam the card again. Rosa Stein watched him with loathing. She knew him to be a murderous liar, but was far too canny ever to reveal her knowledge. Daisy watched him with disbelief, asking herself, Why on earth did my mother marry that frightful man?

"What did you do when she tried to blackmail you?" asked the coroner.

"Well, Your Honour," said Sam leaning forward and becoming quite confidential, "as it happened I ain't a bigamist because my lady and me ain't really married, not in a church, like. We've just got an understanding if you know what I mean. But I was sorry for Em – she looked a wreck and you should have seen her when she was younger! So I gave her a hundred sovs and told her to take herself off."

"She agreed to that?"

"Not really. She got quite difficult because she wanted more. Prison had taught her some very naughty words I'm afraid. She said life had treated her pretty bad and she was going to get her own back but she didn't say how exactly. 'You'll be hearing about me again, Sam,' she said before she went off."

"And did you?"

"Yeah, when I opened the paper and read about her setting fire to her mother's old house. Trust Em, that's just the sort of thing she'd do, I thought."

It was not a surprise to anyone in the court when

the judgement was given that Amelia Portbury had died by accident while trying to burn down her old home. It was likely that the deceased's mind was deranged because of her illness and the tragedies she had endured during her life, said the coroner. By burning down the house where the major event took place, she might have been making some sort of symbolic gesture. It was fortunate that some youths had noticed the flames and raised the alarm in time for no one except the fire raiser to be killed in the conflagration.

"It is a tragic end to a very sad life," he said, standing up and closing the large notebook which had lain open before him during the hearing of evidence.

There was only one main door to the courtroom. When the ushers threw it open, the press and the public rushed to get out, cramming into the narrow aisle between the seats like lemmings.

Sam Portbury felt a hand on his shoulder as he elbowed his way through the mob. The voice of the blond police officer, whose name he had found out was Inspector Trevor Thomson, hissed in his ear, "Sure you're not a bigamist Sam? Absolutely sure? Maybe we'll have to check up on that."

Margaret, Daisy and Alice sat in their seats and let the courtroom nearly empty before they stood up to go. There were tear marks on Daisy's cheeks and both Margaret and Alice put their hands on her arms in sympathy, but she reassured them. "I'm all right really. It was just so sad, the whole thing. A tragedy from beginning to end. Oh Margaret, weren't we stupid!"

Margaret flushed. "I suppose we were but I haven't

changed my mind about the main cause – I still believe in that."

"So do I," said Daisy, "but I'm not going to be so rash in future, and I hope you aren't either."

They were almost through the door by this time. When she stepped into the wide corridor she saw Inspector Thomson waiting, standing with his back against the marble wall, staring at her. Her heart gave a terrible leap. Has he decided to arrest me and Margaret? Does he know the truth after all? she asked herself.

But he was smiling as he stepped forward with a hand extended. "I just wanted to say how sorry I am about your mother, Miss Cavendish. This must have been a dreadful ordeal for you."

Daisy took his hand and as she did so she wondered why her heart was jumping around so much. Why she felt a strange tide of blood rising in her cheeks. To her own amazement she heard herself saying in an almost coquettish tone, "That's very kind of you, Inspector Thomson."

The pair of them stood, hand in hand, smiling at each other as if entranced while Margaret and Alice watched them from a little distance up the corridor. Alice was smiling too, savouring every moment of the meeting, so that she could recount it all to Aaron later.

"Now you know how good I am at picking up on that sort of thing. I was right about Dora and young Bryce, wasn't I? My Daisy and this nice young policeman is another thing that wouldn't surprise me at all. He's a very good-looking fellow and they'll make a lovely pair," she'd say.

CENTRAL 19·8·98